RICK PARTLOW

DROP TROOPER BOOK SEVEN

SHOCK ACTION

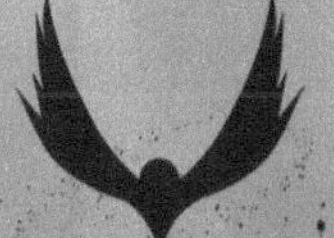

www.aethonbooks.com

SHOCK ACTION

©2021 RICK PARTLOW

CONTACT FRONT
KINETIC STRIKE
DANGER CLOSE
DIRECT FIRE
HOME FRONT
FIRE BASE
SHOCK ACTION
RELEASE POINT

[1]

Jagged mountains stretched beneath us, describing a gently curving S-shape through the center of the northern continent, trapping the moisture to the east, while the west side was an arid brown.

"What's this place called again?" I asked, resisting an urge to lean forward, as if the main display was a physical window rather than a holographic display and I could get a better view by pressing my nose against it.

"Canaan," Kyler Dunstan told me. "Why? You thinking about getting off here and settling down?"

There wasn't the playful snark behind the question that there might have been a few weeks ago. The sarcasm was rote, muted, as if it were an instinct for the veteran pilot but lacking in any enjoyment. He'd taken Baker Gardeck's death hard. Wade Cunningham's too, I suppose, though it was hard for me to remember because he was the only one on the *Yantar* who didn't know that Wade wasn't actually dead.

"If you were," Vicky Sandoval said from my right side, straining against her seat restraints to nudge my arm, "you might want to read the data file." She flicked a finger across the touch screen in front of her station at the cockpit and a data bubble popped up in a corner of the holographic display showing row upon row of statistics. "One point six-five gravities. They grow 'em big down there."

"I don't know." I tugged at the restraints holding me tight to my acceleration couch. "I think I might prefer high gravity to no gravity. I've had enough free-fall to last me the rest of my life."

"Lucky for you the Corporate Security Force station here is a rotational wheel then," Ruthie Amendola chimed in from the copilot's position, the one she'd assumed since Gardeck's death back on Bathala.

The CSF station crawled into view from the right side of the screen, a squat, cylindrical hub, open and glowing bright where the docking bay yawned invitingly. A shuttle slid into the opening as I watched, maneuvering jets flaring along its flanks. Thick spokes jutted out from the center of the hub, running to the flattened rim of the habitation wheel, rotating slowly and methodically, reminding me of the torture wheels they used to break people on in the Middle Ages.

"Yeah," I murmured. "Lucky me."

It had been a long and uncomfortable trip from Bathala, a struggle to watch what we said in front of Dunstan while in private, Ruthie, Vicky, and I had rehearsed our statements over and over, trying to memorize the lie—or, rather the half-truth— that Fleet Intelligence had crafted for us out of the doctored gun camera footage from our Vigilantes. And all of it had been aimed at that space station, at getting us onto it and, more importantly, getting us back off.

The problem was, neither of us was a spy. Maybe Ruthie was, but not Vicky or me. We were grunts. Point us at a problem and we'd shoot it for you. The giant, spinning wheel didn't seem like something we could solve that simply.

"We got clearance to dock," Dunstan said, shrugging. His

smile was wan. "Glad it's you two who get to go explain this shit to the suits. Fucking alien robot bugs..."

"They weren't robots, and they weren't bugs," Vicky ground out. I recognized the irritation in her voice and unlike Dunstan, I knew the dangers it represented. She'd gone over this with him a dozen times since we'd left Bathala orbit. "They were biomechanical drones produced by a nanotechnological factory. And they didn't look anything like an insect. Maybe a scorpion. Or a crab. But not an insect."

"Don't tell me, sweetie," Dunstan snorted. "Tell *them*."

I knew Vicky was as worried as I was because she didn't even bother to threaten Dunstan's life for calling her "sweetie."

———

"Cameron Alvarez. I've heard so much about you."

I took the offered hand and found it soft and mushy and utterly unpleasant, much like the woman behind it. If Investigator Dukanovic was a graven idol to self-importance, then her boss was the goddess of self-indulgence, from the nano-wire weave that kept her hair perfectly coifed to the haut-couture, vat-grown business suit that cost more than an assault shuttle. But the real difference between them came down to the handshake. Dukanovic, for all her paramilitary fashion choices, the black jodhpurs and riding boots and the leather gloves, was a hard woman, cold and decisive. Chief Investigator Trina Wellesley was none of that. She was soft and mushy and utterly unpleasant.

"Nice to meet you, ma'am," I told her with as much sincerity as I could fake.

She'd kept us waiting for nearly two hours, though the anteroom outside her office had an excellent selection of gourmet coffees and finger sandwiches. I'd wondered as I'd downed one tiny cup of coffee after another, whether the two of them were sitting inside, watching us on their monitors and critiquing our table manners.

"Chief Investigator," Vicky said, nodding to the woman with a great deal more respect than she actually felt, if I read my wife's eyes correctly. "I trust our cargo was offloaded safely?"

The "cargo" was the honey in the trap, or at least that was what Fleet Intelligence hoped. There hadn't been much left of the Skrela warrior drones, mostly because they were so damned tough and so hard to kill, but what remained of them had been wrapped up and loaded into the *Yantar*.

"Yes," Dukanovic confirmed, though Vicky hadn't been asking her. She frowned, the expression dramatic, like sliding a serrated knife out of its scabbard. "I can't say that I'm happy at the outcome of your operation, Mr. Alvarez, Ms. Sandoval. It resulted in the destruction of a cargo shuttle and a Corporate Security Force Intercept cutter, a loss of nearly one million in Corporate scrip, and the deaths of two of our people." She arched an eyebrow. "And Zan-Thint is in the wind. We gave him to you on a silver platter, and you and Mr. Cunningham assured us you were up to the task."

I didn't get angry. It wasn't easy, but we'd gamed just about every response we had a right to expect, and this had been one of the more likely ones.

"Ma'am," I said, my voice tightly controlled, not showing any of the resentment I felt and hopefully not the fear, either. "There were three of us in military-surplus battlesuits rigged with makeshift weapons against a full platoon of Tahni battle-suits *and* a swarm of ancient alien battle drones. We're lucky the price wasn't higher."

"Lucky indeed," Wellesley said. She gestured at the two chairs across from her desk. "Have a seat, if you would."

I didn't like it. It was a sign of submission and I didn't do submission well. But I was trying to be a good little spy, so I sat down. The desk was huge, a thing of hand-polished mahogany, either grown in a vat or imported from a colony, and just as expensive either way. I focused on it, on admiring the lines of the thing, wondering if it had actually been carved by hand or simply shaped by a very well-programmed fabricator.

"We're both very disturbed by the loss of life, of course," Wellesley said, leaning back against that incredibly expensive piece of furniture with the seat of her equally expensive suit. "The deaths of...." Her gaze flickered toward Dukanovic in an unspoken question.

"Gardeck and Cunningham," the taller woman supplied, just the barest hint of scorn in her tone, though whether at the thought she would consider the deaths of two such functionaries tragic, or at her boss for not being able to remember their names, I wasn't sure.

"Quite. The deaths of Mr. Gardeck and Mr. Cunningham were tragic. But I am also very concerned about the results. Not only did you fail to capture or terminate Zan-Thint, you didn't retrieve the Predecessor technology that was the main purpose of the operation either."

"It's hard to retrieve an egg after it hatches," I said, trying not to snap at the woman. "The pod opened up. We brought you what was left once we killed them, and if we hadn't, I'm fairly sure those things would have swarmed all over that planet and then spread from there all the way through the Pirate Worlds and into the Periphery by now."

"Yes, I saw the report. And you were able to stop this unstoppable horde due to the timely intervention of Mr. Dunstan, who nearly sacrificed his life and did destroy his star-ship in the process."

"Yes, ma'am." My jaws ached from holding them shut. I wanted to yell at her, to tell her that Dunstan wasn't "Mr.

Dunstan," he was a captain in the Commonwealth Space Fleet, retired, and deserved the respect of using his rank. And Wade was a sergeant and...well, I could have gone on for a while, but Vicky wasn't saying anything and if she could hold her temper with this supercilious stuffed shirt, then so could I. "After that, we had time to program the autopilot on one of the cargo ships at the spaceport to crash it into the base of the volcano and overload its Transition drive. That collapsed the mountain on top of the Skrela pod."

At least that was what the records showed. In reality, Dunstan had crashed Intercept One in a desperate maneuver to avoid a missile strike and the only reason we all hadn't wound up burned to cinders was that Top, Master Gunnery Sgt. Ellen Campbell, had showed up with a company of Drop Trooper to save our asses.

"And you believe what Zan-Thint told you?" Wellesley asked, her eyes narrowing. "About these...Skrela? That they were the ones who killed off the Predecessors?"

"He might have been lying," Vicky admitted.

She had been against telling the Corporates anything that Zan-Thint had shared with us in that volcanic cave, on the grounds that it was better to keep things simple and that the Corporate Council didn't need to know anything more about the lost alien technology than they already did. But Colonel Hachette had reasoned that there was the very real possibility that the Corporate Council already had one or more of the Skrela pods and it would probably be in everyone's best interest if they didn't blunder into releasing a swarm of civilization-killing combat drones onto the Commonwealth.

"He might have been," I agreed, "but to what end? There's no way he could have foreseen what happened. I think he believes what he was saying. Whether it's true or not, well...." I shrugged. "Either he's right or the Predecessors, the race that terraformed dead worlds into living ones and spread life throughout this whole side of the galaxy, decided to launch a whole shitload of doomsday weapons to kill everything they'd built."

Dukanovic's expression twitched into a narrow smile.

"It would hardly be the first time a supposedly civilized race tried to destroy itself." And I couldn't disagree with her.

She clucked and cracked her knuckles, giving me the impression she regretted the fact she couldn't come up with a good reason to just have the two of us disappeared. Which she very easily could have done and there wouldn't have been a damned thing we could do about it.

"We've examined the...." She tilted her head. "...bodies, I suppose. More like body parts. I know you probably thought we were just stuck-up Corporate bitches making you wait to show you how unimportant you are to us and that's probably *also* true." My ears began to redden and I swallowed hard, hoping I hadn't lost the art of keeping my feelings private. "But mostly, neither of us cares to enter a meeting without knowing the facts. We've had your report since you filed it through the Instell ComSat over a week ago, but what we lacked was corroborating evidence."

"Which we now have," Wellesley stepped in, though less with the feel of a well-rehearsed duet than one actor stepping on another's lines. "And they confirm what you said and what we already knew." The hair stood up on the back of my neck at the words. What the hell had they already known? "Stephanie here was ready to give both of you a boot in the ass on your way out of the station and consider herself merciful for not locking you in a cell until your salary covered our losses." I assumed "Stephanie" was Dukanovic, though I'd never been told her first name. "But now, our outlook is different. You've proven quite agile and able to adapt to evolving situations, and that's something we can use."

There was, I noted, no discussion of whether we wanted to remain in their employ. I wasn't sure if that was because they assumed no sane person would turn down the sort of money they were paying us, or if it was because we knew too much already for them to possibly allow us to leave.

"Thank you," Vicky said, her foot nudging mine. Oh, yeah, I suppose they would consider that doing us a favor.

"Yes," I agreed, plastering a smile over the scowl I was hiding. "Thanks."

"We've been considering what to do with you since we received your report," Wellesley continued, pushing off of her desk and standing before us. I had a sense I should stand up now and Vicky beat me to it by a half a second. "You're valuable assets, but the idea of sending you out with just two or three of you in, as you so aptly put it, war-surplus Vigilantes with jury-rigged weapons, is ludicrous. You're both proven combat leaders. So, we're giving you something to lead." She stepped to the door and waited beside it as it slid aside at her presence. "Stephanie will show you."

Dukanovic's mouth worked like she'd bitten into something sour, but she stalked out the door, waving for us to follow. I shot Vicky a doubtful look, but she grabbed my arm and hauled me along with her.

"Good luck," Wellesley added.

I didn't like the way she'd said it.

I don't know if you could rightly say that a rotating wheel space station had bowels, but if it did, we were in them. The storage compartment was dimly lit, swallowed by shadows, not from any disuse or disrepair but because we'd arrived during the CSF station's assigned "night." What a happy coincidence. And how nice of Ruthie to leave this nerve-wracking shit to us when she was the trained spy.

I couldn't decide where to stare, at the shadowy recesses between storage containers for signs that this was all a trick and Dukanovic was bringing us down here to have us executed in some out of the way place where the blood could be more easily cleaned off the floor, or at Dukanovic herself, since I wouldn't have put it past her to shoot us herself. Movement caught my eye in a corner, and I very carefully did *not* jerk around or flinch away, just squaring my stance off in case the worst happened.

"It's zero-dark-thirty, ma'am," a basso voice rumbled. "Couldn't we have done this in the morning?"

The man who emerged from the darkness at the side of the storage room matched the voice, broad-shouldered and square-jawed, and tall enough I could have mistaken him for a Tahni in this light. But his head was shaven clean, revealing the 'face jacks at his temples, something no Tahni would have had. His fatigues were black CSF issue rather than camo Marine, but I knew he had been a Drop Trooper.

"This is a space station, Martz," Dukanovic said without a trace of sympathy. "It's never nighttime." She shrugged. "Or always nighttime, if you'd rather."

The shadows came alive as eight more figures emerged from the darkness, all of them uniformed in the same style of fatigues, all of them sporting the interface sockets. Some had the same sort of ragged edge look as this Martz, a wild gleam in their eyes that spoke of a life lived hard, during the war and past it, while others retained the perpetual boredom of an enlisted Marine between battles. But Martz was their leader, their NCO, of that I was certain.

And as my focus shifted from the rough and ready mercenaries to the murky gloom behind them, the shadows there began to take shape, and that shape was hulking and humanoid and three meters tall. Lined up along the wall, anchored with magnetic locks like prisoners shackled for execution, were ten Vigilante battlesuits, their matte finish dull but unblemished, unmarred by patch or repaint, brand spanking new. Plasma guns were grasped in their right hands like outsized pistols and the missile launchers which had been missing from the suits Wade had salvaged for us were very present.

"First Lieutenants Cameron Alvarez and Victoria Sandoval," Dukanovic said, the introduction perfunctory and lacking enthusiasm, "this is Staff Sergeant Simon Martz and the rest of what we are provisionally referring to as Armor Squad Alpha."

"Alvarez, huh?" Martz grunted, looking me up and down. "Heard of you. Thought you'd be bigger."

"He is," Vicky said, cocking an eyebrow at the bald man. "Where'd you serve, Martz?"

"Second of the 398th, Third Expeditionary Force." The man's chest puffed up. "Served all the way from the start of the war to six months after the invasion of Tahn-Skyyiah."

"Ten years, huh?" Vicky's eyebrow raised. "The two of us were in about eight and we both went from E-1 all the way to E-5 *before* we went to OCS. How'd you wind up topping out at E-6?"

It was still dark inside the cargo hold, but the shade of red that Martz's face turned was still visible.

"Fucking officers," he spat. "Our company commander hated my guts, found any reason he could to ding me, and finally I couldn't take his shit anymore and I told him to go fuck himself."

"Good decision," she murmured.

"You all can get to know each other on the way," Dukanovic interrupted, waving away the conversation like an annoying insect.

"On the way to *where*, exactly?" I asked.

"You'll get your briefing after we load the *Yantar* with your gear and supplies, but the short form is, you're heading out to the Periphery, to a colony called Portent. There's a rhenium mine on the northern continent, the richest anyone has seen in the entire Commonwealth, and the Corporate Council has petitioned the Commonwealth Resources Commission to seize it through Imminent Domain and license it to us to work for the good of the state."

"And why do you need us for that?"

"Because the current owners are contesting the judgement."

"We're not lawyers," Vicky pointed out.

"They're contesting it," Dukanovic clarified, "by selling their rhenium to the highest bidder and using that profit to pay for mercenaries. Our first representatives *were* lawyers, serving the writ. They were chased out at gunpoint. The second was more forceful, two platoons of CSF troopers. That was when they hired the mercenaries, and they proved to be quite capable at their jobs. We lost ten men and women and one of their assault shuttles was shot down."

Outrage at the attempted land grab warred with admiration for the colonists and I had to push them both down to ask a question that wouldn't get me fired.

"Wait a second. Assuming the judgement was legal, why not just call the Patrol? The Commonwealth hasn't been shy about enforcing the will of the Corporate Council before."

"The Patrol doesn't operate in the Periphery," she reminded me. "That's the purview of the military. And even if the military were in a mood to do the CSF a favor, which they are not, they're stretched too thin after the post-war drawdown. Which is why the CSF has moved into so many systems to keep the peace with our own people."

"And you want us to take care of the mercenaries for you?" Vicky assumed.

"And the miners, if they won't listen to reason. That mine is ours and we *will* have it, either with the cooperation of the locals or over their dead bodies."

She was, I thought, as ruthless as Zan-Thint, though less principled.

"And what does this have to do with finding Zan-Thint," I asked her, "or retrieving the last artifact you know he has?"

She sniffed a quiet laugh.

"Nothing, of course. But we have no leads on Zan-Thint or the artifact. We don't know where to send you and we're not going to just stumble around blindly searching for him from planet to planet. When we hear something, you'll be on the front line, don't worry." She eyed me sidelong. "But let me clarify something for you, Alvarez. This is a paramilitary organization, but we are *not* the military, and you don't get to just sit around on your ass and paint rocks while we wait for intelligence on Zan-Thint to materialize. You're being paid to work and there's work to be done."

I had, over the years, gotten pretty good at controlling my anger. You pretty much have to when it's a constant companion, with you ever waking hour. But I couldn't keep the heat out of my voice.

"We didn't sign up just to be muscle. We took this job because we were told we'd be going after Zan-Thint."

I've been told I get a scary, far-away look when I'm angry, but Dukanovic didn't shy away from it, meeting my cold stare with one of her own.

"You signed up to do whatever the hell I need you to do, Alvarez. You're a valuable asset, as Ms. Wellesley said, and the Corporate Council doesn't allow assets to lay fallow." She tilted her head toward me. "We *use* them. And we'll be using *you* however we need you."

She turned toward the exit but paused and spared me an insincere smile.

"Look at the bright side. You and Alpha Squad will be fighting Zan-Thint when we do find him. Think of this as an opportunity to learn to work together."

The door shut behind her, leaving us with the nine members of Alpha Squad. The name bugged me. It didn't follow Marine unit designation protocol, which assigned numbers to squads or platoons and alphabetical designators to fire teams and companies. But I had the sense that was the least of our worries with this bunch.

No one spoke for a moment that stretched out uncomfortably long, and if Martz's glare had been a laser weapon, Vicky and I would have been sliced into bits. Then a perky, red-haired woman stepped forward, smiling broadly and offered me her hand.

"Hi, sir, I'm Karen Fargo," she said, her voice as chipper and cheerful as her smile. "A-team leader. I was a corporal," she added helpfully, "but I never got busted. I was just happy to be a team leader and didn't want any more responsibility than that. I just met everyone else a couple days ago when we arrived on board the station. I look forward to working with you."

I took her hand by instinct, bemused by the relentless upbeat positivity, and she shook firmly, then moved on to Vicky. Martz still didn't look happy, but he settled for a quiet sulk while the rest of the squad followed Fargo's awkward example and came forward to shake our hands.

"Gavin Lynn, B-team leader." He was the very embodiment of nondescript, what we used to call in the Trans Angeles Underground a "Gray Man," someone no one would ever be able to describe if they even remembered seeing him. If Lynn hadn't had the jacks, I wouldn't have been able to think of one distinguishing characteristic he had. "Nice to meet you."

The others were a heterogeny of men and women, short and stocky or tall and thin, but what they shared was the lean and hungry look of people who'd been living their life on the ragged edge, who'd come back to the world from the war and hadn't been able to live in it. Their greetings were polite but perfunctory, an acknowledgement that we were going to have to work together and might as well act as if we didn't want to kill each other.

"Sgt. Martz," I said, addressing the man with the respect I would have given a platoon sergeant back in the Corps, "I assume the CSF cargo handlers are going to come in here and load our gear into the *Yantar*. Would you mind supervising them, keeping an eye on things? I don't trust this bunch of civilians to take care of our armor."

Martz's frown seemed thoughtful rather than upset and I had the sense that he agreed with me and didn't like doing it.

"Right," he said. "I'll stay on top of them. Dukanovic said they'd be coming in to move the gear out in a couple hours." He scowled. "I was *wanting* to get a couple more hours sleep first, but that's shot to shit."

"According to this," Vicky said, holding up the display screen of her 'link, "Portent is a two-and-a-half-week voyage from Canaan. I think you're going to have plenty of time to catch up on your beauty sleep."

"We'll go get the ship ready for the cargo," I said, touching Vicky on the arm and nodding toward the door. "See you all in a few hours."

I wasn't even sure how to get back to the docking bay from where we were in the station, but I walked purposefully and quickly toward the lift banks.

"On a scale of one to ten," Vicky asked quietly as the door opened and we boarded the lift car, "how fucked are we?"

I thought about it for a half a second, stabbing at a random control just to get the car out of there.

"Eleven."

[3]

"Transition in five, four, three, two one…Transitioning now."

Brent Foster's face was a study in earnest professionalism as he leaned forward against his seat restraints and touched the control to discharge the *Yantar*'s capacitor banks through the Teller-Fox warp unit. I was no physicist or drive engineer, so as far as I knew, the thing chanted a spell or sacrificed a virgin to open the wormhole that let us into Transition space. Whatever it did, the blackness of the Goshen system disappeared into the unseeable nothingness and the cockpit viewscreen switched to a simulated projection of our course. The ship's artificial gravity kicked in a second later, which was something else I lacked the hyperdimensional physics degree to understand, why it only worked in Transition space.

Foster turned and nodded to Dunstan, a sharp, precise motion.

"Gravitational field activated, sir."

Dunstan regarded the intense young pilot with a stare of utter disbelief.

"The fuck is it with you, man?" he finally asked. Foster blinked in utter confusion and I couldn't help it, I burst out laughing. Vicky was chuckling beside me, but the young copilot was still nonplussed. "I mean seriously, dude, what do you think this is, the flag bridge of a Fleet cruiser?"

"I...," Foster stammered. "I mean, it was how I...."

"You never flew in combat, did you?" Dunstan's eyes narrowed. "Come on, be honest."

"No." The word was soft, almost inaudible, as if Foster considered it a shameful admission. "I graduated from the Academy just before the final push on the Tahni core systems." The younger man shrugged, obviously uncomfortable with the subject. "By the time I got through flight school, the whole thing was over. I spent a year on security patrols around Tahn-Skyyiah and then they let me out early."

"Oh, great," Dunstan moaned, running thin fingers through thick and decidedly non-regulation hair. "You wanna change his diapers, Ruthie, or are we gonna take turns?"

"Stop being such a shit, Dunstan," Ruthie Amendola snapped, drawing a raised eyebrow from the pilot.

"Since when are you such a live wire?" he insisted. "Ever since we left Bathala, you're all of a sudden all mouthy and assertive? And I don't remember you doing a damned thing but sitting on the fucking ship watching while we all almost got our asses killed."

"Maybe I just got tired of your bullshit," she said, yanking the quick-release on her harness and pushing out of her station. "God knows I've heard enough of it."

She stalked out of the cockpit and I watched her go. Vicky shrugged. Ruthie had been undercover for a while with Dunstan, pretending to be something she wasn't, and I could completely understand how that could get old.

"I'm sure it's going to be fine," I told Foster, clapping him on the arm, remembering the young officers who'd come in at the end of the war, eager to see action and make their mark before it was too late. Plus, he was the dropship pilot, and we would be counting on him to haul our asses out of the fire, so I was hoping to stay on his good side.

"Sure it is," Dunstan said to our backs as Vicky and I followed Ruthie. "I'll just go find Junior here a lollypop to keep him occupied."

"You're an asshole, Dunstan," Vicky assured him.

Ruthie was already ten meters ahead of us, sliding down the railing of the short staircase between the cockpit and the passenger compartment. Alpha Squad was out of their acceleration couches, milling around as if they were waiting for someone to tell them what to do. I scowled, realizing that someone was me. It *should* have been Martz, since keeping the enlisted busy was the job of a good NCO, but he was "smokin' and jokin'," as Top liked to call it, with the rest of the Marine vets.

And did you really think it would be anything else from a ten-year vet who had to make E-6 twice?

"Sgt. Martz," I said, using the tone of voice I'd mastered after OCS, when a junior officer was giving an NCO an order but couching it as a friendly suggestion, "do we have an inventory of how many missile reloads we brought along and what types?"

"Yeah, I'm sure it's in the lading files," he replied, looking up from a conversation with Corporal Lynn, the corner of his mouth turning down as if he resented the interruption. He was, unsurprisingly, not perceptive enough for the whole "order-that's-not-an-order" thing.

"Awesome," I said, smiling like a politician about to pick someone's pocket. "Last time we went out, we had to do some reloading on the run without any techs to help us out and it was one of the most awkward damned things I've ever done. How about you detail a team to check our utility carts and see if we can rig a way to work missile reloads without ground support?"

And if Martz wasn't smart enough to understand *that*, I was going to have to get even more direct, which he'd like not at all.

The big man sighed, like it was an imposition, but then he motioned at Fargo.

"Yo, Fargo, take your team down to the cargo hold and see what you can figure out, okay?"

"Will do, Sergeant," she said, dripping with what seemed like honest enthusiasm, though by the looks on their faces, the others in her fire team didn't share it. "Come on, guys!"

"You know where your compartments are?" I asked Martz once she was gone. He'd dropped back into his discussion with Lynn about the relative merits of different R&R establishments on Eden and he scowled at the further interruption.

"Yeah, I saw the designators on the way in."

"Good. Go ahead and get everyone settled in, then. You said you were wanting to grab more sleep, so feel free if you like. Or there's food in the galley. Once Fargo reports back to you on the loading carts, run whatever she's got by me, but other than that, the next couple days are yours." I smiled thinly. "After that, we're going to start running simulator drills in the suits."

The scowl deepened and I thought I could see smoke coming out of the big man's ears.

"Aye, sir," he growled, and I deliberately ignored the tone behind the words.

"Great. Look forward to working with you."

Which pretty much assured that Martz would go out of his way to avoid me for the foreseeable future and the rest of the squad would be too busy. Vicky hid her grin until we were past them, then let it spread unhindered.

"You really got that whole prick officer thing down," she admitted, smacking me on the butt. "I'm impressed."

"I learned from the best."

I waited until we'd left the mercs behind before speeding up to a fast walk, finally catching up with Ruthie near the small ship's docking bay, which was little more than a sheltered place in the hull with three triangular niches to fit the dropship, a much smaller personal shuttle and the replacement for Intercept One. I hadn't asked Dunstan if he was going to name this one Intercept Two or Intercept 1A, but I was betting he just gave it the old designation.

Ruthie was pulling open the airlock to the repurposed missile cutter when we reached her, and she barely looked up at our approach.

"Are you really upset with Dunstan?" Vicky asked her. "Or is that just a put-on?"

Ruthie made a shushing gesture, then motioned for us to follow her into the smaller starship. The missile cutter was cramped and claustrophobic compared to the *Yantar*, but claustrophobia had never been one of my problems. Ruthie led us through to the utility bay of the Intercept One and shut the lock behind us. She pulled her 'link off her belt and peered at a readout on the instrument for a second before sighing and slipping it back into its pouch.

"I don't know if we're good here or not," she admitted. "I scanned for active monitoring, but that doesn't mean they don't have passive systems. It's the best we can do, though."

"This sucks, Ruthie," I confided in her. "What the hell are we gonna do?"

"I'm afraid you're going to have to be more specific," she told me, cocking an eyebrow. "There are so very many things that suck right now."

"Specifically," I said, rolling my eyes, "what sucks is that we're heading out to some damned wildcat mine to act as the Corporate Council's bully boys instead of doing what we were sent here to do, which was to find Zan-Thint. If we're not going after him, what's the point of being here at all?"

"It's not as if they were going to let you quit," she reminded me. "You were a Marine...."

"I *am* a Marine," I corrected her.

"Then you know the old saying. Improvise, adapt and overcome. We do what we have to do in order to get the job done."

"Is there any way to contact Hachette or Top?" Vicky asked. "We should at least let them know what's going on."

"The only option we have is the dead drop. And to use that, we have to send a message through an Instell ComSat. Which we won't be doing until we drop out for a navigation check in a week."

I bit off a curse and spat it out. I hadn't been crazy about staying on with the CSF from the minute Top had proposed it to us, but I'd accepted that it was necessary to find out what they knew about the Skrela pods and Zan-Thint. This was a huge waste of time we might not have.

"Yeah," Ruthie agreed, presumably with the vociferousness of the expletive. "And there's one other thing. Besides the ship maybe being bugged. At least one of those Marines is a spy for Dukanovic."

I winced at the declaration. I'd had the same thought myself, but it seemed more real and immediate put into words.

"So, what do we do?" I asked again, feeling like a moron repeating the question but yet to receive an answer I could live with. "Do we go along with this? Do what they want and maybe wind up having to kill some poor colonists who don't want their life's work stolen by the Corporate Council?"

"And what's the alternative?" Vicky wondered, spreading her hands in an encompassing gesture, her demeanor cool and calm though she wasn't fooling me. She was as lost and worried as I was, but better at hiding it. "I don't think those muscle-heads out there are going to take too kindly to us scuttling the mission. This is their career now and they don't look like the types who could make money at anything else."

"I'm a field agent," Ruthie reminded us, shaking her head. "Not a politician and not a senior officer, which are pretty much the same thing." She bared her teeth, a cornered animal ready to tear the throat out of the next thing she saw. "I'm a field agent who's been undercover way too damned long pretending to be a dutiful crewmember, a timid little wallflower who's afraid to do anything that's not by the book and it's getting pretty old. But this is the job, and even though you two are new to it, this is how it works. Shit comes up that you're not ready for and you have to handle it on your own. We'll get there and see what the lay of the land is, then we'll make a plan."

I nodded. I didn't like it very much, but I understood the sentiment. It wasn't that much different from what we'd had to do in the Corps.

"What about Dunstan?" I asked. Ruthie made a face like she'd stepped in dogshit.

"What about him?"

"Maybe we should bring him in on this." She looked like she was about to smack me upside the head for even suggesting it and I hurried on with an explanation. "It's not like he's a dedicated Corporate Council type, he doesn't give a shit about them except they pay him to fly. And he's going to be out there in the Intercept One, covering our asses, the biggest weapon we have." I shrugged. "If you offer him a commission the way they did us, he might take it."

Ruthie had calmed down slightly at my explanation, but she still looked angry enough to chew iron and spit out nails.

"Number one," she said, counting her points off on her fingers, "as I said before, I'm just a field agent, I don't have the authority to either read Dunstan in on the operation or to offer him a commission. Number two, it's tough enough just to find an opportunity for the three of us to get away and talk for five minutes without making everyone suspicious. How the hell do you think it would look if we dragged Dunstan off with us? And third and last, are you fucking nuts?" The last was shouted nearly into my face. "The man is an asshole! He may be a damned good pilot, but he'd be just as likely to spill the whole thing out by accident as do us any good!"

"She's got you there," Vicky admitted.

I sighed and nodded.

"Okay, what do we know about the miners?"

"All I know is what you can read in the briefing packet they gave us," Ruthie said, still keyed up, squaring off with me like she wanted to argue. "You can see for yourself."

"Maybe," I admitted, "but whether or not you're just a junior field agent, you're still a hell of a lot more experienced at this than we are."

Ruthie seemed to collapse in on herself as the fight went out of her. She sagged back against the bulkhead of the cutter, then found the latch for one of the emergency acceleration couches and pulled it down off, falling into the seat.

"Okay, from what I can see, the mine isn't your usual wildcat setup like you see in a lot of places. Usually, there's a loose handshake agreement between a few hundred colonists, with everyone in charge of their own particular specialty and if there's any differences, they have to work them out in a big, public meeting." She snorted. "Most of the time, that winds up with a lot of alcohol and a few fistfights. But not this bunch. Nominally, they're a syndicate, but the intelligence report says they're actually run top-down by their so-called 'chairman,' a man named Pavel Konigsberg. He's got a jacket." At my look of incomprehension, she expounded. "A military record. He was in the Marines, the old Special Operations Groups."

My eyebrows shot up.

"SOG? They were disbanded decades ago."

"After they garnered a reputation for utter ruthlessness during the Pirate Wars. Which was where our Mr. Konigsberg received a Bronze Star with a V for Valor...and then got busted from E7 to E5 six months later for using excessive force against an EPW."

I shaped a silent whistle.

"For them to bust someone who just won a Bronze Star," I said, "it must have been something that would have got anyone else a court-martial, not just slapping around an enemy prisoner of war."

"The records were sealed, so I have no idea." She shrugged. "Colonel Hachette could unseal them, but I can't, and the CSF apparently didn't think it was important enough to dig any deeper. Anyway, Konigsberg is apparently the big boss, runs the place with an iron hand."

"What about the mercs?" Vicky asked her. "Do we have any solid intell on them, what their numbers are?"

Ruthie smirked.

"Not from the CSF goons they sent. The only intelligence they were able to share was that the mercs had heavy weapons, armored vehicles, and space assets. And they only knew that because that was what hit them so hard they had to run back with their tails between their legs. We don't even know *which* PMC it is."

"PMC?"

"Private Military Company." Ruthie leaned back in the chair, resting her head on the cushion, her smile twisted and sardonic. "It sounds more respectable than 'mercenary,' and since the CSF is technically a mercenary army all its own, we're all about sounding respectable."

The Fleet Intelligence agent sighed and pushed herself to her feet.

"All right, we'd better get back to the ship before someone comes looking for us." She eyed us sidelong. "I know this is going to be tough for the two of you, but you have to treat Martz and the others normal, like you would if you *didn't* know any of them could be a stooge put in place to keep an eye on you."

"Great," I said, rolling my eyes. "No problem."

"Oh, get off it, Alvarez," Ruthie said, smacking the back of her hand against my upper arm. "I read *your* jacket. If anyone can run a con, it's you."

[4]

"Transponder number A8372CF, classified as freighter *Yantar*, cut thrust and maintain current position relative to orbital insertion. Be advised you are in the crosshairs of our orbital defense grid. You are not on our scheduled arrivals list. What is your business on Portent?"

"Well," Dunstan murmured, easing back the throttle and then keeping his hands safely away from the control yoke, "that didn't take long."

He was, for once, entirely correct. We'd Transitioned barely a half an hour ago and made a leisurely half-g burn for orbit, confident that this place would be like every other Periphery world all of us had been to at one time or another. Lax security, the bare minimum landing transponder, hardly anyone even noticing arriving ships until they requested clearance to land at the spaceport and only then to make sure they paid the landing fees.

Portent was not one of *those* systems. The planet loomed ahead of us, threatening in the jagged edges of its many mountain ranges, its rivers wide and meandering, its seas small and numerous. I knew where we were headed. I'd had plenty of time to study the files we'd been given, particularly since I hadn't been able to talk openly to Vicky or Ruthie Amendola the whole rest of the flight. The southern hemisphere had three continents, but one of them was trackless jungle and the other was mostly barren desert. The one we wanted was about the size of Australia, but dotted with extinct volcanos. In the foothills of the largest was the town of Perfection, our destination.

No one had answered the traffic control call and I realized, belatedly, that they were waiting on me. I had to search the control panel desperately, having never used the comm controls, and thankfully, Ruthie came to my rescue, reaching across from her station to touch the correct control.

"Portent Traffic Control," I said, keeping my voice cool and even, "this is the privateer *Yantar*. We're an independent freighter hoping to negotiate a cargo."

I'd rehearsed the line during the trip, yet it still felt forced.

"Be advised, *Yantar*, that Portent is not generally a destination for outbound freight. We have a shipping contract for our ore. Unless you are bringing goods in for sale, you're wasting your time."

Whoof. The guy sounded young and earnest and was not fucking around at all.

"Roger that, Portent," I said. "We'd still like to take some shore leave, in that case. Been a long flight. Also need to stock up on some consumables. You *do* still sell food and fabricator slugs, right?"

I'd been trying for light banter, but I was afraid it had come across as bitter sarcasm because Portent Traffic Control didn't reply immediately.

"*Yantar*," he said after a long and tense few seconds, "we've had some problems here with Corporate Council hired guns trying to take what's ours. I'm just going to go ahead and tell you right up front, if you're working for the Council in any capacity, you're not welcome here. We take our autonomy seriously on Portent."

Well, shit.

"Roger that, Portent, rest assured, I do not work for the Corporate Council. I came because I heard there might be cargoes to be had, and all I want now is a couple good meals not made from soy and spirulina."

And it wasn't even completely a lie. I wasn't sure why that mattered to me, but it did.

Another pause, too long, and I was about to tell Dunstan to get us ready to spin around and head back for safe jump distance when the reply finally came.

"Roger that, *Yantar*. You're cleared for stable orbit. Follow the transponder signal. If you mean to land, have your shuttle contact the tower. Have a good shore leave."

I muted the mic so he wouldn't here the heavy, relieved sigh.

"Will do, Portent," I said. "Thanks."

Dunstan was concentrating on following their instructions, taking the ship into orbit, but Ruthie, Foster and Vicky were all staring at me.

"What now?" Foster asked the question the others had been too polite to say. "Do we have a plan?"

"We do," I assured him. "But you aren't going to like it."

———

"This is bullshit," Martz declared, arms crossed over his chest, frowning so hard it threatened to pull the rest of his face down with it despite the microgravity. "This wasn't the mission."

"The mission is to acquire the mine for the Corporate Council," I told him, studiously looking away so as not to reward his sulk, concentrating on seating my handgun in its shoulder holster.

I grabbed two spare magazines out of the weapons locker and shoved them into place in the pouch balancing out the other side of the holster, then slipped the leather jacket on over it. Vicky and I had brought some of our civilian clothes along on the *Yantar* from Hausos, but these we'd fabricated en route. They were meant to look like spacer gear, not the rough, practical farm wear we'd worn on the colony world.

"And maybe they didn't share this with NCOs," Vicky put in, shutting the locker door for me, "but you don't just jump in blind without any intelligence. We need to get the lay of the land, find out who's going to fight and who can be bought off."

Or at least that was the excuse we were giving.

"We heard the traffic control when we arrived here," Lynn put in. Neither he nor Fargo had taken part in Martz's tirade, but they were both standing at the corner of the docking bay entrance, anchored by the sticky-plates on their ship boots, watching the show. "It was coming over the PA speakers back in the passenger compartment. They practically accused us of being Corporate Council spies. You really think they're going to tell you anything?"

"They don't have to tell us anything," I said, pushing off from the weapons cabinet toward the airlock for the lander. "All we have to do is play tourist, look around, get an idea of their anti-aircraft capabilities, where the mercenary forces are head-quartered and how professional they are."

"Fucking officers," Martz bellowed, throwing his hands up hard enough that his boots' sticky plates pulled away from the deck and he floated up toward the overhead. "Always making everything more complicated than it has to be!" He pushed off the overhead and refastened himself to the floor.

"Tell us, then, Martz," Vicky snapped, pausing at the airlock to fix the NCO with a glare. "Grace us with your brilliant plan."

"We don't need a fucking brilliant plan!" he snapped. "We need to send down the dropship with the squad suited up and ready to kick ass!"

"And you're so sure that the mercs don't have enough armored vehicles and hardened turrets to take us out that you're willing to bet all our lives on that?" I asked. I wasn't exactly angry, not yet. He was an idiot, or he wouldn't have been busted down from E6 twice.

But Martz grinned as if he'd expected the question.

"That's the beautiful part, we don't go after the mercs. We go after the miners. We drop on the mine, start blowing the shit out of it, trap the workers in there and maybe mow a bunch of 'em down. The mercs would have to come to *us*, and they couldn't move armored vehicles or gun turrets into the mine. They'd come in on foot with maybe some crew-served weapons on carts and we'd slaughter 'em. Bang, bam, boom, job's done, we're paid and out of there."

I stared at him, half in disgust and disbelief and half in honest admiration. The plan was utterly amoral and ruthless, but it *was*, at least, coherent and well-considered. Except for one thing.

"You ever been inside a rhenium mine, Martz?" I asked him. He shook his head and I tried to look superior and intelligent and all, but the truth was, I hadn't either. But I had read the briefing and searched the ship's net for details on the operation. "Rhenium is found in trace amounts in the deposits of other minerals, so a rhenium mine is actually a huge, spread-out place where they did up copper and other shit...and throw it in a fusion torch to separate the rhenium. So the only place down there where there would be miners or technicians all gathered together in a group in an enclosure would be the fusion reactor."

"So?" Martz demanded. "That's as good a place as any!"

Vicky rubbed a hand across her face, not nearly as patient with idiots as she'd once been.

"It's a fusion reactor. You know, big-assed tungsten heat shields protecting everything? There isn't shit we could do to it. They could just run away and hide, and we'd be sitting there shooting plasma guns at big shields designed to stop plasma. I mean, we could blow up their physical controls, but it's a fusion reactor...they have backups, probably remote backups, too."

His face screwed up in a frown, but a scowl replaced it.

"I still think it would work. Whether we did any real damage or not, the mercs would still have to come kick us out. And they couldn't use air assets on us, either."

"It might," I acknowledged. "It's not a bad plan. But we're not going to do it...unless and until we find out that it's the best option. We aren't going in blind and that's the final word."

"Fucking officers. You're soft and you think too much, just like all those other ring-knockers." He scoffed. "They should have put me in charge of this operation, we'd be done already." Now, I was getting pissed. Not that he'd called me soft or overly thoughtful, but that he'd implied I was a ring-knocker.

"In point of fact," I told him, my voice sounding as if it was coming from somewhere far away, like my consciousness was trying to escape the cold rage building up inside me, "neither one of us graduated from the Fleet Service Academy, Sgt. Martz. Lt. Sandoval here enlisted straight out of the Houston Underground. I enlisted straight out of a murder rap in the Trans-Angeles Correctional System."

His eyes widened slightly at that, and I didn't bother to mention that it was only murder because the gangbanger who'd been trying to kill me after I stole his load of drugs had managed to jump in front of a moving train. I didn't like to lie, but the truth was a seasoning, best used in small doses.

"I was looking at fifty years in the 'fridge if I didn't enlist. My second drop was on Brigantia. You ever hear about Brigantia?"

"Yeah," he admitted, almost unwillingly. "I heard it was a rough drop."

I laughed softly.

"You could say that. We lost the whole first wave. Dozens dead, hundreds more injured and out of the fight, stuck behind enemy lines. I fell out of a burning dropship at a thousand meters and the only reason I didn't wind up a thin, fine paste at the bottom of my suit was that I managed to hit a lake. I lost my suit and had to swim out. Hooked up with the civilian militia and they found me a suit after they scraped what was left of the old owner out of it. And together, we blew up the fucking deflector shield generator and let the Fleet take out their defense laser."

"You." He was nodding slowly. "Yeah, I heard of you. I didn't put it together with your name, but I heard of you."

"You heard of Ambergris?" I pressed him. "Tahni military outpost?"

"Who hasn't heard of Ambergris? First, last and only time Marines ever hijacked a Tahni cargo ship and used it to infiltrate an enemy...." His eyes narrowed. "No fucking way."

"Yeah." I nodded toward Vicky. "She was there, too. And Point Barber. And Port Harcourt. And Tahn-Skyyiah. Every single shitty, gut-wrenching, blood-soaked battle of that shitty war. So, you'll excuse me if I'm not impressed by you complaining that I fucking think too much."

Martz bristled like a wild hog, ready to rush at me and establish his dominance, but he stopped with a look into my eyes. I don't know what he saw in them, but I knew what I felt: a total lack of fear. He tried to sneer, but the expression was undercut with uncertainty.

"You're going to get down there," he told us, "and you're going to need us. You're going to regret going down alone."

"Maybe I am," I admitted. "And I'm counting on you to keep an eye on what's happening and pull my fat out of the fire if that does happen."

That seemed to mollify him and he sighed in what I took for resignation.

"Fine. But I'm not sure I like sending one of our pilots down there to be a sitting duck, either."

"Which is why we aren't doing it," Vicky told him. She waved at the airlock. "I'll be piloting the shuttle."

"You know how to fly this thing?" That wasn't Martz, it was Fargo, and she didn't sound skeptical as much as impressed.

"I know enough," Vicky confirmed, "to push the right buttons to let the computer fly it down and bring it back." She shrugged. "This isn't a combat drop. If we have to dodge missiles, we're dead anyway, no matter who's at the controls."

"Fuck it," Martz said, clomping off without a look back. "It's your funeral." Lynn followed him wordlessly, shaking his head, but Fargo hung back.

"Good luck," she said, waving. "I'll try to keep Martz from doing anything stupid. But no promises!"

I waved back, still not sure if the woman was just incredibly, sincerely naïve, or if she was a Corporate spy who just wasn't very good at it. Vicky had headed to the cockpit, leaving me to seal the lock, and by the time I joined her there, she was already strapped in, running through a help menu on the display at the pilot's station.

"It's not too late to have Foster fly us down," I reminded her. "I've never really trusted computers. I didn't even know what a computer was until I got to Trans-Angeles."

"Shh," Vicky hushed me, pointing at the display. "You're

going to hurt her feelings and she's going to wind up crashing us into a mountain."

"Seriously though," I said, strapping into the copilot's position, where I would be as useless as teats on a bore, "all posturing for Martz's benefit aside, are you really sure you can do this? I took the same two-day course you did, and I don't think I could remember how to tell the computer to make me a cup of coffee."

"Lucky for us," she said, smiling with exaggerated sweetness, "that I'm not afraid to read the directions." She squinted at the readout on the help screen. "Shuttle One, engage autopilot system."

"Autopilot system engaged." The voice was female, neutral but not robotic, just animated enough to make you comfortable talking to it.

"Shuttle One, detach airlock and maneuver us out of the docking bay for launch."

Vicky was speaking to the computer like she was trying to train a dog, but if the shuttle's autopilot system minded, it didn't complain.

"Detaching from lock." The loud, metallic clang vibrating through the hull made me jump in my seat and it was a good thing I'd strapped in, or I would have floated out of the chair.

"Secure for maneuvering thrusters," the computer warned, as if it had been spying on me and noticed my reaction.

The bang of the steering jets was softer than usual, softer than any human pilot I'd flown with, but the trip out of the docking niche also took twice as long and I resisted an urge to yell at the collection of ones and zeros to hurry up. Finally, though, the shuttle emerged from the shadow of the *Yantar* and into the blaring white of the system's primary, reflecting off our ship and off the blues and greens of Portent beneath us.

I don't know why the sight of the planet affected me more

from up in the cockpit than it did from back in the passenger compartment, but it did. The image on the screens in both places might have been the same quality holographic projection, but there was a qualitative difference to the experience, an immediacy of hanging out above nothing, ready to fall hundreds of kilometers to the world below.

"Shuttle One is clear of the ship and ready for main thrust," the computer announced, breaking the spell. Vicky shot me a triumphant grin, as if she'd flown the bird out with her own two hands.

"Shuttle One," she said, almost crowing it, "contact Portent Traffic Control for a landing beacon and take us down to the spaceport."

The main engine igniting was an even bigger jolt than the maneuvering jets, but I managed not to flinch this time.

"Oh, ye of little faith," Vicky said, wagging a finger at me.

"If it gets us to the ground safe," I told her, "I'll buy you a beer."

"And if it doesn't?" she asked teasingly, and I shrugged in return.

"Then the damned computer can buy us both one."

[5]

"This place reminds me of Hausos," I said, sucking in a breath of the clean, cool mountain air.

It was mid-afternoon in Perfection and the sky was, as advertised, a perfect, cloudless blue. It was summer in the northern hemisphere of Portent and at lower elevations, I expected it would be hot. But Perfection was high on a plateau, just at the foot of the mountains and it was just cool enough to make the leather jacket I was wearing comfortable.

"Do you miss it?" Vicky asked, stepping down the shuttle's ramp to stand beside me on the tarmac.

Her look was challenging, as if she was daring me to say yes, to admit we'd fucked up when we'd said yes to Wade Cunningham and taken up his offer to work for the Corporate Security Force.

"I liked living there," I told her. "I just didn't like what I was doing for a living." I nodded toward the mountains off to the north, jagged and grey. "This place is beautiful, too, but I don't especially want to be a miner, you know?" I bumped my shoulder against hers. "Come on, let's get into town while we can still catch the miners at work. I don't especially want to spend the night here."

She bumped me back harder, knocking me off-stride.

"You still haven't told me how good my landing was."

"That's because the computer landed the shuttle," I reminded her. "You just sat there singing obscene Marine marching cadences."

"I'll have you know, all my platoon mates in Boot Camp loved the way I sang obscene marching cadences."

I slipped an arm around her waist and grinned.

"You can sing me obscene Marine marching cadences when we're back in our compartment tonight, if that's the kind of thing that gets your motor running, Vick."

"You're lucky I love you, Alvarez," she said, cocking an eyebrow at me. "Otherwise, I'd never let you get away with calling me Vick."

The spaceport at Perfection was surprisingly well built for a Periphery mining world, with over a dozen enclosed landing pads for large cargo shuttles, connected by broad, covered passages to a train station. An electric-powered locomotive was pulling up as we walked into the port facilities, its brakes shrieking in protest as it came to a halt at a cargo ramp. Trucks were already waiting there to load what I assumed was rhenium ore into cylindrical cargo containers and the whole thing had the feel of an insect hive.

"Quite the efficient little setup they've got here," I said. "That had to cost some serious jack."

"So did they."

Vicky nodded off to the other side of the facility, where the walkways and cargo runs intersected in what looked like a customs station. Manning it were a handful of what looked like civilian workers, but backing them up was a squad of infantry in powered exoskeletons. Their gear wasn't exactly cutting-edge

Marine-issue, but it was a cut above anything I'd seen out in the Pirate Worlds, on a level with the Tahni Shock-troopers from the war and I wondered if that was where they'd gotten the armor. It wasn't a battlesuit, not by a longshot, but the powered exoskeletons let them carry heavier armor and weapons and more ammo than conventional infantry. The squad at the customs station was outfitted with heavy Gauss rifles, a generation behind the current issue but better weapons than anyone they'd be likely to face out here, or anything the CSF would have sent to take the mines.

Until now.

I tried not to stare as we waited in line at the customs station behind a pair of spacers who seemed like they would rather be anywhere else, but I did slip a few sidelong glances at the troops, looking for identifiers. And not finding them. Their armor had no unit patch I could see, though they might have worn it on their uniforms beneath the heavy alloy plating. I hoped an officer might come up while we waited so I could find out for sure, but no such luck and we were at the front in thirty seconds.

The woman sitting at the customs station was dressed in plain grey coveralls as if she'd been pulled off the line at the smelting facility to take a shift at the spaceport, and for all I knew, that was exactly what happened. She had the look of agelessness that I'd grown used to in the Corps and missed out in the Pirate Worlds, the effect of the life-extension treatments citizens of the Commonwealth received as a matter of course... or at least citizens who didn't have the bad luck to be born and grow up and grow old and die in the cracks between the mega-cities. I'd seen a lot of old faces in Tijuana in my youth.

"Names, ship of record and business in Perfection?" the woman asked, her stylus poised over the screen of her tablet.

"Alvarez, Cameron," I said automatically, flashing back to

my days going through one line after another, filling out one form after another in Boot Camp.

"Sandoval, Victoria," Vicky echoed my form if not my words and the woman's pen worked at her display with a subdued tapping.

"We're off the freighter *Yantar*," I added. "We came to Portent to see if there's any possibility of picking up a cargo for transport. We need the work."

The woman's blue eyes flashed with sudden suspicion.

"I doubt that would be possible," she said, her tone flat and unfriendly.

"Well, we came all this way," I said, spreading my hands. "Is there anyone we could talk to about it? I'd at least like the chance to make a pitch before we give up and move on."

One of the mercs turned slightly, their darkened visor pointing my way, as if my words or the gesture had drawn their attention to me. They didn't ask any questions, though, and the muzzle of their Gauss weapon didn't raise. The woman leaned over to the man at the next station and tapped him on the shoulder.

"Keith," she said, "these guys want to talk to Pavel."

Keith was a burly, red-faced man with a nose battered by years of wind and cold and a beard that might have last been trimmed sometime around the end of the war. He frowned, eyeing us sidelong.

"About what?" His voice was rough and rasping, matching his exterior perfectly.

"Business," I told him. "Is there any way we can set up a meeting?"

I thought Keith was going to give us a hard time, but he shrugged, not seeming too concerned about it.

"I'll call him, let him know," he offered. "Give me your 'link address and someone will get back with you in a bit."

I nodded and touched my 'link to his when he offered it, exchanging addresses.

"I guess this means we're dating," he cracked, stuffing the 'link into the pocket of his oversized jacket. I chuckled.

"Thanks. Know anyplace we can get a good, hot meal while we're waiting?"

"Sure, go to Betty's Café down First Street." He waved vaguely to the northeast. "Tell her Keith sent you and she'll throw in the first drink free."

"And you'll get your next dinner there on the house, I bet," the woman said, smacking him on the arm.

"Hey, she has good steaks!" the man protested, but we were already moving past the customs station.

They hadn't checked us for weapons, which didn't surprise me, though it might have once. I'd grown up in Trans-Angeles, where weapons scanners and security cameras were omnipresent and even the cops only carried nonlethal weapons. The only guns there were the ones the gangs slapped together out of fabricated parts and threw away if there was any danger they'd be caught with them, because the penalties for possessing a firearm in one of the megacities were far greater than anything else short of murder.

In the colonies, things were different. Oh, on the Core worlds, it was still illegal to carry a gun in the city, but every farmer out in the sticks had a shotgun. And once you hit the Periphery, well, it was just best to assume that everyone you met had a gun on them somewhere. And in the Pirate Worlds, they would probably have a rifle hanging off their shoulder in the middle of dinner. Here, not so much, but it was still enough to make me watch every wandering tourist and miner, checking their jackets for tell-tale bulges.

"Is food all you ever think about?" Vicky asked. "Every time we touch ground anywhere, you make straight for the nearest restaurant."

"One thing I learned in the Corps is to never turn down a chance at real food." I shot her a grin. "You're just too used to the soy and spirulina shit that the government handed out in the Underground...and the Marines."

"Or maybe you just got spoiled with fresh meat and vegetables every day back on the farm. You liked the fringe benefits of farm life, just not the hard work."

She was teasing, but it did strike a nerve.

"I didn't mind the work," I protested. "It was kind of soothing, even. But after a while, it felt too much like being retired. And I'm not ready to retire."

"Obviously."

Perfection might have had a proper spaceport, but the town itself wasn't that different from any other small-time colony. It was laid out before us like a checkerboard on the rise stretching out from the plain of the spaceport, the largest building a huge apartment bloc looming eight stories tall in the center of town. I'd seen the like before, a communal living space for the miners. Farmers and ranchers were spread out on colony worlds, but miners always packed together to save money on transportation, climate conditioning and construction. It was more convenient, too. If you needed a doctor, the clinic wasn't dozens of kilometers away, they were just down the elevator. If you wanted to go into town, it was a ten-minute walk instead of a two-hour drive.

I couldn't have lived that way, not anymore. It was too much like the life I'd left behind. But it did make the layout of the city easier to reach. Lots of places, we'd have had to hire a taxi or hop a bus out of the spaceport to get to the downtown area, but in Perfection, it was a short walk, albeit uphill. As much time as we'd spent on spaceships lately, I didn't mind it.

The streets weren't labelled, nor did they have transponders for the mapping functions on our 'links, so we had to stop and ask for directions twice, which went against the grain. Thankfully, Vicky was there to do it because I would probably have kept wandering for an hour, searching through the exterior signs for stores and signs until I saw Betty's.

The streets weren't crowded and I saw very few spacers, far less than most colony worlds. Probably because of what the Traffic Control had told us, that they had an exclusive contract for taking out the ore. That meant that the only freighters coming in would be unloading, cutting their traffic in half. Lots of locals, though, most of them wearing work clothes, which I thought was unusual since it was afternoon, until I realized they likely worked round the clock on shifts.

None of the other buildings were taller than two stories, but they lacked some of the homey, hand-built character I remembered from Hausos. Instead, everything here had the appearance of being thrown up quickly and cheaply and patched over with plaster.

Betty's Café was no different, cement block covered with stucco and painted a forest green that matched the pines outside the town, a mural hand-painted across the front wall showing a bear—a grizzly, I thought, though I wasn't an expert—holding a flag with a mountain emblazoned on it. The same flag flew from a thirty-meter poll in the courtyard of the communal apartment building and I gathered it was the colony's symbol.

"Weird," I said, nodding toward it as I hesitated by the front door of the place. "I don't ever remember a colony with its own flag before. Not even out in the Pirate Worlds."

"I don't ever remember a colony telling the Corporate Council to go fuck itself either," she pointed out. "Come on, let's go get you a steak."

If the city was unique in some ways, the interior of Betty's Café wasn't one of them. It was every family-run diner on every colony world I'd ever visited, during and after the war. The tables weren't plastic because plastic required petrochemicals and a production plant or else it had to be shipped in as interstellar cargo, which would have been cost-prohibitive. They were wood, as were the chairs, because it cost nothing but time and effort to cut down a tree. The counter was polished granite, something else that was next to free. On Earth, it would have been the worst sort of conspicuous consumption, insane opulence you'd expect to see from the President of the Commonwealth or one of the Corporate Council executives in their vacation homes outside the megacities where they could pretend they were living in a bygone age and there'd been no nuclear war and environmental crisis and people could just take whatever they wanted from the Earth without repercussions.

No, no, I'm not bitter or anything.

It was about halfway between lunch and dinner local time and the flashing sign just inside the door invited us to seat ourselves, so we picked a booth in the corner, where we could see the door, and both sat with our backs against the wall. When the waitress came to our table, she eyed us beneath a tilted brow.

"You two waiting for someone else?" she asked.

"No, ma'am," I assured her. I grabbed Vicky's hand and held our intertwined fingers up demonstratively. "Just newlyweds."

Vicky snorted a laugh, but soft enough I doubted the other woman heard it. The waitress shrugged, flipped a foldable tablet over in her hand and pointed at the menu displayed on the wall beside our table.

"You two know what you want?"

"If he knew what he wanted," Vicky murmured, "we'd probably be back on our farm."

I nudged her knee with mine, trying to ignore the jab.

"I want a steak," I told her. "T-bone, or the closest thing you have to it. Medium, with a baked potato and a vegetable salad."

"I'll have the roast pork," Vicky decided, jabbing a thumb at the menu. "With rice and beans, please."

"Oh, and Keith sent us," I said, remembering the bearded customs agent.

"Did he?" the waitress asked, scowling. "Well, I'll let you eat here anyway because we're not busy, but I can't guarantee no one'll spit in your food."

She stalked off and I sat back against the wooden slats of the seat.

"I never thought I'd miss remote ordering and robot waiters."

"No way they'd have them out here," Vicky said with a shrug. "Not when people are so much cheaper than robotics."

"We've always been expendable."

She didn't reply, but I knew she was reliving the same memories that I was, seeing the faces of our brothers and sisters who hadn't made it through. I'd watched movies where veterans of the war would be filled with guilt over the enemy they'd killed, but that was bullshit. I never lost a minute's sleep over any of the Tahni I'd killed during the war, and if I was being honest, not one of the humans I'd killed since. If they hadn't wanted me to kill them, they shouldn't have been shooting at me.

No, the nightmares that woke me up at night, that had driven me to drink more than was healthy, were about the people I hadn't been able to save. It had gotten better since I'd started operating again, but I was sure it would never go away completely no matter if I lived to be five hundred years old.

"Steak medium." The waitress smacked the plate against the table as if it owed her money. "Pork roast."

"Where's my...." I let the words trail off as the waitress stalked off again. "...salad?"

"Whoever this asshole Keith is," Vicky said, slicing off a bit of pork, "I think it's safe to say Betty is no fan of his."

"Remind me to keep my mouth shut next time," I sighed.

"I always do, but you never listen."

"At least the steak's good."

"I always eat here myself when I'm in town."

I hadn't heard the footsteps and given the man's size, that was quite the testament to how quietly he moved. He was nearly two meters tall and a good one hundred kilos, most of it muscle. The stains on his coveralls and the callouses on his hands spoke of a working man, but there was something about his chiseled features and the set of his grey eyes said that he was in charge.

He stepped forward, looming over us and I fought back an urge to pull my gun, knowing it was too late for that.

"I'm Pavel Konigsberg," he said. "I understand you're looking for me."

[6]

"I'm Cam Alvarez," I said, finally gathering my wits together, raising from my seat to offer the man a hand. His grip was firm without being crushing, and I sensed he was a man who had no need for such dick-measuring contests because he already knew he was the biggest dick in the room. "This is my wife and business partner, Vicky Sandoval. Our freighter, the *Yantar*, is in orbit with the rest of the crew."

"What?" Konigsberg asked, arching an eyebrow. "They weren't interested in shore leave and a good meal?"

"Eventually," I told him, using the line I'd rehearsed. "But when we're making a new deal, we like to come down first and introduce ourselves." I smiled. "Some of our guys don't get off the ship too often and I didn't want them getting wasted and starting a fight in one of your finest bars to be the first impression you had of us."

"A smart businessman," Konigsberg said with a nod. He waved at the door. "Look, if you want to make your pitch, we're gonna have to walk and talk. I have to get back to the smelter. We got an unscheduled service going on and I have to be there for the restart in case anything goes wrong."

"Sure," I said. "Let me just pay for our meal."

"Don't worry about it," he assured me, then motioned to our waitress. "Ronnie, their dinner is on me, okay?"

"Anything you say, Mr. Konigsberg," the woman waved at him, smiling broadly. Either the man was popular here or she was scared shitless of him, and also scared shitless of showing she was scared shitless. I was hoping it was the former.

We had to jog to keep up with his long strides and for once, I actually wished I was taller, something that had never occurred to me when I was in a battlesuit. The streets were more crowded than when we'd entered the restaurant, foot traffic so dense I was sure there had to be a shift change going on at the mines.

They all parted for Konigsberg, though, most of them with nods of deference. And appreciation. I thought I was a good enough judge of people at this point in my life to be able to tell when respect was being feigned, and even if someone with a good poker face might have been able to fake it convincingly, a whole town's worth of people wouldn't have been able to manage it. The man had popular support, which killed the first idea I'd come up with when I'd read the mission brief. I definitely wasn't going to be able to incite some sort of worker's uprising against the man.

"Where are you two from?" Konigsberg asked, his voice booming over the buzz and bustle of the street.

"Earth," I told him. "The cities. The Underground." I had to project the words to make sure he heard, and I missed a step and had to jog again to catch up to his unrelenting pace. "How about you?"

The truth was, I knew where the man was from since I'd read his file, but I couldn't let that on, and it was a natural response. Plus, I figured maybe if I got him talking, he might slow the hell down so I could catch my breath. I was a Drop Trooper, not Force Recon.

"Oh, I'm from back on the dirty blue basketball myself," Konigsberg admitted. "New Brussels Development Corridor." He chuckled. "Not from the Underground, though. My parents were mid-level Corporate Council Project Managers. But that was a hell of a long time ago."

"Must have been nice," I mused. Both to be middle-class and to have living parents, though I didn't specify.

"It had its drawbacks," he told me.

I would have asked what those were, but then we were walking up a hill so steep it was all I could do to keep up the step-and-a-half it took to match one of his. Even Vicky was huffing and puffing, though she took conditioning more seriously than I did. We were heading perpendicular to the apartment building, up into the hills and panic surged in my chest at the thought we might be walking all the way up to the mines, because there was no way I could keep up this pace for that long.

The trams dispelled that notion and relief replaced the panic. They were nothing fancy, just sheet metal boxes with metal benches inside, two of them running side by side on a pair of single tracks heading up the hill toward the mines. The hum of electrical motors was almost drowned out by the clack of the rollers in the tracks, and I guessed they were centrally powered from lines running either through or beneath the rails. It was a surprisingly centralized and efficient method of transport for a Periphery colony, but I wasn't complaining.

I thought Konigsberg might command his own personal car, but we sat down on a bench at the back, just two rows from a cluster of miners in grey jumpsuits. They all greeted the big man politely but then went back to a bawdy conversation about the night the four of them had spent in town on their last weekend off.

I shut them out, trying to get the lay of the land. It was a good five kilometers up to the refinery from town, and another five or six past that to the mines. They were scars on the mountain, gouges and pockmarks from heavy, automated digging machines creating new saddles and valleys and passes where they broke the rock down and crushed it to powder.

"That's some set-up you have here," I said, trying to keep my expression neutral, not letting the vague sense of distaste the place gave me show through.

"Isn't it?" Konigsberg agreed, pride unmistakable in his voice and the gleam in his eyes when he stared at the mine. "I tell you what, I could search for a thousand years and not find a place like this." He slipped into a didactic tone, like he was lecturing a classroom. "You know, rhenium is one of the few elements you just can't find in most asteroid fields. It's created by volcanic activity, and even then, only as a byproduct of other elements...copper, for instance. That's what we have here." He gestured upward at the mines. "Bunch of extinct volcanoes. All we gotta do is tear down that mountain a bit at a time and run it through the refinery and boom! One of the rarest elements in the galaxy filling up our train cars and our cargo birds and we're all fucking rich. That's what makes it perfect for an operation like this. No massive investment in ships or space habitats, no overhead costs for life support, no constant importation of food and water. It's all on a habitable planet with arable land." He snorted. "Habitable? Hell, it's *beautiful* here. I'd fucking pay to live here."

"Does it bother you at all?" I blurted the question before I could suppress it. Vicky kicked me in the ankle, but it was too late. At Konigsberg's confused frown, I went on. "I mean, like you say, this place is beautiful and you're kind of, you know, grinding it down to the nub. Does that ever make you feel bad?"

"I'll tell you what, if this was back on Earth, it might," he admitted, answering quickly enough that I was sure he'd given the question some thought before I'd ever asked it. "But worlds like this are all over the Cluster, and the government...." He mashed the word together, pronouncing it like *gummint*. "...has already turned most of the Core worlds into fucking nature preserves where you can't cut down a tree or turn over a Goddamned rock. And this...." He motioned out the window of the tram toward the mountain. "...ain't nothing compared to what the Corporate Council does to any world they get their greedy little hands on. I seen some things...." He shook himself like a dog getting excess water out of its fur. "Anyway, you wanted to make your pitch, so now's the time."

I glanced at Vicky. We'd rehearsed this whole spiel on the ship and had agreed that she was better at it than I was.

"Mr. Konigsberg," she said, launching into it with the enthusiasm of a budding entrepreneur, "we're partners in Semper Fi LLC, a shipping start-up owned and managed by veterans. Together with the rest of the crew, we jointly own the freighter *Yantar* outright and if we can get a steady business going out here, we have other freighter crews who've committed to join the company as contractors."

"That's wonderful," Konigsberg said, not quite sarcastic or snarky but definitely in the same neighborhood. "What does it have to do with me?"

"It has to do with your rhenium mine, sir. You have one of the very few independent rhenium refinement facilities in the whole Commonwealth, and we have a buyer who'll pay top dollar for as much of it as you're willing to sell."

The big man eyed her with a skeptical sidelong look.

"I already have a buyer who pays very well for everything we can produce."

"We'll top it," I interjected, putting a hand over my heart as if making a promise. "I guarantee it. And if we need to start small and work our way up as you increase production, we'll take whatever we can get. Our buyer is *very* eager to establish a relationship, not just for what they can get now but for future considerations."

"Are they now?" Konigsberg crossed his arms over his chest and settled back like he was setting in to watch a show. "They sound almost too good to be true. I don't suppose you'd care to be telling me who this mysterious buyer is, would you?"

I smiled, imitating a naïve beginner thinking he was being sly.

"No offense, Mr. Konigsberg, but if we tell you who it is, you could just go make this deal yourself and cut us out. Not that we mistrust you, but we don't really know each other yet." I shrugged. "Of course, if you want to have some quid pro quo, we'll tell you who our buyer is if you tell us who your current buyer is. That seems like a good way to build trust." And a good way for us to find out what this whole thing was really about, which was the whole point of this subterfuge.

"An interesting idea, Mr. Alvarez, Ms. Sandoval. But my client values discretion above anything and I'm sure I'd have to get their permission before I shared any of their information with an outsider." He waved the idea away. "But tell me, what's the advantage to me? I mean, I have a reliable customer, no problems, pays on time every time. Why do I need *your* business?"

"You have a reliable customer *now*," Vicky pointed out. "Nothing lasts forever. Do you really want to put all your eggs in one basket? If anything goes wrong, well...rhenium will always sell, but how many months will you be looking at no new income?"

I saw where she was going with the line of the argument and I took it up.

"We saw those mercenaries you have working for you. They don't look cheap. Not if they're good enough to keep out the Corporate Security Force. You think they'll stick around if you can't pay them for two or three months?"

Konigsberg stared at me through slitted eyes, silent for a few seconds longer than I was comfortable with.

"You seem very well informed."

"We wouldn't have come here to make a deal with you," Vicky pointed out, "unless we'd done our due diligence first. That would be an insult to you."

"We aren't coming empty-handed, either," I added, deciding now was the right time to spring it on him. I fished the dataspike out of my pocket and reached it across the row to him. "Fifty thousand in Corporate scrip. A token of esteem from our buyer." In reality, it was the entirety of our discretionary fund from Dukanovic, but what she didn't know wouldn't hurt her.

Konigsberg took the crystalline data-storage lattice from me, tossing it up and down in his hand casually, like it wasn't more money than most people would make in ten years.

"Contingent on me accepting the deal, I suppose?"

"That would be very unprofessional of us," Vicky told him. "The funds are a gift, to show how serious we are about this deal."

He tilted his head to the side, as if trying to look at the dataspike and us from a different angle.

"Well, now, that's one nice gift. You could just about buy another starship with this spike."

"Without this deal," I said, "we won't be able to keep the one we have running. And if we steal our client's money, we'll never be able to do anything but tramp loads or smuggling." I shrugged. "It's hard enough to make a living as an honest trader with the Corporate Council trying to freeze all the independents out."

The words came naturally enough, just like I'd practiced, but they tasted sour on the way out. I was, I told myself, helping the man. If I hadn't come down here and lied to him, the alternative would have been to drop down in force and blow up his shit, and if I'd refused, Martz would surely have done it. But it felt wrong. This wasn't the life I wanted to be leading.

Konigsberg nodded and slipped the dataspike into his breast pocket.

"I appreciate that," he said. "I can't guarantee anything, not until I sit down and run the numbers. We put out pretty much the maximum we can currently manage right now, so to squeeze out any extra is going to take some infrastructure investment." He grinned. "It's all fine and good to talk about expanding our distribution, but if I drop major investment into pumping out more supply and your buyer flakes off, well...like you said, those mercs want to get paid. And they have the guns." He shrugged. "Most of the guns."

"I understand. How long do you need?"

He closed his eyes, and for a moment I thought I'd offended him with the question, but something about his expression told me he was concentrating, calculating.

"Give me till tomorrow morning. I should be able to give you an answer by then, barring some unforeseen problem with the restart."

The tram stopped and I abruptly realized we'd arrived at the refinery. I'd been so wrapped up in our negotiation with Konigsberg that I hadn't been paying attention to the changing scenery outside. The facility was cyclopean, carved into the hillside and built from giant blocks of granite, the ramps leading to the train tracks slabs ten meters across. It looked impossible, the work of ancient gods, the way the pyramids had seemed to later generations stumbling across them the first time. But like the Egyptian pyramids, the reality was that this was the easiest way to build a facility this large when you had unlimited fusion power and plenty of granite to work with.

"You're welcome to come on in and observe the restart," the big man invited, grabbing one of the vertical supports and pulling himself to his feet. "It's pretty dry work unless something goes wrong, but you did ride up all this way...."

I looked to Vicky and she shrugged assent.

"Sure," I said, standing and following him to the tram's exit. "It'll give us an idea of your production capabilities."

Which was happy horseshit. What it would really give us an idea of was what kind of man we were dealing with. And more importantly, it would help me put off having to decide what the hell I was going to do.

———

"Boss!" the fat man bellowed as we walked into the control room. "I was wondering when you were going to haul your lazy ass up the mountain! What? You get tied up counting your money and forget about us poor working stiffs?"

I stared at the man for a beat, trying to get a read on him. His face was jowly and florid, his beard bushy and shot with grey and he was bald. Not with a depilated head the way some people chose out of a sense of fashion, but with hair that thinned out the farther up it went. And I hadn't seen his like since I'd left Tijuana. Oh, there were people in the Pirate Worlds who hadn't gotten the anti-aging treatments handed out like candy to Earthers, even in the Underground, or in the inner colony worlds, but they weren't fat. Almost no one got fat in the

Pirate Worlds. And no one got fat by accident in the Commonwealth, not when most people's genes were tinkered with before birth and for those who hadn't, there were easy treatments to lose unwanted weight.

There'd been times and places when intentional obesity had been a style among a certain class of people, but it had gone out of fashion well before I was born. And I had the sense just from looking at the man that he wasn't making a statement, that this was just who he was. Sitting behind a station in the reactor's control room, he nearly overwhelmed the leather-wrapped seat, but his fingers were dancing across touch screens even as he shot us a leer.

"And who are your friends?" he asked. "You already trying to replace me?"

"Cam, Vicky," Konigsberg introduced, seemingly unoffended by the man's irreverence, "this is Oscar Wendt, the biggest pain in the ass on the whole planet." His smile seemed genuine, just like everything else about the man. "And my best reactor tech, unfortunately. He can afford to treat us all like shit because he knows we can't replace him."

"And you're wondering," Oscar said, his brown eyes boring into us, "what the hell is with me, aren't you?"

"I...," I stuttered, at a total loss for words. Vicky didn't even try.

"Don't worry about it." Oscar made a sound that might have been a snorting laugh or possibly he was choking to death. "Everyone asks eventually. It's genetics, nothing to be done about it."

"Okay," I said, and would have been happy to let it die there, but he went on as if I hadn't spoken.

"I was born on Thunderhead in the Pirate Worlds, no fancy prenatal gene selection there, but plenty of background radiation. My parents managed to scrape together enough money for passage out, but the only place I could get a full genetic makeover is back in the Core colonies and I'm not on the citizenship roles."

"I keep telling you, Oscar," Konigsberg insisted, "we are going to get that equipment out here. Another year or two of production and we'll have the jack to pull in a fully equipped med lab."

"Yeah, yeah, I ain't holding my breath, mostly because I'd probably pass out."

"What's the status on the restart?"

The question seemed to shift Oscar's gears from bluff and bullshitting to business and he swiped his fingers over a holographic display, sending an image streaming across to the main screen on the back wall. A few heads turned but the other workers and technicians went back to their tasks when they saw what it was. I didn't even know enough to be disinterested in it. It was some sort of technical projection, that was all I could tell.

"Everything's by the numbers so far," Oscar said, and I had to take his word for it. "Ready for ignition whenever you give the word."

"And the slag buildup didn't weaken the shielding?"

"Well, if it did, we'll be the first to find out."

Konigsberg rolled his eyes and slapped the fat man on the shoulder.

"Okay, Oscar, get it started. I'll stand over here and try to look like I know what I'm doing."

"Yes, sir, boss. I'll do my best to make you look good, as usual."

"Tell me something," I said to Konigsberg after he'd stepped away to let the technicians do their work, "you were in the Marines, right?"

Vicky nudged me in a silent warning not to go there, but it was too late.

"I was," the big man said, chuckling. "A hell of a long time ago. Long before this last ugly business." The smile ran away from his face at the memory. "Back during a war that might have even been uglier, if you can believe it."

I did. What I'd heard about the Pirate Wars from Captain Covington wasn't pretty. The Belt Pirates and every other bandit and outlaw in the Commonwealth had banded together in an attempt to seize the Periphery colonies for their own. They'd believed themselves justified, believed they deserved a home among the new worlds we'd discovered. Maybe they were right, but the Commonwealth government didn't see it that way.

"How'd you end up in mining, then?"

"Well, that's a long story, but the short version is, I mustered out and came home and found out my marriage had fallen apart while I was busy killing bad guys. I couldn't go back into the Corps and I didn't want to stay there, so I signed up for a Corporate Council apprenticeship at a mining facility." A derisive snort. "I hated it. Couldn't get out of there fast enough. But I learned what I needed to know."

He glanced over at me, eyes darting in a familiar way, the way I'd seen from so many others. He was looking at my implanted interface jacks.

"You were Drop Troopers, right?"

"We were," Vicky confirmed.

"Didn't have those battlesuits when I was in. We had powered exoskeletons for our line Marines, kind of like what the Tahni had with their Shock Troopers. I was in Force Recon. Same then as it is now, what we could carry on our back."

"Some people believe," I said, treading carefully, but needing to know the man, "that the Belt Pirates got a raw deal in the war. That they were screwed by the Corporate Council, forced out of their mining claims and given no other choice except either working for the Council mines or going outlaw. What did you think?"

He regarded me with a cool, neutral expression.

"Some people believe," he countered, "that the second war with the Tahni would never have happened if it hadn't been for the squatter colonies. And that the squatters wouldn't have had the Transition drive ships to get there if it wasn't for the fact that the Corporate Council decided it was more profitable to sell those ships on the open market instead of keeping them under government control. What do you think about the Tahni, Cam?"

I shrugged.

"No one thinks they're the bad guys in a war. Whether they're human or Tahni. You can get someone to kill for money, or status, or power...but you can only convince them to die if they think they have God on their side. Whatever version of God they believe in. But when the first shots are fired, it doesn't matter who's right, it only matters who's left. But there was a guy named Hemingway I read once, a guy who wrote way back in the early Twentieth Century. And he had it right. 'Once we have a war, there is only one thing left to do. It must be won. For defeat brings worse things than any that can ever happen in war.' The Tahni might have gotten screwed, but someone was gonna win and someone was gonna lose."

"Then I guess that's how I feel about the Belt Pirates. They tried to take something for their own, something they thought they deserved. It didn't work out so well for them." He grinned lopsidedly. "I'm hoping it works out a bit better for us."

Green lights flickered across the control panel, drawing Konigsberg's attention away.

"Aw right!" Oscar crowed, hands going up in a touchdown motion. "We have restart! And nobody got blowed up or irradiated!" It all seemed a bit anticlimactic to me, but what did I know about fusion reactors?

"Awesome. Get the scoops running again and have the techs power up the electromagnetic filters. I expect us to be back at target output by this time tomorrow." Konigsberg turned back to us, spreading his hands apologetically. "Sorry, duty calls. Can you two find your way back to the city or should I have one of our people escort you to the tram?"

"We'll be fine," Vicky assured him. "Thanks for hearing us out."

"We look forward to hearing your decision," I added.

"Yeah," Konigsberg said, laughing softly, waving to us as he turned to head off deeper into the facility. "I do, too."

[7]

"I like him," Vicky said as we stepped off the tram back in Perfection.

"I do, too," I admitted. "And it worries the hell out of me."

Twilight had deepened into full night by the time we reached the town, and, for all the modernity and high-end amenities of Perfection, adequate street lighting apparently wasn't one of their priorities. I had come prepared this time, though, having learned my lesson the last time we wound up on a small colony without our suits, and I slipped a pair of night vision glasses out of my jacket pocket and put them on. They were commercial models, not military, which meant they wouldn't synch up with the sights of my pistol or act as a rangefinder, but at least I wasn't tripping over my feet on the way out of the tram. Vicky, of course, had hers on already.

"Yeah," she agreed. "This would all be a hell of a lot easier if Konigsberg was a dickhead and all his people hated him."

The night vision filters in the glasses weren't quite up to the level of the ones in my Vigilante, mostly because the battlesuit had room for a much more sophisticated and powerful computer system to run the imaging software. The imagining system in the Vigilante could make an overcast night look like noonday, but the through the glasses, it could have been twilight except for an unnatural green tint to the light, and everything had a flat, artificial quality to it, like I was a step removed from reality.

"You know, something about this doesn't make any sense," Vicky said, shaking her head.

"Just one thing?" I snorted.

"The rhenium. Who the hell would be buying this much of it? Besides our fictional patron, that is."

"From what I researched on it during the trip," I said, "it's used in almost every piece of military equipment, from Gauss rifles all the way up to Transition drives. Who *wouldn't* want it?"

She sighed in what I took for exasperation.

"In that sort of quantity? I mean, the military isn't buying it because they buy their equipment already assembled from the Corporate Council. And the Corporate Council isn't buying it because that's why we're fucking here. So, who else is trying to build a fleet of ships? Because that's the only reason you'd need this much rhenium. There's no industrial project you'd use it on this big of a scale."

"The cartels," I suggested. "Maybe one of them is trying to build their own fleet, get a leg up on the others."

Vicky went quiet, her frown thoughtful, and I scanned around us carefully, not wanting to get so wrapped up in the conversation that I let my guard down. There wasn't much traffic on the street at this hour, probably because the shift change, and dinner had both passed, and tomorrow was a normal workday. The businesses we'd walked by earlier were closed now, even the restaurant where we'd eaten. The only places I saw with lights on were bars and brothels and I was a bit surprised they had the latter here. Not that the oldest profession didn't follow humans wherever they went, but Konigsberg had struck me as a no-nonsense, all-business type interested in efficiency and keeping everything running smoothly. Brothels usually invited organized crime, not at first but eventually, because there were never enough people available to do the job willingly to meet the demand.

"It can't be the cartels," she decided. "For a couple reasons. First, there's no reason for it. None of the cartels has anything resembling a real warship. Maybe a lighter."

"A lighter what?" I wondered, which earned me a scowl.

"A lighter is a converted freighter. Something like the *Yantar*, but designed for battle with makeshift armor and weapons jammed into it. That's all I've ever heard of the cartels having. They wouldn't *need* a whole fleet to overwhelm the others, just one or two dedicated warships. And for the other reason, there's no way they could get together the techs and the machinery to build a fleet without the other cartels hearing about it and teaming up to pound them down."

"Then who?" I asked, throwing up my hands.

"Exactly. And maybe it doesn't matter, maybe it's totally unrelated to why we're here, but do you really believe that?"

"No. The Corporates don't do anything by accident."

"What are you going to do," Vicky asked me, "if he says yes to this proposition? Because I hate to break it to you, but we do *not* own a small shipping company and unless you're holding out on me, between us, we maybe have enough to buy one load of rhenium and I don't know what the hell we'd do with it."

"Oh, I like that," I said, shooting her a baleful glare. "What am *I* going to do if he says yes. Like this was all my idea and you didn't contribute at all."

She laughed and pushed at my shoulder.

"Well, you're the one Dukanovic put in charge. You're always the man with the plan. And better you than me."

"Shit."

I ran a hand through my hair. I needed to get it cut. Not that I looked like a dirty hippy or anything, but now that I was back in the saddle of a Vigilante, I liked to keep my 'face jacks clear. My hair was straight, like my mother's. My brother Anton had curly hair, like Dad. I'd always envied him when I was little, though I couldn't honestly remember why.

"Okay," I said, walking as I talked, "what we do is, when we hear back from him, if he says no, we tell him that we're up shit creek because we're out that money, and we ask him for an intro to the mercs, to see if they're hiring. That way, we can get a read on them, find out how well organized they are. If he says yes...."

This was the hard part. Because honest to God, there was part of me that kind of wanted to blow off Fleet Intelligence and the CSF and just go haul fucking rhenium for Konigsberg. It would be less boring than farming and have fewer moral conundrums than my current profession.

"If he says yes," I went on, my mouth working only a half-second behind my brain, "then maybe we have to consider taking the load of rhenium on board and taking it back to Dukanovic along with a counter-offer. Maybe if we point out to her and that stuck-up, vapid asshole Wellesley that they can still have their rhenium for just a little more than it would cost to build their own mine and ship in their own people, they'll pull their heads out of their asses and try to act like real human beings for once."

She cocked an eyebrow at me, skepticism written all over her expression.

"Seriously? Your plan is to try to convince Corporate Security Force executives to act like human beings?"

"You're right," I admitted, putting a hand to my head as if it was about to explode. "Okay, then how about this, if we...."

I'd lost track of where we were, knowing only that we were

headed in the right direction to get back to the spaceport and our shuttle. I only knew we were walking through a section of shops closed for the night when I caught the motion out of the corner of my eye, somewhere in one of the narrow alleys between buildings. I didn't think much of it until I noticed the four tall, burly figures coming up the street toward us.

They shouldn't have been. I might have been distracted, but not so distracted that I would have missed a cluster of four people coming all the way from the other end of the street, a good kilometer straight down the boulevard downhill from us. No, they had to have cut over from another street just to get right there in front of us and I couldn't think that was a coincidence.

And they'd done it at just the right time. There was no side street, no alleyway for us to retreat into, which just left behind us.

"Vicky," I said softly, my hand going under my jacket, feeling for the hard polymer of my pistol.

"I see it."

I skidded to a halt and turned back the way we'd come...and stopped again. Behind us were four more dark, bulky figures, closer this time but still fuzzy and imprecise. It took me a second to realize they were wearing camouflage body armor, designed to be hard to pick up on infrared and thermal. Their features were blank singularities of darkness, the featureless visors of combat helmets, and each of them carried a rifle at high port and suddenly, my handgun seemed incredibly inadequate.

I touched Vicky's arm and shook my head, letting my hand fall away from my weapon. We weren't going to shoot our way out of this one.

"Who are you?" I asked. It was an unnecessary question, but one I had to ask to keep up appearances. "What do you want? We don't have any money on us."

"You need to come with us." The voice was robotic, stilted, filtered through the external speakers of the helmet, and I couldn't even be sure which of them was speaking. I knew that every single one of those rifle muzzles was pointing straight at us, though.

"Who are you?" I asked again. It was inevitable that we were either going to do what they said or die, but I didn't want to give in too easily. That held a danger all its own, as I'd found out when I was a kid in the homes.

The one who'd spoken stepped up closer, the bore of his rifle only a few centimeters from my face. This close, I could see that it was a Gauss rifle, which was high-end equipment for mercs. The electromagnets running along the inside of the barrel were like an inside-out nautilus shell, and the slug it shot was big and fast enough to turn my head into a red mist. He reached under my jacket and pulled out my handgun, tossing it back to one of the troopers behind him, then did the same with Vicky.

I didn't hear the vehicle until it was nearly on top of us. It was electric, which was unusual for a Periphery colony, where most of the trucks and personal vehicles were fabricated from old designs to run on alcohol or methane. But then, this wasn't a truck. It was an armored personnel carrier, the like of which I'd seen in the Marine museum on Inferno, though never in battle. They hadn't been used since the Pirate Wars and not much then. The thing was lozenge-shaped, six-wheeled with an electric motor inside each axle, a coil-gun turret riding heavy at the rear while missile launch pods hugged the sides and it certainly brooked no arguments.

It rumbled to a stop in the street behind us and the side door swung downward, forming a staircase. The light inside was dim, but it seemed as bright as day compared to the darkness of the city.

"Get in," the mercenary ordered, apparently not inclined to answer my questions.

I shared a look and a shrug of resignation with Vicky and ducked into the troop compartment of the vehicle. A single, unarmored soldier waited inside, his face squared off and humorless, a pistol in his hand pointed at us. He waved us wordlessly into a bench seat against the right-hand hull and we sat. The bench was hard, unyielding, built for troops in armor and not my decidedly unarmored ass.

The rest of the mercenaries filed in behind us, their boots clomping hollow on the metal decking, and the one who'd taken our weapons sat down across from us. I knew it was him because of the E6 sergeant's chevrons on the chest plate of his armor. He lifted his helmet's visor, revealing a rounded, soft face that didn't match his hard, businesslike voice or the harsh, blue eyes staring us down.

"You want to know who we are?" he asked as the door shut with a metallic finality. The car lurched away, carrying us to an unknown fate. "We're Extreme Measures PMC. And what I want from you is for you to keep your fucking mouths shut until someone asks you a question." He nodded towards us. "You understand?"

"I copy five by five," I assured him. Vicky nodded silently.

There was nothing to say, anyway. We were fucked.

———

I wasn't sure how long we were in the vehicle. Time drags when you're sitting on a hard, metal bench with guns pointed at you, not allowed to speak. But it was certainly longer than ten minutes and less than half an hour. The city wasn't that big, and I had the sense we weren't going towards the mines, which meant we were out past the spaceport. I couldn't really recall what was out there, if anything. I could have checked the maps I'd downloaded to my datalink, but I didn't imagine the unpleasant NCO across from us would have like me pulling out my 'link. And I had reasons for not reminding him that he hadn't taken it yet.

As long as it seemed to take, it still came as a surprise when we stopped. The car was well-maintained, but it was still decades old and jolted fitfully on its suspension when the driver hit the brakes. I had my feet planted solidly on the deck and still almost slid right into Vicky before the car rocked to a stop. The NCO didn't move until someone had worked the door open and the rest of the squad had disembarked. Only then did he motion for us to get out.

I still couldn't tell where we were, not only because of the darkness of the night but also from the glare of the spotlights pointing outward from the walls. They were local stone, but impressive for their height and thickness despite their primitive construction, three meters tall and probably a meter thick, solid enough to mount a coil-gun turret at each corner, right alongside the floodlights. The gate we'd come through wasn't stone, though. It was solid metal, though I couldn't tell if it was steel or tungsten or even something more sophisticated like BiPhase Carbide.

The bunker was definitely shaped from stone, the gaps filled in with sandbags. A pair of guards stood at the front door of the bunker, wearing the same powered exoskeletons I'd seen at the spaceport. I wondered why the troops who'd come to grab us hadn't been wearing it, but decided maybe it was just too big and cumbersome to fit into the APC. The rest of the squad milled around, as if they'd decided we weren't dangerous enough to need them to watch us, but they didn't especially want to go inside for fear someone would find them something to do.

I sniffed a silent laugh. Whatever else they were, they were still grunts.

"Inside," the sergeant instructed us, motioning with his rifle.

I didn't ask any questions, remembering his warning. The bunker's hardened, metal door was left open and we pushed through a black curtain hung across the doorway. The interior was divided into rooms by other curtains, most of them closed and inscrutable. One was being held open by a woman in a tank top and fatigue pants, her hair buzzed a centimeter off her scalp. She regarded us with the sort of curiosity she might have about a new species of bug that had crawled into the building right before she killed it. I looked past her, into the room and saw that it was some sort of bunkhouse. I imagined the others were probably the same.

Past them was a storage room, not concealed by curtains, just piled high with cargo containers. A couple were propped open, revealing spare magazines for Gauss rifles in one case and prepackaged meals in another. And on the other side of the storage chamber was a command post. It had the same look as every command post on every forward operating base I'd ever been at during the war, with prefab chairs and tables recycled over and over from one battle to another, and portable display screens hung on special, quick-takedown boards designed to hold them. The screens were tuned to what seemed to be security camera views of the spaceport, staring at our shuttle.

Seated at one of those prefab tables was a slender, narrow-shouldered man with almond skin and jet-black hair, his eyes as dark as the shadows of the night outside. Captain's bars in subdued gold decorated his shoulder epaulettes and a compact pistol rested high on his left hip, and I got the idea that one was as much a symbol of his authority as the other. He sat watching us in silence, trying, I supposed, to look menacing and I was thinking about asking if we were going to get on with this when a pair of heavy chairs were dragged into the room behind us with a scrape of metal on concrete.

The NCO pushed us down into them and another merc trooper grabbed my hands and pulled them back behind me, securing my wrists to the vertical slats of the chair back with zip ties. I tensed up instinctively, glancing over at Vicky, wanting to resist, to keep them from doing the same to her, but I forced myself to relax. We were unarmed and surrounded by armored mercenaries and all I'd accomplish by starting a fistfight was to get myself smacked in the head or maybe shot. Or maybe get *both* of us shot. I didn't try to pull away when they tied my ankles to the chair legs, despite the feeling of utter helplessness it gave me. Which was, I figured, the idea.

The captain still said nothing, his dark eyes boring into us, and I had a sense that he was daring us to speak first. This was a power game for him, and I could have given him what he wanted, smarted off to him and let him show how big of a man he was by smacking me around. It wouldn't be the first time. But making him uncomfortable, taking him away from what he wanted might be a better way to get him to spill some intell he didn't want to give away. I just sat there and stared back, keeping my face carefully neutral, hoping that Vicky would do the same.

She did not.

"What the fuck is this all about?" Vicky demanded. I glanced out the corner of my eye, saw her shooting the captain a fierce glare. I'd known her for a long time, knew her better than anyone else in my life, but I still couldn't tell if the glare was genuine or if she was just playing the game, sticking with her role. "We had a nice conversation with Mr. Konigsberg and made him a legitimate business proposition. Does he know what you're doing here? You *do* work for him, don't you?"

Okay, she's playing her role. Which is understandable, if a bit inconvenient because...

The mercenary officer was fast. One eyeblink, he was sitting motionless, and the next, he was up, his foot planted in the center of Vicky's chest, pushing her backward. She grunted as the breath went out of her, then again as her chair smacked against the concrete floor. I lurched forward, knowing I couldn't accomplish anything but trying to at least deflect his attention away from her. I didn't mind getting smacked around a little, but I was sure I wouldn't be able to handle the same thing happening to Vicky. My chair slid two centimeters at my surge against the zip ties, and then the captain's sidearm was out, its barrel just a hand's breadth away from my face.

I said nothing.

"You will not speak," the officer said, addressing Vicky though the barrel of his handgun didn't waver from my face, "unless spoken to. When I do ask you a question, I expect an immediate answer. Failure to comply with these rules will result in pain. Any attempt to resist will result in summary execution. Lest you think these threats are idle bluff, that I would not dare to do these things, I would remind you that Extreme Measures Private Military Company is the only armed military force on this God-forsaken ball of rock and dirt. There is no police force to speak of, there's no Commonwealth military presence, there's no Patrol cruiser stopping by to press charges." He shrugged and smiled thinly. "Theoretically, it would be possible for us to be charged and tried in a Patrol Circuit Court, but for that to happen, you'd have to be alive to press charges."

The NCO had moved behind Vicky and he hauled her up by the back of the chair, setting her back up in front of the officer. Her face was red, her breath coming harsh and heavy, but I didn't think she was badly hurt.

"I am Captain Dhoni, the commanding officer of this particular detachment of Extreme Measures. For you two, that means I am the arbiter of your life and death, whether legal, illegal or extra-legal. The difference will be no difference to the outcome of your situation, so you'd be best to abandon that train of thought. Am I clear?" He cocked his head toward us expectantly. "That was a question, so you may answer."

"Yes," I said immediately.

Vicky didn't speak at first and I glared at her, wondering if she was *trying* to get shot. Finally, she sighed.

"Yeah, it's clear." She still sounded resentful, and this time, I was sure it was real.

"Wonderful," Dhoni said, sliding his pistol back into its holster. "Then let's get down to business. I want to know who you are and who you work for."

I didn't give Vicky a chance to get recalcitrant. We'd already told this story once; the key was to just keep consistent.

"We told Mr. Konigsberg who we are," I said. "I'm Cam Alvarez and this is Vicky Sandoval. We're vets, both of us. We served in the Marines during the war, then we took our separation bonuses and bought into a shipping startup with some Fleet pilots. We're part owners of the *Yantar*, a freighter up in orbit. We came here to make Mr. Konigsberg an offer to sell a percentage of his rhenium output to a buyer we have lined up."

Dhoni sniffed a laugh, pacing back and forth in front of us, hands clasped behind his back.

"It would be easy to buy such a story. But I think it's far more likely that you're here as spies for the Corporate Council."

"Why the hell would the Corporate Council send us here to buy rhenium from you?" Vicky demanded.

Dhoni leaned in cat-quick and grabbed the arm of her chair, shaking it as if he was going to toss her backwards again.

"That does not sound like an answer. You do not ask me questions."

Vicky badly *wanted* to say something back, but she shut her mouth, staring daggers at him. Dhoni straightened and stepped back over to me, leaning in nose to nose.

"What are your partner's names? Quickly."

"Dunstan," I said instantly. "Kyler Dunstan. He's our pilot, former Fleet Attack Command missile cutter pilot. The crew chief and cargo handler is Ruthie Amendola. Copilot is Brad Foster. He's the minority owner, bought in for ten percent. That's everyone for now. We did have another Marine vet with us, a guy named Wade Cunningham, but we've been trying to make this work for a year and he couldn't wait anymore, so we bought him out."

"And that's it?" he asked, raising an eyebrow.

"That's all the owners," I insisted. "We have a few cargo handlers we hired for this trip in case things worked out, but they're gonna get dropped off after the job is over."

"Describe them for me."

I frowned, shook my head.

"Umm...Dunstan is tall, kind of long-ish hair and...."

"No." He scowled and made a "get on with it" motion. "Describe them as *people*."

I blinked, trying to figure out what he wanted. He was trying to trip us up, of course, but I was prepared for questions. I wasn't ready for the way he was whipsawing back and forth.

"Dunstan's an asshole," Vicky declared, surprising me. There was still resentment in her tone, but also the grudging cooperation from someone who'd been thoroughly intimidated. Which I *knew* was an act, because there wasn't much that could intimidate Vicky.

"Thinks he's God's gift to women and the best pilot in the Fleet, even though they didn't offer him a position after the war, just processed him out. He resents that and instead of admitting he just wasn't that good an officer, he blames it on them. Brad is a stick-up-his-ass type, by the book, not an ounce of imagination in his whole fucking body." She shrugged. "Ruthie's nice, but she's as boring as a safety lecture. Boring enough that she even makes me miss Wade, even though he was a huge oaf."

I stared at her in frank admiration, and I thought Dhoni was doing the same.

"All right," he said, and I thought I sensed disappointment in the words.

He'd *wanted* us to be spies. He wanted an excuse to kill someone. Mercenaries had a bad reputation, but I'd tried to go into things with an open mind, sure that there were hard-working, honest vets out there who couldn't fit into civilian society, kind of like me, who had turned to gun-for-hire work to make a living. They were probably good people, who wouldn't go along with anything they didn't believe in. This guy wasn't one of those. Captain Dhoni was one of the officers I'd met during the war who wanted the brass for the power it gave them over others, the kind everyone hated to serve under.

"I am prepared to believe you're who you say you are," Dhoni told us. "I just need to check on the company you're supposedly working for. Who are your buyers?"

"We signed a Non-Disclosure Agreement," I said. "If we reveal our buyers, the deal's off, and that won't just hurt us, it'll cost your boss a shitload of money."

"Oh, I think you can count on me to be entirely discreet in my investigation," Dhoni assured me, the smirk on his face giving me an idea of how sincere he was being.

"It's not up to us," I insisted. "Don't you understand, if we do this, we're done. We're finished. It's all over."

"Interesting choice of words," Dhoni leered. "Sgt. Reindl!"

"Yes, sir?" It was the NCO who had brought us here. At least I had a name for him now.

"If they don't answer my question to my satisfaction in the

next ten seconds, I want you to begin breaking things. Start with fingers and we'll work our way up. The woman first," he added. "I have an idea that Mr. Alvarez is a soft touch when it comes to his wife. She seems to be made of sterner stuff."

Reindl hesitated, and through his open visor, I thought I saw a flash of doubt in his eyes, but it wasn't enough to make him disobey orders.

"Yes, sir."

He walked behind Vicky and slung his rifle, fingers flexing as if he was loosening up for a workout.

"Have you even checked with Konigsberg?" I asked desperately. And it wasn't that I was afraid to give him a fake answer, it was more that I didn't have a good fake answer to give him. I'd been trying to think of one for several minutes now and I kept running into the same problem we'd had figuring out who Konigsberg's buyer was. None of them made any sense. "Have you asked him if he wants this? Because I can guarantee he doesn't."

"Go ahead, Reindl," Dhoni nodded to the NCO. "The fingers."

"No, wait!" I yelled, jerking against my restraints. "All right, it's a shell company! I mean, they wouldn't tell us who they really were, just a dummy corporation. But we checked it out, because we didn't trust they'd pay the balance for the load without knowing who we were dealing with." I winced, hoping he'd have less trouble believing this than Vicky had. "It's one of the cartels from the Pirate Worlds. We traced the funds to La Hondonada. It's the *La Sombra* cartel."

Now there was interest in Dhoni's face, belief.

"And what," he asked, "would *La Sombra* want with a load of rhenium?"

"The same as everyone else," I said. "They want to use it to build their own warships. They're tired of trying to squeeze territory from the other cartels. They want to take their own part of the pie here in the Periphery."

Dhoni nodded slowly.

"This," he said, "I can believe."

I let the breath I'd been holding escape in a sigh and slumped in my chair. Vicky was staring at me with doubt in her expression, probably because she thought it was a dumb story, but apparently, Dhoni had bought it.

"Unfortunately," the mercenary captain said, "now that I know exactly who you represent, well...." He spread his hands helplessly. "I am tasked with not only keeping Mr. Konigsberg's operations secure from current physical threats but from potential future ones as well. Right now, our sole concern is the Corporate Council. The Patrol won't bother with us way out here, and the last thing the military wants to do is clean up the Corporates' mess. So, we're in a good situation...unless we do something incredibly stupid like entering into a business relationship with a Pirate World cartel."

"Fine," I said, "just let us go and we'll take off and not bother you again. I wasn't really comfortable working for those guys anyway. We'll just go."

"Oh, I wish I could believe you, Mr. Alvarez." He said it as if he meant it, but there was an inhuman cold behind those eyes, the sort I'd seen in the faces of some of the worst killers in the gangs of the Trans-Angeles Underground.

"No, you don't," I told him, dropping the pretense, straightening in my chair. "You're looking for an excuse to kill us. You have been this whole time. You don't give a shit about Konigsberg or his business. And you probably don't much give a shit about this Extreme Measures outfit, either. I know you don't own it because if you did, you'd be worried about its reputation and you're not." My lip curled into a sneer. "You're not a soldier, you're a killer. That's why you're here."

Dhoni didn't seem to take offense. He stood straight, regarding me with cold detachment.

"You might be right, Mr. Alvarez. But in a few minutes, it will have ceased to matter to you. Right along with everything else."

"Do it here?" Reindl asked him.

"No, I don't want to have to clean up the mess. Take them to one of the old quarries outside town. That way, when Mr. Konigsberg asks me, I can tell him they were alive the last time I saw them, and I won't even be lying."

[8]

I didn't make a move when Reindl cut our zip ties, though I wanted to. But we were inside, surrounded by their people, and we wouldn't have made it three steps before someone shot us down. So, we acted resigned and accepting, allowing our hands to be re-fastened behind our backs. Vicky didn't speak and, from the glare she was giving me, I wasn't sure if she'd speak to me again even if we got out of this.

Yeah, I know. I panicked and went with the Pirate World story because I was afraid they'd hurt you.

I didn't look at her glare, though, tried not to look at anything, just kept my eyes downcast and played the defeated and condemned man heading for an inevitable execution as Reindl pushed us ahead of him toward the bunker exit. When we were outside, we'd have to make our move. It would be tough, but I'd done the old trick I'd learned as a kid, and flexed my wrists to create more space inside the flex cuffs. Theoretically, I should be able to yank my hands out, though I'd be leaving a little skin behind. I didn't know if Vicky had done the same and I couldn't count on her to have her hands free.

Just a few steps to the door and I tried to make the most of them, my thoughts churning.

The honest truth was, we had next to no chance in the courtyard. The walls were high, the guards alert, their weapons long-ranged with good night-vision optics. Our best hope, I realized, was to wait until we were in the vehicle and outside the walls. It was where this Sgt. Reindl would be the most alert, but he'd also have the least support.

Good, I had a plan. Now if I just had some way to pass it on to Vicky. I thought she'd come to the same conclusions I had, but then again, I'd thought that during the interrogation and it hadn't turned out to be the case. I tensed slightly when we passed through the door, knowing there was a chance she'd make a break for it and ready to back her play if she did.

But she didn't, and I hoped that meant she was waiting for a signal from me.

"You want the APC, Sarge?" one of the mercenary enlisted troops asked Reindl when he saw us emerging from the bunker. The private was younger than us, young enough that I wondered if he'd missed the war entirely, though I supposed it was possible that he'd enlisted for the final year or so of it.

"Naw," Reindl told him. "Just bring me around the rover."

The kid jogged off to retrieve the vehicle and Reindl looked between the two of us, not quite as hostile and merciless as when he'd grabbed us in town. He glanced around, and I thought he was making sure no one would overhear.

"Look," he said softly, leaning into us to keep anyone else from catching the words. "I'm sorry about this. I ain't got nothing against either of you and if it was up to me, I'd cut you both loose."

"It *is* up to you," Vicky hissed. "Take us out of here in your vehicle and let us go! We'll get in our shuttle and no one here will ever see us again!"

There was shame in his eyes, but not enough of it.

"I'm sorry. I need this job. It's my last chance. I got nothing else left."

"Shit man," I told him, trying to keep my voice down. Alerting anyone else that we were trying to subvert him would have just forced him to double down on killing us. "I know some people...guys in Fleet Personnel. I can get you back in the military if you want."

I was kind of lying. The only "people" I knew were Colonel Hachette and Top, and maybe they'd get him back in the military or maybe they wouldn't. But I'd lie every day and twice on Sunday to avoid a bullet to the back of the head and a one-way trip to a rock quarry.

"Ain't no way they're letting me back in the Corps. Not after what happened."

I was about to promise him the moon, but he took a step back from us and my gut dropped. We'd lost him. Vicky looked as if she was about to say something else, not ready to give up, but then the rover pulled up beside us, its ancient suspension creaking as the driver braked a bit too hard.

"You sure you know how to drive this thing, Garcia?" Reindl asked, pushing me forward and waving at Vicky with the barrel of his rifle. "I don't want to wind up turned over in a ditch somewhere."

"Oh, sure, Sarge!" the driver replied, motioning for him to get in. "I'm from Aphrodite and we got all kinds of manually operated cars there. My dad taught me how to drive when I was like twelve."

"At least it ain't been that long ago, then," the man murmured doubtfully. He yanked open the rear passenger's side door of the vehicle and nodded to us. "Get in you two before I get one of our boys in an exoskeleton to throw you in."

Vicky muttered curses at him as she awkwardly stepped up

onto the running board and fell shoulder-first into the seat, then scooted across before straightening up. I tried to learn from her example, hopping in, using momentum to make sure I was all the way inside the cab before I fell back against the seat. I kept my hands clasped together so I wouldn't give away how loose the cuffs were, enduring a faceplant against the hard plastic for the sake of maskirovka. The worst part wasn't the dull ache from hitting my cheek on the seat, it was the fact that it was sticky, and I didn't want to know from what.

Reindl scooted in beside us, which was disappointing. I'd hoped he'd make a rookie mistake and get into the front passenger's seat. Instead, his rifle muzzle was about a centimeter from my chest, and I began to worry his finger might stray too close to the trigger and if we hit a bump....

The rover wasn't as cutting-edge as their APC. It was a locally fabricated all-terrain vehicle fabricated from materials found here on Portent. An internal combustion engine growled beneath its hood when Garcia pushed down on the accelerator, probably fueled by alcohol distilled from the grain crops I'd seen from the air. Inefficient and probably a maintenance hog, but cheap, both to make and to fix. Gravel spat out from the rear tires as Garcia took us through the gate.

I squinted against the floodlights, formulating an estimate now that I'd seen the place from the outside. It was big enough to house about fifty troops and their gear and vehicles, no more. That wouldn't be the only Extreme Measures outpost on the planet, not even the only one in the city. I would have been willing to bet they had at least a hundred troops here, maybe twice that, if putting a nominal captain in charge of them meant anything except an empty rank and title.

I'd held out hope when we'd begun this clusterfuck that we could somehow get out of it without a fight, but after meeting Captain Dhoni, I wasn't so sanguine about that possibility.

Konigsberg seemed like a reasonable man, but Dhoni was not, and it wasn't at all a sure thing that Dhoni would go along with it if Konigsberg ordered him to stand down.

And, of course, there was the whole business of us trying not to die in the next few minutes.

"Turn right at the intersection," Reindl called up to the driver. "Then it's a straight shot for about twelve klicks."

There were taillights ahead of us on the gravel road, another vehicle far ahead, but I lost sight of them when they went over a rise. Aside from the one car, the road was deserted, and the only sign we weren't alone on the planet with the mercs was the glow coming off the mining facility in the far distance, up the mountain.

"We can pay you," I offered Reindl. It was useless, or at least I was fairly sure it was, and I was usually pretty good at reading people, but you miss one hundred percent of the shots you don't take and, if nothing else, it might help us to catch him off guard. "We have some discretionary funds we set aside for shit like fuel and food and equipment. Ten thousand in Corporate scrip. It's yours, along with a ride to whatever planet you want, if you take us back to our shuttle."

We had no such funds, in fact. I'd given Konigsberg the last of our operating expenses, which might have been short-sighted of me.

"Or if it's a job you want, you could work with us," Vicky offered. "We're looking for another partner. You could be security chief for the operation."

She was really getting into this, I thought, not without some admiration. Improvisation under pressure wasn't easy.

"Or you could just keep working for that nutcase Dhoni," I said, "watching him drive away customers because he just wants to kill people and break things. How many PMC's do you think go under every year because they're just a bunch of overgrown kids playing soldier?"

"Hey, that ain't right!" Garcia said plaintively from the driver's seat, half-turning, his frown almost a pout. "You can't talk about the captain that way!"

"Shut up, Garcia," Reindl snapped. Then he jabbed the muzzle of his rifle into my chest and I grunted at the sharp pain in my ribs. "And you shut up, too! Captain Dhoni didn't want a mess in the bunker, but he wouldn't give a shit about blood in this junk heap of a car. Keep your mouth shut or I'll see if I can put one round through the both of you and save fucking ammo!"

I took him at his word and sat in silence for another five minutes, the only soundtrack the rasp of the tires on the gravel and the occasional thump as they pounded over weather-worn ruts in the road. It was going to have to be soon, I decided. If we waited until we got to the quarry, he'd be on guard, and Garcia would have his gun out, wouldn't be distracted by driving. Trying hard not to move my upper arms, I worked my right wrist back and forth, trying to squeeze it out of the cuffs.

Get my hands free, grab the gun barrel. The length of the rifle was a weakness. If Reindl had been more experienced with transporting prisoners, he would have slung the rifle and pulled out a handgun. The problem was going to be his armor. It would make disabling him hand-to-hand almost impossible, except he had his visor up. Small target, but it would have to do. I'd go for the eyes because it would force him to take his hands off the gun, then I could use it to shoot Garcia.

As plans went, it wasn't horrible, but it did have one drawback: I was a Drop Trooper, not a commando. Aside from some training in Boot Camp and a few sparring sessions for physical exercise in garrison, the only experience I had fighting was from trying not to get my ass kicked in Trans Angeles and it usually wasn't against anyone with a gun or body armor. Reindl had probably been Force Recon, though he might have been Fleet Security. Force Recon was way more into that unarmed combat shit than the Drop Troopers were. He had training, experience, and a good ten kilos on me. I'd have to be really fast and hope surprise, as Captain Covington used to say, was a force multiplier.

Something went pop-pop-pop-pop in the distance, a nondescript sound that I couldn't identify except that it had the distinctive cadence of a weapon discharging. I hadn't even caught the clunk of the rounds going through the car door, but I noticed when the slugs exited Garcia's body, left to right across the front seat of the car, spraying blood like some abstract work of art on the interior of the front passenger's side.

Reindl stared at the carnage in the front seat, wide-eyed, frozen into inaction for a second, and it would have been easy for me to do the same thing, because I sure as hell hadn't expected it. But I'd also been thinking about escaping, about how and when to get free, where to strike, and another saying Captain Covington had been fond of was "fortune favors the prepared mind."

I ripped my right hand free of its restraints, barely feeling the sting of the skin being scraped off, and grabbed at the barrel of the rifle. Reindl tried to fight me, but I threw all of my weight against the side of the barrel and wedged myself between him and the gun, then lashed out, raking my fingers across his eyes.

Reindl screamed and the gun discharged, ripping through the air inside the car with a wave of static electricity that stood my hair on end, the tungsten slug spearing through the front windshield as if it wasn't even there. I kept my hold on it, kept leaning into it and kept clawing at his eyes. Until the rover rolled into a ditch and threw all three of us into a pile wedged against the rear of the front bench seat. I saw stars and that was about *all* I saw with Garcia's body slumped against the control yoke, blocking out the lights from the dashboard, but my fingers tightened on the barrel shroud of the Gauss rifle, keeping its muzzle pointed downward at the floor of the car.

Something hit me in the side of the head, hard and unyielding, and I winced but didn't let go. It was Reindl, trying to strike out at me, but lacking the leverage to get a really good punch. He couldn't get up, either, because I was across his chest and Vicky was sprawled over his legs...but her hands were still restrained and I couldn't let go of the gun to go for his eyes again. And at some point, he was going to try to reach his pistol, or a knife, and then we'd both be dead.

Someone ripped the door open and my feet, which had been propped against it, fell out into nothing and I went with them. And so did the Gauss rifle. It didn't come free because it was attached to Reindl's armored vest by its sling, but it pulled out of his hands, which left me hanging partway out of the car by the receiver of the weapon. And staring up at the ugly face of Sgt. Simon Martz.

"I told you," he said gruffly, "that this was a stupid-ass idea. Fucking officers."

———

"Not that I'm not grateful as all hell," Vicky said, rubbing at her wrists, "but how in the hell did you guys happen to be here?"

"We didn't *happen* to be anywhere," Martz growled, twisting around in his seat, taking his eyes off the road long enough for the battered old rover to rumble into the grass and dirt for a few seconds before he pulled the steering wheel back to the center. "I *knew* you two would wind up in trouble. I decided about an hour after you landed that I wasn't going to let you get this operation scrubbed by getting yourself killed, so I got Ruthie to track your 'links and had that pretty-boy Foster drop me off in the cargo bird."

"And I made him take me along," Fargo said cheerfully from the front passenger's seat. "Because you don't run a rescue mission alone."

"And because no one else wanted to go," Martz added. "They don't know either of you from Adam, and didn't see the point in risking their asses to save yours."

"With that kind of esprit de corps," I commented, rubbing at the nascent bruise on my cheek, "it's a wonder none of you are still in the military."

"Well, we might not be fancy-assed officers, but we managed to steal this piece of shit car, figured out where you were taken, then we stuck around long enough to watch them stick you into that car and drive you out."

"Who took the shot?" Vicky asked.

"Oh, I did," Fargo told her, and my eyebrows shot up. "I was on the battalion marksmanship team three years in a row. I'm actually better with a sniper rifle than I am in a battlesuit."

I nodded, reevaluating the woman.

"Thanks for saving our asses."

"You're welcome," Martz muttered, and I resisted the urge to inform him I hadn't been speaking to him.

"Did you find the information you needed?" Fargo asked, perkiness undeterred by the acrimony between Martz and the two of us.

"We did," I told her. "But the news isn't good. I was hoping we might be able to turn some of the residents against Konigsberg, make our jobs easier." Which wasn't *quite* what I hoped, but it would work better with the hired muscle. "But they're all intensely loyal to him. And then you have Captain Dhoni and Extreme Measures PMC, and they're the cherry topping on this pile of horseshit. Dhoni is clinically insane and wants nothing more than to get a chance to kill someone."

"What's so insane about that?" Martz demanded. "Why else would anyone become a mercenary?"

I ignored him.

"So, even if we got Konigsberg to do the smart thing and give up the mine, Dhoni wouldn't care, he'd just start a fight with us anyway."

"Bring it on!" Martz insisted. "A straight-up fight is better than this bullshit sneaking around."

"We have one advantage anyway. They don't know what happened to us or Reindl, and if we can keep it that way...."

"Umm, guys," Fargo said, her head cocked to the side. "Does anyone else hear that?"

"What?" Martz snapped.

And then I heard it, too, a buzzing sound above us, a mosquito flying past my ear...but it wasn't by my ear, it was out the open window of the car, and it was a hundred meters above us.

"That's a hopper," I said, putting my head out the window, the chill wind slapping me in the face. The mercs had taken my night vision glasses and I couldn't see anything against the clouded black of the night sky.

"It doesn't mean anything," Vicky said, no conviction in her voice. "They could just be locals heading for the spaceport."

It was true, the lights of the port were glowing off to our west, the featureless blur of the clouds lit up and clarified, the ridges and curves turned into mountains hanging in the sky. They *could* just be flying mine employees out from the facilities to the spaceport for a business trip, and I'd almost convinced myself that was the case until they opened fire on us.

[9]

"Shit! Shit! Shit!" Martz screamed like it was an order, but I barely heard him over the explosions.

I didn't know what they were firing at first, just saw the flares of light and the spray of dirt and heard the rattle of stones bouncing off the side of the car, though I wasn't sure if that was from the blasts or Martz jerking the car to the left and right in reaction to the shots landing on either side of us. I hadn't fastened my seat restraints, mostly because it was dark in the cab and it hadn't seemed worth it to hunt for them, and the violent maneuvering threw me against Vicky and the passenger side door, alternatively, making me wish I'd taken the time to strap in.

"Grenade launcher," Fargo guessed, sounding much, much cooler and calmer about it than I was. "Bolt-on, I think. No computer guidance or they would have hit us already. They're just eyeballing it."

"Can this thing go any faster?" Vicky asked, jamming her foot into the seat to brace herself and leaning over the front bench. "Eyeballing it or not, they're not going to keep missing much longer!"

"Get my rifle," Fargo said, gesturing urgently behind me at the cargo compartment.

Another chain of explosions ripped into the road ahead of us and the windshield splintered into a spider-web of cracks, as if the gunner in the hopper was urging me to do what Fargo said. I didn't need the encouragement. I threw myself over the rear seat, hitting the padded floor of the cargo compartment with my right shoulder, my legs still hanging over the rear bench, and began feeling around for the purported rifle. It wasn't hard to find since the case was a meter long and fifty centimeters across of hard metal and I'd landed on top of it, but I had to run my fingers down the length of it from either side before I could find the latches.

I swung my legs into the cargo compartment and scrunched up out of the way to allow the case to swing upward. I could barely see the weapon in the glow from the running lights outside the rear window, and I wondered why Martz hadn't turned them off, but I decided that wouldn't help much since the hopper probably had IR and thermal sights for the gun. It still would have made me feel better.

The rifle was long and lean, with an adjustable stock and a fat, cylindrical scope mounted atop it, a box magazine already loaded to the front of the pistol grip, and I couldn't immediately identify what sort of weapon it was in the dim light.

"I got it!" I called up to Fargo.

"Good!" Martz yelled, then reached over and touched a control beside the steering wheel. The rear window popped upward, letting in a rush of cold, night air from outside. "Shoot that fucking thing down!"

"I'm not the one who was on the fucking battalion marksmanship team!"

"Mag is loaded," Fargo told me as if I hadn't spoken, "round is chambered, safety is on. Scope will light up when you put your eye to it."

I didn't try to argue with her, realizing that it would take too long for her to switch places with me, and we likely didn't have that long. The hopper had veered away from the roadway, probably hit by an updraft, but it was coming back in line and no one could be a bad enough shot to miss from that distance. I twisted into a seated position in the back of the rover, nearly pulling a hamstring in the process, but finally I had my legs underneath me and the rifle resting across the edge of the rear window.

The scope worked as advertised, turning night into day, finally revealing the details of the hopper. Fargo had been right in her guess. It was a commercial model, an old one, beat up and patched, the sort of thing I expected to find on a place like this where nothing was ever thrown away. The grenade launcher was jury-rigged, but professionally done and I knew it had to be the mercs who'd done the work, and them who were flying it.

A targeting reticle appeared floating across the image and I realized I hadn't bothered to ask Fargo what the hell I was shooting. Oh well, it didn't matter. One thing was just as likely to work as another. The safety was in the usual position and I flicked it onto fire, then past it to full auto because why the hell not? I settled the stock into my shoulder just in case there was recoil, then touched the trigger.

There was a kick so I knew it wasn't a laser, but no bang, no hiss of rockets, just a snap-crackle-hum and the whip-crack of multiple rounds breaking the sound barrier. It was a Gauss rifle, which I suppose made sense for someone in the marksmanship unit. Although being on the marksmanship unit in a Drop Trooper battalion was sort of like being the smartest kid in the remedial reading course. I hadn't fired a Gauss rifle since Boot Camp, but it was just like riding a bicycle. Or so I'd been told. I'd never ridden a bicycle.

The hopper wasn't armored, and the airframe had no defense against tungsten slugs travelling at three thousand meters per second. I couldn't see the holes even through the scope, but I knew I'd hit it when it slewed violently left, going into a wobble. I kept firing, trying my best to stay on target and wishing the damned thing was a laser after all, because then I could have walked the rounds onto the target, but the best I could do was count on the dancing reticle. The round counter had started at fifty, but it rolled downward quickly and I let it, keeping the trigger depressed until it hit zero.

The hopper was see-sawing back and forth, and above the rumble of the rover's internal combustion engine, I could hear the whine of the aircraft's ducted fans taking on a higher, more desperate tone. I'd hit something vital, something in the engine and maybe something in the pilot as well. I kept the scope up to my face, feeling around with my left hand, trying to find a spare magazine without lowering the rifle, but as my hand finally closed around the metal box of the extra mag, the hopper nosed over and crashed not fifty meters behind us.

The vibration shook the rover through its suspension, a cloud of dust rising into the sky though there was no explosion. The hopper, even out here on the Periphery, used electrical motors, because no one would have been crazy enough to trust an internal combustion engine for powered flight. I doubted it made any difference to the crew inside her, though. They were just as dead.

I pulled the rifle back inside the window and switched out the magazines by rote, putting the weapon on safe and handing it up to Vicky before I climbed back over the seat.

"Nice shooting, sir," Fargo said, and I was glad the darkness hid my frown. Her saccharine sweetness was starting to grate on me.

"How the hell did they find us so quick?" Martz growled. "No one saw us take out the car they were transporting you in!"

"They tried to radio them," I surmised, taking the Gauss sniper rifle back from Vicky and holding it barrel down between my legs. "When they didn't get a response, they sent out the hopper looking for them. It probably wasn't too hard to guess that the only other car on the road was the one who'd killed their people."

"And what will they do when they find out they can't contact their hopper?" Vicky asked, staring out her window at the night sky as if another threat was about to jump out of it.

"Let's get on your fucking shuttle and get out of here," Martz suggested, "before we have to find out."

As much as I found Sgt. Martz a disagreeable person, I couldn't disagree with that.

———

"*Yantar*," I repeated into the replacement 'link Fargo had thought to bring for me. "Come in, *Yantar*."

"Why are we sitting here?" Martz groused, shifting in his awkward crouch like it was hurting his legs. "The shuttle is right fucking there! Why don't we just drive up and get in the damned thing? I don't see anyone down there!"

I glared at him, giving him the same look my brother had given me as a kid when I'd suggested something stupid. We'd gone off road the last two kilometers and parked the rover at the edge of the landing field, concealed under a stand of cottonwood trees just a kilometer or so from the *Yantar*'s passenger shuttle.

"Yeah, I don't see anyone either," I agreed. "Am I the only one who's bothered by that?"

"What do you mean, sir?" Fargo asked. She had her sniper

rifle back and was scanning slowly across the field with the scope. "I'm not getting anything on thermal or IR either."

"They *know* who we are, Fargo," Vicky told her. "They know where we have to be going. Why would they leave our only means of escape sitting out there unguarded?"

"Then what the hell do you suggest we do?" Martz demanded. "We can't just sit out here forever."

"That's why I'm trying to contact the ship," I grated out, waving the 'link at him, half-wanting to wave the pistol I'd borrowed from Fargo in his face instead. "If we can reach them, they can launch Intercept One to cover our flight." He started to say something else, probably something stupid, and I interrupted him by calling the ship again. And finally, Ruthie Amendola answered me.

"Cam, this is the *Yantar*." Her voice was strained, as if she was boosting at high gravity, and I had a sick feeling in the pit of my stomach, a suspicion that was exactly what she was doing. "We got trouble! Mercenary assault shuttles and at least one cutter gunship are heading our way! We're breaking orbit at max gees and heading for the belt! Dunstan's out there and we should be able to hold them off! Find a hole and crawl into it and we'll come back for you as soon as we can!"

And then she was gone. I looked up at the others. The conversation had been on the 'link's external speaker and Vicky's face had gone grim. Martz was cursing way too loud, and Fargo had paled, though it seemed impossible with her complexion.

"We still need to get to the shuttle," Martz insisted. "They're busy chasing the *Yantar*, which is probably why they're not guarding the bird. We can use her to hop over to one of the other continents and hide there until it's safe to come out, until we can get the dropship down here with our suits."

Vicky shot me a look and shrugged.

"He might be right."

I shook my head, but there was only one way to answer the question.

"All right, I'll go down and try to get to the shuttle," I told them. "*If* I can get in, and *if* they let me take off, I'll touch down at this end of the field and pick you up. If not...."

"If there's a problem," Vicky insisted, "we'll come down in the rover and get you."

"I'd rather you just hauled ass," I told her. "But I know you won't do it, so there's no point in arguing about it."

"I've taught you so well," she observed, the corner of her lip turning up in as much of a smile as I was going to get under the circumstances.

"Fargo," I told the corporal, "you got the sniper rifle. Cover me. If you see anyone or anything coming my way, shoot it."

"Will do, sir."

I thought about high-crawling, but it was a paved landing field, and it was a kilometer...it would have taken forever, and I would have been in some sad shape when I got there. So, I went for option two, walking right across the field like I owned the place. It had gotten me into a lot of places I shouldn't have been back when I'd been living off the con in Trans-Angeles.

My shoulders were squared, my stride purposeful, though I did keep the gun in my hand, swinging freely at my side. The mercs had to have people out here. Maybe if they were watching, they'd think I was one of them.

Or maybe Martz is actually right and they figured they'd just cut off our route of escape and not have to bother to guard the shuttle. Or, maybe, even more likely, they just haven't gotten their people here yet. After all, we were closer.

Yeah, I decided that was probably it. We'd just beaten their ground forces here from their base because we had a head start. The thought gave my step an extra bounce and I restrained myself from jogging just in case any port personnel were watching. I couldn't be sure the theory was correct, but if I wasn't getting shot, it was a good indication.

It was only a kilometer, but it felt as if it took an hour to walk it, and I did speed up to a jog the last hundred meters, hounded by the conviction that time was running out and I had to get on the ship *now*. The ramp began to lower at the touch of my palm on the security plate and I clambered up into the cockpit, urgency gathering in my gut like a debris field congealing into an asteroid. Sitting in the pilot's seat seemed unnatural and I felt lost for a long moment, trying to remember what the hell I was supposed to do and wishing I could recall the commands Vicky had used to set the thing up for voice control. For some reason, that was considered a mortal sin among Fleet types, somewhere south of necrophilia, and I'd been afraid to ask Dunstan to tell me how to do it.

There. There was the main menu control, the one I'd seen Vicky using. I scrolled through to computer-assisted pilot mode, which was something else the ex-Fleet pilots loathed. Not quite a mortal sin, but a venial one, something along the lines of lying to your mother about being a necrophiliac. The choices were simple, self-explanatory enough that even a M/arine grunt could figure them out.

Start turbines, start take-off sequence.

Head for orbit? Yes or no? No.

Please show desired course. I traced a line on the map overlay with my finger to the edge of the field where the rover was parked.

Land at desired destination? Yes or no? Yes.

There, that simple. The turbines spun up and I urged them on with encouraging thoughts, wondering if I should get out and push. Remembered pain from the car ride made me fasten the seat restraints and by the time I had them on, the belly jets were roaring, lifting the small aerospacecraft off the tarmac. The lurching motion set my teeth on edge with the gut-deep conviction that someone other than me should have been in the pilot's seat, human hands guiding the controls. It was atavistic and old-fashioned, I know, something I'd picked up in the military. Civilian crews, especially commercial ones, were happy as hell to let a computer do the boring work—it cut down on the number of pilots they had to keep on the payroll. The military never trusted computers to make life-or-death decisions, and neither did I...when I had a choice.

If we lived through this, I was determined to get Dunstan to teach me how to fly a shuttle without active computer assistance. Hell, I had the jacks, I might even be able to get their firmware programmed to include flight interface. I'd heard about other retired Marine Drop Troopers doing it, though I'd have to be sure they didn't mess up my ability to interface with a Vigilante.

One thing I really needed remedial lessons on was reading the sensor display. It wasn't anything like the tactical readout inside my Vigilante's helmet HUD. That display was meant to be simple and easy to read on the run, because there were just too many potential distractions inside a battlesuit without adding another. This, though...it was easy enough to tell *what* things were, but not *where* they were. So, when I saw the bogie coming over the horizon, I had no trouble at all determining that it was a shuttle. The avatar was universal throughout the military and in commercial spaceflight. But I had to scan from top to bottom and left to right and then diagonally to find the readout that told me the distance the unknown aerospacecraft was from my position and what direction it was heading.

Twelve kilometers. And it was coming right for me, adjusting its course as I moved across the mapping screen. *Shit.*

The shuttle was landing almost before it took off, because

one kilometer was barely a footstep for the thing, and the second it began descending, I was out of my seat and running for the belly ramp. One kilometer was a footstep, and twelve kilometers was just a hop across the street, and I had to get off this damned bird right the hell now.

The shuttle jolted and swayed as it settled into the suspension of its landing gear and I nearly went flying off my feet, only managing to stay upright by grabbing a handhold in the utility bay and nearly dislocating my shoulder. I had seconds, but I had to do one thing before I left the shuttle. The weapons locker was locked, of course, but it opened with a touch of my hand to the ID plate and I scooped up a double armful of whatever I could grab and then dove down the ramp headlong.

"What are you doing?" Martz demanded as I nearly ran into him on the way down, stumbling, feet slapping into the tarmac.

My breath was coming in sharp gasps, and it was a struggle to get the words out, but I had to.

"Enemy shuttle on the way," I told them, the muscles in my arms twitching with the load of carbines and ammo pouches. "Run!"

"What about the rover?" Martz yelled at me, still standing at the foot of the ramp.

I let him and didn't stop running, zipping right past the rover and heading up the hill into the trees. Vicky was following me and if the others didn't care to, well, I wasn't really close enough with either of the others that I'd feel guilty about it if they got themselves killed. But they had come down and saved our asses from the mercenaries....

I skidded to a halt, checking behind me. Fargo was only ten meters back and sprinting to keep up, still carrying her rifle, while Martz was chugging along twenty or thirty meters behind her, only a couple hundred meters from the shuttle. The scream of the turbines was rolling over the landing field, echoing inside my head and I knew what was coming.

"Hurry up, Martz!" I yelled.

I don't know why I turned my head and fell into a crouch. Maybe it was an instinct, a premonition, or maybe I just had a feel for how close the enemy bird was and a memory of the effective range of the weapons it could carry, but when our lander blew up, I was facing away, my eyes squeezed shut, and I could still see the light of the proton cannon like I was staring into the noonday sun. Heat washed over me, dry and crackling, the door of an industrial oven the size of a building opening, taking my breath away, and that was just the proton beam. When the metallic hydrogen in the shuttle's fuel tanks went up, the whole landing field shook.

The flash was nearly as bright as the proton beam, but the shockwave made me forget all about it. I'd already been in a low crouch, but I was suddenly flat on the ground and didn't remember falling, dirt and gravel smacking into me like a sandblaster. I squeezed my eyes shut and ducked my head, waiting for the storm to pass, but the second it did, I was getting my feet underneath me, knowing the mercenary shuttle would be making a pass around the landing field to make sure he'd gotten all of us.

I tried to yell and couldn't hear myself, couldn't hear anything except a shrill whistling that seemed to come from everywhere and nowhere. Vicky was beside me, a small cut oozing blood over her eyebrow, and I grabbed her by the arm, pulling her to her feet and then shoving a pulse carbine into her arms along with a bandolier of spare magazines. I pushed her toward the trees, then ran back to Fargo and Martz. The woman was up on one knee, her teeth gritted in determination I hadn't expected from her, and she took my hand when I offered it.

"Run!" I yelled, and this time I heard it, just a little.

I wasn't sure if she did, but she got the point and stumbled after Vicky while I checked on Martz. The big man had rolled onto his side, but he was lolling, his eyes glazed over and his mouth open and gasping like a landed fish. My fingers closed around the casualty handle on the back of his tactical vest, and I dug my heels in and dragged him on his shoulder.

There wasn't time. I knew it as certainly as I knew my own name, knew that the Extreme Measures shuttle would be back around before I could get him into the woods, and they wouldn't even need a direct hit with that proton cannon, just a near-miss, anything within fifty meters, and we'd both be burned to a crisp, dead before the flash had the chance to reach our optic nerves. I should have left him, but I couldn't do it. He was an asshole, but he'd come for me and Vicky when we were in trouble, even if he'd only done it so he could tell me that he'd told me so.

Then Vicky and Fargo were beside us, grabbing Martz and helping me to lift him to his feet. The two pulse carbines slung over my shoulder clattered against each other and smacked me in the side of the head, but I ignored the sharp pain and pulled the big man by the handle. He was lurching and stumbling, but at least he was moving. The trees ran a race against the approaching whine of the shuttle's turbojets to see which one would reach us first.

The trees won and darkness swallowed us.

[10]

"You know this is all your fault, right?" Martz demanded, smacking the palm of his hand against the receiver of the pulse carbine that I'd been considerate enough to bring for him from the now-defunct lander. He let out an overly dramatic sigh and leaned his head back against the bare rock wall of the cave. "I should have just gone with my first instinct and fucking stuffed everyone in their battlesuits and gone and completed the fucking mission on my own without your worthless ass!"

"He did go back and pull you out of there when he could have let you die, Sergeant," Fargo pointed out, incessantly upbeat.

I didn't know how she managed it. To call what we were huddled inside a cave was to cheapen the word. It was more an indentation in the side of a rocky hill, just enough to keep us out of sight of satellites or drones or overflying hoppers, with a floor of cold mud and an infestation of some improbably hardy mosquitos. I had my jacket's hood pulled over my head and the face warmer pulled up to the bridge of my nose and was honestly feeling too warm, but I'd decided I would rather sweat than itch. And we'd had to run nearly five klicks to find it. It was a damned good thing our 'links could map out our location, because I had no idea where we were.

"I wouldn't have *needed* him to pull me out if we'd done what I said and just gone down and kicked some ass!"

"Look," I interrupted, not only tired of his bitching but concerned he was getting way too loud, "maybe you're right. Maybe I should have just done it simple and gone in shooting. But as an officer, I remember very well how many times we got butt-fucked by bad intelligence or no intelligence. Don't tell me you didn't see the same thing."

Martz made a face, then shrugged as if unwilling to give up his grudge.

"Yeah, but it didn't fucking work, did it? We're fucked now!"

"No, we're alive and we're still free," Vicky told him. "And we're armed. What we need to decide is what to do now."

"I'll tell you what I think we should do," Martz said, emphasizing the words with a raised finger. "We need to get out of his fucking muddy hole in the wall and go back into town. We find a house somewhere, break in and hold up there until that dickweed Dunstan can get back here and pick us up."

"Wouldn't work," I told him, shaking my head. He looked as if he was going to yell loud enough for every drone in a twenty-klick area to hear it, so I went on before he could. "Most of the mine workers live in a communal apartment building. There's some housing in town, but not enough that no one would notice if we broke into one. And given what we know about Captain Dhoni, I wouldn't bet against him dumping a few mortar rounds in our lap and not worrying about collateral damage."

"Or just having that damned shuttle blast us with its proton cannon," Vicky agreed. "Maybe we should try to get a message to Konigsberg. As far as he knows, we're still legit. If we told him what Dhoni did, he might call him off."

"What's the point in that?" Martz grumbled, swatting at a mosquito that had landed on his cheek. "Our mission ain't to make googly-eyes at this Konigsberg, it's to seize his fucking mine!"

"The point," I said, "is to get the mercenaries off our backs long enough to get us back on the *Yantar* and back in our suits. If we can con the guy into getting that done, I'll kiss his ass and offer to shine his fucking shoes."

"Do you think it would work, sir?" Fargo wondered.

"I think he'd *try*." I shrugged. "The problem is, I don't know if Dhoni's the kind of dog he can call off."

"He *is* a bloodthirsty bastard," Vicky agreed. "But what does that leave us, then?"

"Maybe the mines," I suggested.

"You just said we couldn't count on Konigsberg," Martz reminded me.

"Not going to the mines to talk," I clarified. "They do run a night shift, but from what I could see, it's a much smaller crew. There's bound to be unused buildings, business offices, bunkhouses, break rooms, computer centers, maintenance buildings...someplace we can break in and get some food and water. Hell, I even saw some of the mercs stationed down at the mines. If we can find the right place, we can get transportation, maybe a hopper or even a long-range flyer and get out of the area."

"Not bad," Martz acknowledged. "That might actually work."

"And maybe," Vicky mused, "we could even find out who he's selling his rhenium to."

"Why the fuck do you care?" Martz demanded. "That's not our fucking job. We're just here to kick them out and take the mines."

"It's easy to talk about taking the mines," I shot back, "but those Extreme Measures troops are well-equipped and well-trained. Vets, most of them. You know how much it costs to hire an outfit like that, Martz?"

"Why would I?"

"I looked into it when I found out we'd be dealing with mercs. Just to see what kind of opposition to expect. Konigsberg and Dhoni both made it sound like Extreme Measures was working for the mine, but there's no way. Even with what Konigsberg is pulling in, he couldn't afford to keep an outfit like that on retainer indefinitely. He could afford some cartel muscle from the Pirate Worlds, but Extreme Measures has their own space assets. That's hundreds of thousands of dollars in Corporate scrip or Tradenotes, hiring a company like that long-term, months at a time."

Martz's face screwed up in confusion and I rubbed at my eyes. It was like dealing with a child. Worse, since children have an imagination.

"Konigsberg isn't paying the mercs," Vicky spelled it out for him. "His buyers are."

"Okay," Martz acknowledged, palms upward, "but who the fuck cares? Why does that make a difference for us?"

Which wasn't a bad question, but he wouldn't like my answer, that I was working for Fleet Intelligence investigating the Corporate Council and needed to know. Luckily, I had an alternative narrative already thought up.

"It makes a difference because we're *not* mercenaries, Sgt. Martz. We're permanent employees of the Corporate Security Force, which means our stars and our fortune is tied to whether our bosses in the Corporate Council think we did a good job. And if Konigsberg's buyers are flush enough to hire high-quality mercs *once*, what makes you think they aren't going to do it again after we get rid of this bunch? Just have them sweep right in here and take everything over? You think the Corporates are going to station us here permanently? No, they'll have a bare minimum of CSF troopers to control the population. And if that happens and we didn't do anything about it, who do you think they're going to blame?"

"Fucking officers, always worrying about who's going to get blamed and shining their brass for the high command." Martz sneered. "You do whatever you gotta do, but don't expect me to save your ass again if you get into the shit playing your stupid games instead of doing the job we came here to do."

"Noted," I said, using the cover of the darkness to roll my eyes. "We'll stay here until it gets light, then try to find someplace a bit more comfortable to spend the rest of the day. We'll head for the mines at sunset."

"Jesus, we're gonna spend that much time fucking around in the woods?" He waved away another cloud of bugs, cursing under his breath. "I'm gonna go take a leak."

He pushed away from the cave and stalked into the blackness of the early morning.

"Go with him, Fargo," I told the woman. "You've got the only night vision here," I reminded her, nodding at the scope on her rifle. "Make sure he doesn't get lost."

"Right," she said, following after the man.

"Maybe you can hold it for him when he pees," Vicky added quietly after the other woman had left. She shook her head. "I don't trust either of them. But I think I trust her less. No one is that fucking cheerful and upbeat all the time. She's gotta be a Corporate plant, someone Dukanovic sent to keep an eye on us."

"We'd be dead if they hadn't pulled our asses out of the fire," I reminded her. "This is a Corporate Council mission, and I have to think they want it to succeed."

"Yeah, that's the other thing," she said, huddling under her jacket from the zero-dark-thirty chill and the persistent insects.

"We know—well, we *think* we know—why the rhenium mine here is so important to whoever's buying it, that they're building their own fleet somewhere. But why the hell is it this important to the Corporate Council? I mean, think about it, Cam. The CSF has shitloads of hired guns. How many of us do they have? Vigilante-qualified Drop Troopers with interface jacks? You think they have more than just the one squad of us?"

"Probably not," I admitted. "Dukanovic made it sound like Wade was taking a huge gamble buying those surplus suits."

"But they send us here." She shrugged. "Maybe it's a test, just to see how well we do leading their people, but I have to think this place is important to them for some reason besides just another source of rare metals. You really think the Corporate Council is hurting for rhenium?" She put a hand on top of mine and squeezed. "What aren't we being told?"

"I guess we'll find out tomorrow."

<hr>

"Man, I ain't spent a night and a day sleeping in the fucking woods since Boot Camp," Martz said, scratching at the back of his head. "There's a reason I went into the Drop Troopers instead of Force Recon, you know? Because I like sleeping in fucking beds, not under a damned tree."

"Martz, I gotta hand it to you," I said, dusting dead leaves off the back of my jacket, then picking one out of my hair, "you have a talent for bitching unparalleled by anything in my military career. You bitch more than any three Spec-4's I ever served with."

The primary star was still on the horizon, but the rolling hills and the thick stand of pines blocked it out, throwing this stretch of woods into deep shadow and giving us what I knew was a false sense of security. No drones or dismounted patrols had found us here, but it hadn't been the darkness that had saved us. They probably thought we were all dead in the shuttle explosion. Or at least that Vicky and I were dead. They likely didn't even know Martz and Fargo existed. But beside giving us the illusion of invisibility, it would also make the opposition less likely to be looking for us. It *shouldn't* have, but that was just how we humans worked. Darkness made us want to pull a hole in around ourselves and huddle by the fire and pray to the old gods that the leopards wouldn't come hunting for us.

"And I bet you never bitched about anything, right, Alvarez?" Martz scoffed. "You always been a *stoic*, genteel officer type, huh?"

"I never bitched," I informed him, "because I've always understood something you apparently don't."

"Yeah?" he asked, stepping up nose to nose with me, his breath hot and rancid. "And what's that?"

"That nobody fucking cares." I pushed him away, my nose wrinkling. "You didn't bring any chewing gum with you, did you, Martz?"

"How far is the walk?" Fargo asked. She was examining the action of her rifle with meticulous care and I had the sense that the weapon belonged to her personally rather than the CSF.

"From here," Vicky answered, checking the display on her 'link, "it's fifteen kilometers to the outer perimeter of the mines. Twenty to the refinery. Gonna take longer because we can't use the roads, but I've been seeing some trails through the woods here. Maybe game trails or maybe from off-road trikes." She cocked her head upward. "Moon should be close to full tonight, too. Shouldn't be too bad."

"Fargo," I asked, "how comfortable are you with walking point?"

"I can do it if you want, sir," the woman said, agreeable as always. "If you want the real truth, though, I'm not that good in a umm...non-urban environment."

I sighed. I'd gotten out of the Marines as an acting company commander, in a captain's slot, even if I'd lacked the actual rank. Why the hell did I keep getting put on point?

"All right," I told her, draping the sling of my pulse carbine around my neck and right shoulder, carrying the weapon across my chest. "Follow me. Keep your interval and keep looking at that night-vision scope. If you see anything, call out distance and direction and if you think it's a threat, just go ahead and shoot it." I glanced back at Martz. I didn't want him behind me, but I also didn't want him riding drag with no one keeping an eye on him. "Martz, you're after me, Vicky you're watching our six. You've got the mapping program pulled up and I want you to guide me over my earpiece. Everyone clear?"

Martz didn't appear happy with the setup, but then, I hadn't really seen him look happy so maybe I just didn't know what to look for. But no one said anything, and I nodded curtly.

"Then move out."

The trail through the woods was broad and well-defined for a game trail, and I had to agree with Vicky that it was probably used by the locals for recreational off-roading. I'd never heard of the concept until I got to Hausos, and still didn't quite understand the appeal, but then, I'd basically been deathly afraid to go outside until I was almost twenty-one years old, so it wasn't a pursuit I was likely to take up for pleasure. I did appreciate it at the moment, since I really didn't want to keep climbing over fallen timber in the dark. We'd had to do way too much of that finding the clearing twelve hours ago at the first grey light of dawn, and I had the cuts and bruises to prove it, including a knot on my shin that throbbed with every step.

Motion flickered to my left, the gentle crackle of leaves and underbrush a veritable crescendo in the wooded echo chamber, and I swung the pulse carbine around, almost touching the trigger.

"Deer," Fargo said, her eye affixed to the scope on her rifle. "Just a deer."

I let out a sigh and lowered the muzzle of my weapon.

"Shoulda shot it," Martz suggested. "I'm fucking starving."

I cocked an eyebrow at him.

"I saw you eating that protein bar last night, not that you offered any of us a bite."

"I'm a big man!" he protested, tapping a finger against his chest. "I need more fuel to run this engine."

I wish he hadn't brought up food, because that late lunch at the café yesterday afternoon seemed a long time ago now and my stomach was growling. There'd been a time when regular meals were a fantasy and I'd considered myself lucky to snag a faked ID code that would last long enough to get me access to the government food dispensers for a few days. But the Marines had fed me consistently if not extravagantly, and once we'd taken up farm living on Hausos, fresh eggs, pork, chicken and steak had left my stomach conditioned to expect regular support.

Head in the game, Alvarez. Dinner's going to have to wait.

But sundown wasn't. The shadows had closed in and the glow filtering through the pines went from gold to red to grey in minutes, and I began picking my way along the trail carefully until my eyes adjusted.

"We're heading north in a kilometer," Vicky told me.

"Is there a trail?"

"Since these aren't exactly established city roads," she informed me, "and this place is too backwoods for dedicated satellite mapping, so I'm going off dead-reckoning and I'm sure this dinky little map wouldn't tell me."

There was a trail, branching off from the main one, and if it didn't head straight north, it was close enough for government work, particularly since we didn't know exactly where we were going. The trail we'd been following had stayed fairly level, but this one angled upward, way too steep for my aching quads.

"We seeing anything yet, Fargo?" I asked, using the question as an excuse to take a break.

She stepped up closer to me on the trail, nearly tripping over a root, and raised the Gauss rifle to her shoulder.

"I'm getting some sky glow ahead," she told me. "Could be the mines."

And about an hour later, over three sets of exhausting hills, it was, and I was just about too tired to feel happy about it. I took a knee and pretended to be studying the lights gleaming on the next hill over while I caught my breath. The moon was low over the eastern sky and yesterday's clouds had rolled away, and under the milky pallidity of its glow, the commercial road from Perfection was a white streamer stretching around the curve of the hill. No vehicles spoiled the illusion. Nothing moved at all, not so much as a night flying bat or owl, though somewhere deep in the night, kilometers away, the rumble of earthmovers carried over the hills.

"There's a building," Fargo announced. Her foot was propped up on a rock, her knee supporting her elbow, steadying the front stock of her rifle. "At the top of the hill."

"I can see the lights," I said, exhaustion sucking away my patience. "Does the scope show you anything useful?"

"The hill is two kilometers away," she said, no offense at my tone evident in her voice. "The building is about thirty meters by forty, single story. It has satellite dishes and laser line-of-sight relays on the roof. No weapons emplacements. No vehicles outside that I can see. No one walking around. There're floodlights in the parking lot, but I don't see any lights on inside the building. It might not be occupied."

Martz stepped up beside her and tried to look over her shoulder, and Fargo jerked away from the intrusion, finally showing something besides polite accommodation.

"That's an awfully big 'might.' Maybe we should watch it for a while longer."

"What?" I asked him, taunting just a little just because he pissed me off. "You afraid of a few mineworkers?"

He sneered and shot me a bird.

"All right then." I straightened and smacked him on the shoulder. "It's just another two klicks. Let's Charlie Mike."

[11]

"Hey! Is anyone there?"

I felt like a huge idiot walking through the parking lot of the mining company office, and I was going to feel even sillier if someone popped out of the building and shot me. But there were only so many ways we could approach the building, and since none of us were any sort of special operations commandos, that ruled out sneaking up and trying to rappel down from the roof or any such shit. And since this was my plan, I would be the one to take the risk.

"Is anyone home?" I repeated, yelling louder as I grabbed the railing of the ramp up to the entrance. "Hey man, our rover broke down and I need some help!"

I felt incredibly naked without my laser carbine, but I'd left it with Fargo both to sell the story I had ready about being a mine employee whose vehicle had broken down and because her sniper rifle wouldn't be very useful at close range. I still had the Gyroc pistol I'd borrowed from her, tucked into my belt at the small of my back, under my jacket, but I was no sort of fast draw even under the best of circumstances.

If I'd known how much time I'd wind up spending hiking

around with a gun in my hand, maybe I would have tried harder to get into Force Recon back when.

The front door of the sheet metal building had a cheap, pot-metal feel under my knuckles, the knocking a hollow thump. A light shone from inside, dim and green-tinted, probably chemical strip lighting, but that was it. I couldn't see any working lights or computer displays through the narrow window built into the door.

"Hey, come on! Is anyone here?"

I grabbed the door handle and pulled, expecting it to be locked. I wasn't disappointed. The lock wasn't anything complicated, no ID plate, no retinal scanner, just a simple, magnetic seal with a reader I assumed would take a code from a company 'link. I didn't have one of those, but I did have the one Fargo had brought for me.

"We're clear up here," I said. "But the door's locked."

"On my way," Vicky said, her voice quiet in my ear.

All three of them came around the side of the building and I bit back a curse.

"Weren't you two," I waved a hand at Martz and Fargo, "supposed to stay out there and keep watch?"

"If they have drones out here," Martz argued, "it's gonna look damned suspicious the two of us creeping around in the bushes with guns."

Which I couldn't argue with. I did wish he'd brought the objection up when we were planning all this, not just blow me off and do what he thought was right, but another thing that would have looked damned suspicious was the four of us standing around the front door with guns, arguing like idiots.

"Take out the lock," I said to Vicky, backing away.

Vicky held the carbine up to the door lock one-handed, her other hand covering her face as she looked away, and pulled the trigger. I'd shielded my eyes from the flash, but it was still bright enough to cast shadows, and the thunderclap of the superheated air rushing back into the evacuated tunnel burned through the atmosphere from the laser echoed three times around the empty parking area. If any drones *were* around, they'd know where we were, but we had no other way into the building.

The shot had blasted the magnetic lock out of the door, white-hot bits of metal from the destroyed mechanism scattered over the landing at the top of the ramp. I pulled the Gyroc pistol and pushed through the door. There was a sort of mud room at the front of the building, and I supposed they needed it when it rained or snowed here, to hang jackets and stash their overshoes, though it was empty now. Through it were banks of monitors, their displays turned off for the night, and three doorways.

I checked each of them, finding two bathrooms and a single, private office with a data terminal, a cot and the sort of cheap, knock-off holotank that were all you could get out here. It wouldn't last three years without constant maintenance, or so I'd been told when I asked about buying one for our place on Hausos.

"What's all this stuff do?" Martz wondered, motioning at the banks of inactive monitors.

"Detects stupid questions," Vicky shot back, pushing the door shut and pulling a chair up to hold it that way. "Is there anything useful in here?"

"In here," I said, waving them over to the office.

The walls were decorated with active holograms of some powerball team called the Storms, and I'd never heard of them. To be fair, though, I hadn't the opportunity or inclination to follow the sport in my youth. What was important to me was the flashing icon on the data terminal that covered the top of the desk. I waved a hand over the screen and it flared to life, asking me for a security ID and daring me to try to access the system without one.

"Damn," I murmured. "Should have figured they'd have security, even out here in the boondocks." I shot Vicky a hopeful glance. "You know anything about information systems?"

She squinted at me doubtfully.

"How long have you known me, Cam? Do you recall me ever showing any interest in software security?"

"Well, I didn't know you were into alien conspiracy theories until a few months ago," I argued. "Anything's possible."

Karen Fargo sighed, handing off the pulse carbine to me and fishing in the pouches of her tactical vest until she came up with a small, rectangular device I didn't recognize and unfolded a dataspike connector from the side of it.

"What's that?" I asked her.

She didn't answer immediately, leaning down over the desk until she found the receptacle for the dataspike and plugged the device into the data terminal. The security screen flashed twice and then disappeared into the spinning wheel animation as the system chewed on whatever she'd fed it. I was about to repeat the question when a generic business user interface popped up, replete with menus and suggestions for tasks it could accomplish.

I stared back and forth between Fargo and the display, frowning in confusion.

"It's a cracking module," Fargo said, as if that explained everything.

"And how the hell did you get it?" Vicky wondered.

"The CSF has a bunch of them, in the armory, you know, locked up." She shrugged. "When you sent me and Gavin to requisition the small arms for the operation, I grabbed a little of everything and, I think, three of these?" She shrugged. "The other two I put in your tactical vests, but you didn't wear them when you went down on the lander."

"Well, that was...foresightful of you," I said, and she beamed with the compliment.

"Thank you, sir!"

Only I wasn't sure if I meant it as a compliment. Karen Fargo was entirely too helpful for someone who'd gotten out of the Marines as a corporal and went to work for the CSF because she couldn't find a job anywhere else. I was having enough problems with Martz without having to worry about her being a mole.

"Kiss ass," Martz murmured, leaning over the desk to get a better look at the display, as if making an effort to remind me that he was the asshole, and I should stop thinking about Fargo.

I shouldered past him and began scrolling through the menus, looking for something that would jump out as important. Martz and Fargo were both trying to crowd in and kibbutz, while Vicky watched them with her arms crossed, glaring.

"Fargo," I said, "since you seem to know what you're doing, can you go check out the terminals out there in the main room and see if any of them are hooked up to the communication dishes? I'd like to see if we can get a message to the *Yantar* without hooking our 'links to the satellite relays."

"Sure, will do."

Martz scowled as she left the room.

"I don't trust her," he declared. "Ain't nobody that cheerful all the fucking time."

"I totally agree." I leaned over conspiratorially and whispered to him. "Do me a favor, go keep an eye on her, make sure she doesn't do anything hinky."

Martz nodded, following Fargo out of the office. Vicky waited until he was all the way out the door before she let her straight face break into a smile, her shoulders shaking with silent laughter.

"Well done, Lt. Alvarez," she said quietly, leaning her

shoulder against mine and examining the screen. "What have we got here?"

"There's a folder labelled 'shipping invoices.' Let's see if it has any notes on who it's being shipped to."

The operating system was as old as the computer, no holographic projectors, no haptic controls, just a touch screen, but at least it was simple and intuitive. I tapped on the folder and it exploded outward into row after row of files marked with dates and times that I took to be rhenium shipments. I picked one at random and opened it, bombarded with numbers that washed over me like they were in another language.

"There," Vicky said, pointing at a section of the file down near the bottom. "The subfile that says 'notes.' Open that one." I did.

Shipment 05162232 offload from B-Train 0730, launch scheduled 0900.

"That was three days ago, if I'm reading it right. Go back." I did and she pointed to another folder, this one on the upper left-hand side. "That one. That should be the latest."

A bunch more incomprehensible numbers, but yeah, there was that notes file.

Shipment 05192232 offload from A-Train 0630, launch scheduled 0845.

"That's tomorrow morning," I said, shaking a finger at the words on the screen.

"Yeah, but what's the significance of that?" she wondered. "What can we do with it? You think we can cross-reference it with other records?"

"We can try," I said, shrugging. "There's a search function. Let's look for shipment numbers."

The search led me to a list of invoices, payment receipts and a bunch of other shit that made my eyes start to go out of focus, but I scrolled through every bit of it, searching for any reference to the buyers. But that was all they were referred to as, just "the Buyers."

"Damn," Vicky murmured. "Don't these people believe in competent record-keeping? How can they run a business this way?"

"It's pretty damn easy when you only have one customer and they don't want anyone to know who they are. Maybe Konigsberg doesn't even know who they are."

"You think someone like him would really make a deal and not know who was paying him?" She scowled doubtfully. "He doesn't seem the trusting type to me."

"This kind of money," I said, waving at the figures listed on the invoices, "could buy a shitload of trust."

"You guys find anything in here?" Martz asked, coming back into the office with Fargo in tow. "Because we can't unlock any of the controls out there without that cracking module. They're all security coded."

"Kind of," I said. "We know when the next shipment of rhenium is going out."

"And what good does *that* do us?"

I shared a look with Vicky. I saw it in her eyes when she understood what I was saying and she shook her head, not in disagreement but in resignation.

"Two things," I replied. "One, it gives us a way off this planet. The rhenium is going to be transported by train from the refinery to the spaceport. The train is automated, and I'd bet it doesn't have much security. After all, who'd try to sabotage a train filled with ore? Each load isn't that valuable by itself and damaging the train would only delay production for a few days."

"What about getting from the train to the cargo shuttle?" Martz's look was thoughtful rather than dismissive, so at least there was a chance of talking him into this.

"I saw the train being loaded on the ride up to the refinery.

The rhenium is stored in disposable metal cargo pods. All we have to do is get inside one of them and they'll load us right into the hold of the shuttle. Our main worry is going to be if the hold is pressurized or not."

"Most cargo shuttles have pressurized holds," Fargo said. At curious glances from Vicky and me, she expounded. "I tried to get some work on a freight hauler before I was recruited by the CSF. Cargo shuttles are made for versatility. They need to be able to haul cattle, seedlings, even passengers sometimes."

"All right, then," I said, clapping my hands together as if I was about to start digging an irrigation trench back on Hausos. "We sneak on the train, conceal ourselves in a cargo container, and then—and this is the most important part—we get out and take over that shuttle *before* we dock with the freighter, because even if the shuttle's hold is pressurized, the freighter's won't be. And once we get onto the freighter, we'll know who's buying the rhenium."

"We're not going to be able to fly the freighter ourselves," Fargo warned me. "Like I said, I worked on one. Those kinds of ships, even less...reputable kinds, let's say, have biometric locks or at least security codes set up with the crew's 'links. We might could get access to some of the secondary systems, but not navigation or engineering."

"All we'll need is communication," I assured her. "We've got our own ship. We just need to get somewhere they can pick us up."

Martz nodded, thumping the desk.

"Not bad, for an officer. How long will it take us to make it to the train station?"

"We could get there in a couple hours on foot," Vicky said. "But we'd get spotted. Even if they don't have any drones up, even if the mercs think we died in the shuttle, they're going to be on alert and watching the roads."

"Yeah, that's the one part I don't have figured out," I admitted. "We can't walk in there without getting spotted, but I don't know how we can get a ride."

"Wait a second," Fargo said, jerking a thumb behind her. "I was looking at those terminals out there and thinking about it, and this place has got to be an uplink for their space assets. I mean, look at it, it's got a LOS relay and a satellite uplink, and you've got access to their business files. This office is the highest spot of all their structures according to the maps. They use it to beam data upstairs to their satellites and use the relay system to get messages onto ships heading for one of the jumpgate systems with an Instell ComSat."

"For what?" Martz wondered.

"Banking," I guessed. "Even a wildcat outfit like this needs to manage their finances. Unless their rhenium buyers are into barter, they have to get paid in Tradenotes or Corporate scrip."

"But what's your point?" Vicky asked her. "What does it matter if this place is a satellite uplink for their financial transactions?"

"It means," Fargo told her, the smile on her face nearly beatific, "if we get up on the roof and start breaking shit, they're going to have to send someone to fix it. Not tomorrow, but right now."

"And they're going to have to come out here in a rover or a cargo truck," Martz realized, snapping his fingers. "Fargo, I take back every nasty thing I ever said about you. You're a fucking genius."

"Thanks, Sgt. Martz," she said, grinning broadly...until it faded into childlike disappointment. "Wait...you said nasty things about me?"

I sighed.

"Later," I told her. "Come on, let's find some tools." A thin smile crept across my face. "And do some damage."

[12]

"Hey!" Martz said, bursting through the rear door of the uplink building as if he had urgent news.

"What is it?" I turned, long-held instinct keeping the muzzle of my pulse carbine pointed down the gravel road instead of swinging it around to follow my eyes. "Did you see anything the other direction?"

"No, man," he insisted, then brought his hand out from behind his back, his fist crammed full of shining, silver wrappers. "But I did find a whole bunch of ration bars in the desk drawer of that office! Either of you two want some?"

Vicky's sigh was nearly inaudible, and she didn't leave her position laid out across the back porch of the building, her pulse carbine pointed back the way we'd come, but I could read her thoughts as clearly as if she'd yelled them at me. *Moron.*

But I was still pretty damned hungry.

"Yeah, thanks, man. Leave us a few, if you don't mind."

Busting the satellite dishes and the laser LOS relay had been a calorie-intensive endeavor, and it was all I could do to keep my eyes open. Every now and then, I snuck a look at the wreckage, sending up a small prayer that there would be some hard-assed slave driver riding herd on the night shift who'd force his people to come out here well after dark and fix the smashed equipment instead of waiting till morning. Vicky never did, though, being so much more pragmatic than I could ever hope to be. And not at all religious.

The ration bars were pretty basic, one step up from cardboard, but they were better than the empty pit in my stomach and I sighed with relief as I downed the second. Vicky waited until I'd finished eating and taken a swig of water from the bottle that we'd found in a storage closet inside the office before cocking an eyebrow at me questioningly.

"Are you done?" she wondered. "I wouldn't mind grabbing a bite, too, but I don't intend to inhale the food, so I wondered if you could keep watch for me."

I raised my hand in surrender, properly abashed at my sloppy eating habits, then settled the foregrip of my pulse carbine against the porch railing and watched the night. The gentle rustle of the ration bar wrapper drowned out the sounds of the surrounding woods and even the distant grumble of automated digging machines tearing into the mountain.

"I don't like this," she said. I shrugged.

"Yeah, it's pretty bland," I admitted. "But beggars can't be choosers."

"Not the food, you doofus," she sighed. Then she paused. "I mean, yeah, those rat bars sucked and they're probably ten years old, but I meant I don't like *this*." I glanced at her and she twirled a finger around us. "All this. I feel like we're just barreling ahead and not even considering whether we're doing the right thing."

"If we're working for the CSF, we're probably *not* doing the right thing. But they're not the only ones we're working for," I reminded her. "Like Ruthie said, we have to improvise, adapt, and overcome."

"I hope she's all right. Shit, I even hope Dunstan is all right. And not just because if they're dead, we don't have a ride out of here."

"We've been in worse fixes. We'll be all right." I didn't really believe it, and I knew she wouldn't believe it either, but it felt like it was important for one of us to say it, to get the positive vibes out into the air.

"Your lips to God's ears," she said, then fell silent.

"I don't know how much God's listening to me at the moment...," I started to say, but she held up a hand to stifle my reply.

"There's a vehicle coming."

She had better hearing than I did, because it took me another few seconds before the mild growl of an alcohol-fueled engine reached my ears, and even then, I couldn't tell from which direction it was approaching. I was about to ask her when I saw the muzzle of her carbine pointing up the road, towards the refinery.

"We should get back inside," I told her. "If they see us out here, they're going to turn around and call for help."

Her mouth was a hard line, but she pulled off the wall and went for the door. I shut it behind us and watched from the narrow window beside it while Vicky shut off the interior lights.

"Martz, Fargo, we have a vehicle approaching from the north," I called back to them, using my 'link to avoid shouting. "Watch your sectors. If they come up our way, we can take care of them. If they circle around the front, they're yours. If they're unarmed, *try* to take them prisoner without shooting them."

"What difference does it make?" Martz scoffed.

"Unless the Council wants to bring in all its own workers and equipment, they're going to have to work with these people," I said. "It'll be easier on them if we don't have any bloodbaths. Save it for the mercs. You can kill all of them you want and no one'll blink at you."

His sigh rasped in my ear, even more unpleasant than it would have been in person.

"Fine."

"And we can trust that about as far as we could throw him," Vicky murmured.

"Maybe we won't have to," I told her. "They're pulling up on this side of the building."

They'd brought a cargo truck rather than the rover I'd expected, its bed covered with canvas, flapping in the wind. The truck's design was probably two centuries old, copied and fabricated over and over from one decade to another on one colony after another because it was easy to make from local materials. The men and women inside the cab could have been from any of those decades, dressed in stained, grey work clothes, their faces sharing the same resentment as any working stiff who got called out of bed after midnight by their boss to go fix someone else's fuck-up.

I could make out three of them through the front windshield, their faces lit up by the floodlights, which seemed manageable.

"When they get out," I told Vicky, "you and I run out quick, get guns in their faces and make sure they don't have time to call for help."

"Right." She didn't complain, but I could sense the impatience in her voice, the unsaid addition of, "yeah, I heard you the first three times."

The truck hesitated, and I was sure it was about to pull up right outside the back porch...but the gears shifted with an awkward grind and it lurched forward again, rolling right across the back of the building, turning slowly down the driveway circling around it.

"Shit." I keyed my 'link. "They're coming around your way."

"I see 'em."

Across the building, the rumble of the truck's engine died and doors squeaked open. The low murmur of indistinct voices traveled through the distance and the walls between us, though their meaning was lost. I knew I should be paying attention to the road outside, in case they'd sent more people, or mercs as security, but I kept glancing back through the break room to the main area where the displays glowed dimly, still deactivated. I couldn't see the other door, couldn't see the mud room or Martz and Fargo, no matter how much I shifted back and forth in my position.

"Just go," Vicky urged me. I frowned, regarding her with narrowed eyes. "I'll watch this side and call you if I see anything. Go."

"Love you," I told her, heading back through the office.

"Damn right you do."

The voices were closer now and each step I took brought their words closer, their meaning clearer. Two men and a woman, her voice shrill and cackling, someone who'd been out here on the rough edge too long.

"This is just the sort of bullshit he would do!" she insisted, as if I was catching one half of an argument en media res. "You watch, he had his little twatwaffle girlfriend Angela bust up our shit just so he could roust us all in the middle of the night! He knew we were on call!"

"Oh, come on, Rosie," one of the men said, his tone longsuffering, if weary. "Even Rafferty isn't that big of a prick. And even if he was, he's a lazy prick. That would take way too much work."

"Besides," the second guy added, a hint of a slur to his words, "Angie's too high-maintenance to get up on the fuckin' roof and wreck a satellite dish."

"Well, *someone* did it!" the woman bellowed. "What? You think a fuckin' bear climbed up there?"

I slowed to a cautious walk as I came up to the entrance to the mud room, knowing that was where Martz and Fargo would be waiting, but not knowing if the workers would actually come in that way, or at all. Would they have to? I was no sort of communications tech, and had never worked on anything electronic other than the innards of a Vigilante battlesuit or an auto-harvester, so I wasn't sure if they could fix the damage we'd done just by replacing the outside hardware.

"You two get up there and start working on the dish," the first male voice I'd heard said, loud as if calling back to someone, and close, coming up the steps to the mud room. "I'll make sure the systems are up and running so we can get them connected and get the hell out of here."

Shit. This was the worst of all possible worlds.

"Vicky," I hissed into the pickup for my 'link. "Two of them are going up to the roof."

"You want me to head out there?" she asked.

"Not yet. If they see you, they could still call back to their office. Wait for my word."

The door to the mud room was free-swinging on a kickplate, and I put a hand against it, waiting until I heard the curse from outside.

"What the hell...?" The technician had seen the blasted lock on the door. There'd been nothing we could do about it, which was why them coming around to the front had been a bad thing, not just for them, but for us too.

Martz moved, yanking the door open, and I pushed through into the mud room at the exact same time, coming out right behind Fargo. Martz grabbed the man by the front of his shirt and yanked him inside, and I had just enough time to catch a glimpse of a pale, jowly face and an unruly blond beard before the former NCO had the technician in a choke hold, cutting off the blood from his carotid artery. The guy struggled fiercely for a few seconds, hands clawing at Martz's arm in futility until he went limp, his eyes rolling back into his head.

I let him hold the choke for another five seconds before I tapped him on the shoulder.

"That's enough. Let him loose. Get flex cuffs on him and gag him."

Martz looked as if he was going to argue with me, so I assumed the sale, pulling the unconscious technician out of his arms and lowering the man to the floor, motioning for Fargo to hand me the flex cuffs I knew she kept in a pocket of her tactical vest. I zipped them around the man's wrists and ankles, then motioned again.

"Give me your knife."

It was nothing special, not a monomolecular blade or a vibro-shiv, just a handy utility knife, but it was sharp enough to slice right through the technician's sleeve, and I used the tough, thick stretch of fabric to gag him, finishing just in time as he was beginning to stir.

"Get his 'link and see if he's wearing an ear bud or a throat mic," I told Fargo, handing her back the knife.

"I thought you were going to watch the other side," Martz said, something low and menacing in his voice.

"Thought you might need an extra hand." I smiled thinly. "Fargo, drag him back inside and keep an eye on him." I touched my ear bud. "Vicky, we're going out now. Head out the other side and make sure neither of them makes a run for it."

"If they do, she needs to shoot them down," Martz said, eyeing me with doubt in his expression. "You think she can do that?"

"I think she could shoot about anyone she thought deserved

it," I assured him, then motioned at the door. "After you, Sergeant."

I'll give him this, no matter how upset he was with me, he moved with a purpose, bursting out the door and vaulting over the railing on the front porch, heading for the truck. Both of the other workers were still there, around the back at the tailgate for the bed, trying to pull out replacement parts for the gear we'd damaged. The man was rail-thin, his long hair stringy and unkempt, the woman thickly built with an active tattoo running up her forearm and under her rolled-up sleeve, a powerball player in full armor, his arm outstretched, slamming the metallic pilota into the magnetic goal over and over.

What was it with these people and powerball? I didn't think anyone outside the core worlds cared about the damned game, but apparently it was hot shit here.

They'd parked the truck close to the building, and there was only enough room for us to move single file between the two, and Martz was in the lead. Which meant that, when the man stepped into that gap, his arms filled with a heavy satellite transceiver dish, Martz ran into him full tilt, knocking them both to the ground...and leaving me blocked out.

The woman screeched at the top of her lungs and took off running in the opposite direction. I yelled out a curse, since being quiet didn't matter anymore, then touched my ear bud again.

"Vicky, we got a runner, heading your way!"

And then I ran up to help Martz, because there was no way I was going to get to that woman in time to stop her and because I trusted my wife. And I didn't trust Martz to subdue this guy without killing him. The skinny man was down, the satellite transceiver crushing him beneath its weight and Martz's, but the former NCO was trying to pummel the technician in the head, the power of his blows limited by a lack of leverage.

"Stop!" the mine worker was yelling. "Don't hurt me!"

I pushed Martz to the side and shoved the crystalline emitter of my pulse carbine into the technician's face.

"Put your hands behind your head and roll onto your stomach," I told him. "Now or I'll put a round through your head."

He couldn't move fast enough to comply, and I nodded to Martz.

"Cuff him, hurry."

The big man grunted, glaring daggers at me for having pushed him aside, but he did as he was told.

"Vicky!" I called. "Did you get her?"

"I got her," came the reply, even and calm. "She's alive, but she's going to have a sore jaw."

"Haul her inside. We'll meet you there."

———

"What do we need to talk to him for?" Martz asked plaintively. "We need to get the fuck out of here!"

"For once, I agree with Sgt. Martz," Vicky said, looking at me askance. "Let's get out of here before they send someone else."

"And go where?" I asked, being gentle about it because it was Vicky and not just Martz. "Do any of you know how to get on that train? Other than just walking up to it while they're loading the cargo? Because I don't think that's going to work."

"Now you tell us," Martz grumbled.

I ignored him, staring into the eyes of the man strapped to the office chair in front of me. I had been there myself not so long ago and felt a bit of empathy for the innocent technician when I saw the abject fear in his eyes.

"I double-checked," Vicky assured me. "I got his 'link and ear bud and he doesn't have any other comms on him."

"Pull out his gag," I instructed.

"You bite me," Vicky warned the man, wagging her finger like an elementary-school teacher, "and I'll break your jaw."

He didn't seem interested in biting, but he did start babbling as soon as the gag came out.

"Where are my friends? You didn't kill them, did you?"

"They're right outside," I assured him. I nodded to Vicky and she pulled the door to the office open to show the man the other two technicians trussed up on the floor, Vicky standing over them with her Gauss rifle at the ready. She shut it quickly, before any of the others could see what was happening in the office. "And they're going to be fine, as long as you cooperate with us."

"What do you want?" he stammered. He was not what I would have thought of as a hard case, which worked out better for us. "Who the hell are you guys?"

"We want to know about the A-Train heading out this morning. What do you know about it?"

"The...what? The train?" He blinked, confused either by the line of questioning or maybe from the lingering effects of a rear naked choke. "I don't know nothing about the trains, man! I work on communications and networking!"

"You know where the tracks run, don't you? You know where it's loaded, how long it takes?"

"Well yeah, kind of. I mean, it runs every day. It goes down the west track, the one on the far side of the refinery. Everyone knows that. It gets loaded up at the refinery and then heads down the tracks to the port. It takes maybe forty minutes, I think."

"Does it ever stop along the way?" I asked him. "Any road crossings? Track changes? Anything?"

"I mean, there's one crossing, I think. Up where the earth

movers sometimes have to move from one dig to another. But that's it, that's the only place it might stop."

"Where's the crossing?"

"Umm, I mean, I don't have the longitude and latitude, man!" he protested, his shoulders moving like he would have shrugged if his hands hadn't been tied behind his back.

I rubbed a hand over my eyes, the exhaustion hitting me like a wave, but the meaty sound of a fist striking flesh snapped my head up, with Vicky's outraged shout hot on its heels. By the time I opened my eyes, Martz was already shaking out his right hand and the technician's head was rolling back, blood streaming from his nose.

"Goddamnit, Martz!" I yelled, pushing him away.

"We ain't got time for this fucking around, Alvarez! We need to get out of here!" He grabbed the technician by the front of his work shirt and shook him. "Tell us where the crossing is or so help me God, I'll pound your face into fucking hamburger!"

"All right, man! Don't hurt me! Please!" The technician was cringing away, turning his head. "It's like, down the main road from the refinery to town, like a bit over halfway...I don't know how far exactly, but it's maybe a twenty-minute drive."

"How do we make sure the train stops?" I asked, still glaring at Martz but deciding to take advantage of the technician's fear while I had the chance. "Is there a driver? Or does it just detect vehicles across the track and stop automatically?"

"There ain't no driver, man," he said, squinting at me and then wincing when it hurt his nose. "I mean, Jesus, what are we? Fucking cavemen? It's all automated."

"There you go," Vicky said, nodding. "We can use their cargo truck. It should be big enough to register."

"What about them?" Martz said, nodding toward the bleeding technician and then motioning at the door. "We can't leave them here. Someone might check on this place before the shuttle takes off and then we're fucked."

"We'll leave them gagged and tied together in the woods a klick or so down the road," I decided. "By the time anyone finds them, we'll be in orbit."

Martz snorted in derision but didn't argue with me and I took it as a win.

"Get him in the back of the truck," I said, then yanked open the door. "Fargo, let's get them up. We've got a train to catch."

[13]

"This may be the worst date you've ever taken me on," Vicky yelled into my ear.

I still barely heard her over the steady *thump-thump-thump* of the wheels on the track. I'd have thought being inside the ore container would have muffled the noise, but instead, it seemed to amplify the sound until it was a drumbeat inside my head, trying to pound its way out. Getting onto the train had been childishly simple, just a matter of stopping the cargo truck on the tracks and then waiting until the train stopped. I'd waited until everyone else had climbed on board before I moved the vehicle out of the way and I'd imagined that I'd have to run to catch up with it, but the automation software must have had some sort of fail-safe that left it sitting there for a good five minutes.

Which had been convenient, since it gave me plenty of time to clamber into the maintenance hatch on the cargo container, but now was making me paranoid as hell. Would the train report the stop to the mine offices? Would someone stop us and check the train before we got to the spaceport? Did they have sensors on the locomotive that told them someone had opened the door? Maybe they already knew we were on board and the whole thing was a trap.

The only good thing about the ceaseless racket was that I didn't have to listen to Martz gripe about how uncomfortable it was. And I knew he would, because it *was* really damned uncomfortable. Rhenium slugs were piled meters high inside the cargo container, leaving us barely enough room to crouch, hunched over near the maintenance hatch, which we'd left cracked open enough to ensure an airflow.

"I don't know," I yelled back in her ear, trying to sound more confident than I felt, "I recall our first date being on a Tahni military outpost."

"Only you would consider a military operation a date, Alvarez."

"Hey!" Fargo said, leaning in toward us to be heard. "Is it just me or is this thing slowing down?"

I listened for a second and realized that the rhythm of the clacking of the wheels had changed, slowing from a kicking club beat to something more classical.

"She's right," I told Vicky, shifting positions to get closer to the hatch.

I pushed it open a few centimeters and the grey light of dawn leaked inside, but all I saw was the sky...until the train's brakes began to squeal, and the curved hemisphere of a heavy-lift cargo shuttle peeked above the body of the train car.

"We're at the spaceport," I told them, not having to yell because the noise of the train had begun to lag with its speed. "Get ready, brace yourselves."

I waved at Vicky to join me as we jammed ourselves into a corner of the cargo pod, wedging against each other and the metal liner. Vicky was cringing in anticipation and the look on my face probably mirrored hers. We both knew what was coming next, and knew it wouldn't be pleasant.

It wasn't. The cargo arm was invisible behind the grey, metal walls, but I pictured its grasp, a giant, robot crab leg with a pincer twenty meters long. The metal of the cargo pod rang like a gong when the claw grasped it and then the ride began. Rhenium slugs weren't the most comfortable cushioning to begin with, but when they began to shift and roll like the tide, trying to wash us away, to bury us in one side of the container or the other, I began to have serious doubts about the soundness of my plan.

"Fuck!" Martz blurted, echoed by a cry of pain from Fargo as the wave of metal pellets crashed into them. I would have cautioned them to keep quiet, but I was too busy trying to keep my head—and Vicky's—above, well, if not water, then something that could drown me just surely.

I hadn't taken up swimming until the Marines had put me through drownproofing, and hadn't been a big fan since I had to swim up from the bottom of a lake on Brigantia. But I would rather have been dumped into that lake a thousand times before trying to swim through that ocean of ore again. The crush of it kept threatening to bury me with each jolting movement of the pod, tentacles of metal circling my ankles and calves and trying to pull me under. Panic flared inside my head in surges of red and I wondered if the agoraphobia I'd overcome less than ten years ago was about to be replaced by well-earned claustrophobia when finally, the capsule thumped solidly into a stable resting place.

I pushed out of the pile of rhenium pellets, gritting my teeth at the stream of the things that had made their way down my collar. Everything had been plunged into complete blackness and I knew we were out of the open day and inside the cargo hold of the heavy-lift shuttle, fastened securely into a magnetic anchor.

"Is everyone okay?" I asked, my voice sounding intrusive and alien in the sudden quiet.

"Can we get the hell out of here now?" Martz wondered.

"Not yet." I checked the local time on my 'link. "Unless you want to be plastered all over the cargo hold in about ten seconds."

"Oh, God, not again," Fargo moaned, proving not even the most sanguine optimist could be thankful for what we were about to receive.

The distant whine of the turbines was our first warning, but there wasn't much we could do other than lie flat and motionless on our bed of very expensive metal beads. When the jets ignited and the hand of an angry god pressed down in vengeful rage against my chest, I discovered the hard way that rhenium was not a quality replacement for the gel in an acceleration couch.

Darkness closed in around the edges of my vision and then swallowed me completely.

————

"Cam. Wake up, Cam."

Consciousness swam just out of reach, a disembodied voice in the utter blackness, and I was lost in a dream of butterflies, their wings fluttering against me, a feeling that was not quite the sensation of raindrops falling, not quite snowflakes against my skin. Drier, warmer, more substantial and yet somehow infinitely lighter at the same time. It was a feeling totally apart from any experience of reality I'd ever had, convincing me with its ethereal quality that I was lost in a dream.

Light shone on my face, blindingly bright, revealing the stark truth. I was still in the cargo capsule, but the pressure from the boost was gone, as was the pressure from Portent's gravity, and the rhenium pellets danced around us in a microgravity ballet like something out of one of the holographic displays in a museum demonstrating particle collisions on a subatomic level. They lacked weight and their individual mass wasn't that great, which turned what had been a suffocating tide into a cloud of feathers.

"We're in orbit," Vicky told me. "Boost cut out about a minute ago."

Martz and Fargo were floating free, surrounded by their own personal ring system of metal pellets, and both were just beginning to stir, overcome by the g-forces of our orbital insertion, just as I had been.

"Why didn't you pass out?" I asked Vicky, pushing away from the wall towards the hatch. The question came out more petulant than I'd intended, as if I resented the fact she was able to stay conscious. And maybe I did.

"Because I'm tougher than any of you wussies," she told me, arching an eyebrow. "And don't you forget it."

"You guys up?" I asked Martz and Fargo. "We need to get out of this pod and into the cockpit before this thing docks."

"I'm good," Martz insisted, even though his eyes didn't seem to be focusing on anything in particular. "I'll be fine."

"Ready when you are, sir," Fargo assured me. She had her Gauss rifle tucked under her arm, her other hand steadying her against the bulkhead.

I whispered a prayer as I worked the fastenings on the hatch, hoping God was listening after all these years. If they stored the capsules the way they were designed to be stacked, the hatch would always be kept clear in case they needed to adjust the load during acceleration. But we weren't exactly dealing with Corporate Council shipping firms here and they might just shove as many of the pods into the shuttle as they possibly could, and to hell with safety regulations. I hadn't mentioned that worry to the others because I figured they had enough to think about already, but it weighed heavy on my mind when I yanked down on the latch.

Either God was smiling at us or Konigsberg ran a tight ship all the way into orbit, because the hatch opened, swinging outward freely and bouncing back before I arrested the recoil with an open palm. I hissed out a relieved breath.

"Nervous?" Vicky murmured near my ear.

"You know me so well."

I grabbed the edge of the hatchway, pushed my carbine ahead of me and yanked myself upward into the cargo hold. There was no up or down in free fall, of course, but most space-ships were organized either along vertical or horizontal lines relative to their axis of travel. Shuttles and smaller starships designed as airfoils intended to fly in an atmosphere were gener-ally built horizontally, but heavy-lift shuttles were the excep-tion. They were massive spheres set into a base of multiple atmospheric jets clustered around the main plasma drive, meant to take off and land vertically.

And if I'd been up in the cockpit, my eyes and my inner ear could have aligned using that vertical orientation to make it easier to deal with the free fall, but the cargo hold was a different thing altogether. The cylindrical cargo pods were anchored together in clusters of magnetic brackets, projecting up and out at an angle like the disc florets of a sunflower, with the shuttle's reactor shielding at the hub.

Thank God we'd come out in free fall because if there'd been any sort of gravity, I never would have been able to climb up from the bottom of the anchors to the catwalk at the top. In free fall, it took only a gentle push off from the side of the cargo pod to send me flying thirty meters up. I could have tried to skirt the edge of the cargo pods, take it slow, but I'd never had the patience for commando shit, so I just barreled forward, counting on speed and surprise to take the cockpit.

As it turned out, either approach would have worked.

"What the hell?" Martz said from behind me as I stopped myself against the railing at the rear of the cockpit. "There's nobody there!"

And he was right. The cockpit was empty, the displays shifting from one view to another, with no one to watch them.

"It's under computer control," Vicky declared, braking herself with a hand against my shoulder. "Either from the ground or the freighter. Makes sense. Especially if the buyers don't want any contact with Konigsberg people."

"Shit," I said, almost spitting the word. "If that's so, we aren't going to find out anything on this shuttle. We have to get onto the freighter. And if there's no crew, they won't be leaving the thing pressurized."

"Suits," Fargo said, pointing at the lockers around the edge of the catwalk, at the utility airlock. Without elaborating, she propelled herself along the railing, speeding toward the lockers as if her life depended on it. Which it did.

I scanned the displays, looking for a sensor readout, some sort of transponder signal.

"Can you figure out how close the freighter is?" I asked Vicky, hoping she'd paid more attention than I had to how the docking procedures worked.

"That's it," she declared, stabbing a finger toward one of the screens, to a green avatar moving across a projection of the planet. She floated across the bridge, catching herself on the back of the acceleration couch at the pilot's station, eyes darting from side to side as data streamed across the top of the screen. "It's coming fast, decelerating to match orbits. We don't have much time."

"Suits!" Fargo yelled from across the breadth of the spacecraft, in counterpoint to her earlier repetition of the word.

She was pulling them from the locker, the sort of beat-up,

generic vac suits I expected from an outfit like this, probably bought surplus from a Corporate shipping outfit.

"Hurry!" The metal of the handrail was slick against my palm, burning with friction, and I didn't try using it to arrest my momentum, swinging my feet around and taking the bulkhead with my boot soles. I hit hard and gritted my teeth at the pain in my knees, but I didn't waste breath on cursing, just grabbed one of the suits and tried like hell to remember how to get one of the damned things on.

They'd taught us, of course, in the Corps. We were on troop carriers more than half the time, and if there was an emergency, we couldn't count on being able to get to our Vigilantes, so everyone received training in spacesuit use, but that had been years ago. I fumbled with the catches, not nearly as nimble and practiced as I'd been when my squad had gotten first place in the safety drills, then forgot that I had to take my boots off before I put the suit on and had to start all over again.

"You're slow, Alvarez," Vicky taunted playfully, already lowering her helmet onto the suit's neck yoke.

I beat Martz, anyway.

"Check the air in the tanks," I warned, following my own advice, tapping the monitor on the suit's wrist. "These things are pretty old and if the shuttles are usually automated, they might not maintain them."

My own tanks were half full, which was a huge safety violation, but would be enough for our purposes.

"Everyone good?"

"Mine are full," Fargo announced.

"Fuckers only left a quarter tank in mine," Martz said.

"Still more than me," Vicky said, sounding even more put out than Martz.

I grabbed at the locker to pull myself over to her and checked her readout. Then let loose the curse I hadn't wasted on my knees free when I saw she had less than an eighth of a tank of air.

"That's maybe twenty minutes," I estimated. "Is that going to be enough?"

"If it isn't," she said, "then I'll be the first to know. There's fuck-all we can do about it now."

An alarm sounded from the cockpit, one I hadn't heard before, but I was pretty sure what it meant. I pulled my helmet on and locked down the neck gasket, checking to make sure the others were doing the same. I'd barely got the green light on the helmet's pressurization indicator when the maneuvering thrusters banged against the hull, throwing me towards the port side of the bulkhead. I grabbed at the utility locker with one hand and Vicky with the other, keeping her from slamming into the bare metal. Fargo grabbed at her own handhold, but Martz went flying and I thought he was about to break his neck, but he somehow managed to spin in mid-air and hit the bulkhead feet first.

The alarm changed tones, and this one I did know. Everyone who'd ever served on a ship knew the vacuum alarm. Air was flowing out through the vents in the wall, back into the storage tanks, the hum of the fans slowly fading as the interior of the shuttle went into hard vacuum. I was still holding onto Vicky's hand and I shot her a look, her face visible through the clear plastic of her helmet's visor. She had twenty minutes.

"Get to the cargo lock," I said. The suits probably had helmet radios but we hadn't trusted them, had left our 'link ear buds in place. "They're going to come in through there and we have to beat them to it."

The lock was already opening, a curved strip around the center of the hold, thirty meters tall and just as wide, sliding aside ponderously, folding into the inside of the hull. Through the gap was darkness, but in the darkness was light, the glaring floodlights of the freighter shining through from the yawning maw of its cargo cradle. I couldn't see the whole ship, but I knew the design. The cradles were fitted flush with the hull, each of them capable of holding ten of the freight capsules, but they'd have to come over in transfer vehicles to grab them, skeletal frames with rocket engines and power loaders attached to grab the cargo.

I pushed off the edge of the catwalk, the metal grating of the flooring and staircase only useful when the shuttle was on the ground or under boost, and dove downward at the source of the light. The shadow told me I was too late. The rockets of the maneuvering jets made no sound in the airless void as the thing poked into the cargo hold, its loader arms spread out and seeking the closest of the capsules. There was no way the crew wasn't going to see me, so I didn't try to hide.

There were two of them, faceless behind the mirrored visors of their suits, and maybe I was wrong, maybe they were inno-cent workers, hired to haul freight for some anonymous buyer and they didn't know anything...but there was only so far that I could take this and still keep my hands clean. I'd known that when I'd accepted the assignment to work for Fleet Intelligence. No one liked spooks because they had to make decisions just like this.

I brought my pulse carbine to my shoulder and shot them both.

There was no flash of light, no sound, no ionized gas to advertise that the laser had fired or to trace its path. Just a slight shudder inside the ignition chamber as the Hyper-Explosive cartridge detonated, pulsing its heat through the lasing rod, focusing it through the crystalline emitter. And then an instant's glow of vaporized plastic and metal on the chest of a spacesuit, the death spasms of whoever was inside. I shifted my aim and fired again, and the second one died in the dark silence.

Fuck. I wanted to scream it, wanted to find Colonel Hachette and Top and punch them both in the face for bringing me into this. But I forced down the heat and the anger and replaced them with the same sort of cold calculation that had slipped over my thoughts back in the Underground when the difference between life and death was keeping my head.

I hit the skeletal framework of the transfer vehicle and held on, using it as a perch while I stared past it at the freighter. Inside the cargo cradle, shining with the interior light from the square porthole at the center of it, was an airlock, the same airlock the crew had come through. Fifty meters away.

"This way," I told the others.

I braced myself and sprang away from the transfer sled, through the cargo doors and out into open space.

[14]

I'd been on an untethered spacewalk once before, though I'd been in a Vigilante at the time, and I hadn't been a fan even then.

This was much worse, despite the fact I only had to cover fifty meters. I had nothing to use for propulsion if I missed, nothing to prevent me from sailing off into space, tumbling in orbit until I ran out of air. I didn't miss, of course—the freighter was huge, even compared to the cargo shuttle, and the shuttle was nestled in the niche in the hull that formed the cargo cradle. There were two more transfer sleds moored inside the cargo cradle, waiting for crews to come out and use them, sliding by me in a blur, so close I could have brushed my fingers against their frames on either side.

The airlock rushed up at me, threatening to slam into my face and this time, to spare my knees the fresh insult, I took the impact with my left shoulder. The air gushed out of me in a pained grunt, and I would have bounced right back into space like a pinball if there hadn't been a handhold built into the hull beside the lock for just such emergencies, and even then, I was barely able to grab it in time. I kept a grip on the handhold and reached out to haul in Fargo, making sure she had one hand on the safety handle before I let her go.

"Get that lock open," I told her, bracing myself for Martz, who was coming in hot. Asshole must have just pushed off as hard as he could and forgot he was going to have to stop at some point. "Feet or shoulder, Martz. Don't hit the fucking hatch head-first."

"I know how to move in null grav," he insisted, so I let him do it his way.

The best part was, he still had his line to me open, so I could hear it when he yelped with the pain as his boots impacted the hull and he wound up with his knees beside his ears. I grabbed his arm to keep him from ricocheting away.

Vicky was last and the most graceful in her technique, probably not least because she got to watch the three of us screw it up first. I was about to congratulate her when Fargo interrupted.

"Got it!"

The outer hatch was sliding aside, the interior of the airlock flashing red to remind us it was in a vacuum. Once upon a time, I might have considered the warning unnecessary. After all, who would come into an airlock in a spacesuit and then forget they were in a vacuum? Then I joined the Marines.

These Marines, at least, didn't need to be told to get into the lock. No one wanted to be outside any longer than necessary. Fargo had gotten us in, but I didn't need her cracking module to open the inner door—all that took was yanking down the physical lever mounted on the bulkhead. No touch screens in a vacuum, and usually no easily pushed buttons either. Things had to be big and deliberate when you were working in a vac suit.

The internal lights flashed red as the outer hatch closed,

then yellow as air began flooding the lock. There was a small porthole set in the inner hatch, but all I could see through it was a bare patch of deck in the utility bay. There could have been a squad of mercenaries waiting for us on the other side of the lock, ready to blow us all to hell. But we were fresh out of choices. I checked the heels of my boots, something I hadn't had time to do back on the shuttle, and found they were fitted with magnetic anchors for work in free fall, so I anchored myself to the deck and held my pulse carbine at the ready, waiting for the inner door to open.

"We don't know these are bad guys," Vicky said, like my conscience sitting on my shoulder.

"If we don't go in hard," I told her, "they could seal off the cockpit and dump us right into the lap of whoever's behind this shit. Call me suspicious, but they're building their own fleet of warships. Somehow, I don't think they have good intentions."

She didn't respond, which bothered me even more. But then the door slid aside, and all our choices were made for us. Two figures in full vac gear were just turning from open lockers in the utility bay, probably getting ready to cycle through the lock and board one of the other two transfer vehicles. One stray transmission from them over their helmet radios, and the mission would be FUBAR. The cockpit crew could jump us into Transition Space, seal us off, force us to surrender, or just deliver us to their bosses.

They didn't get the chance to say a word. There was no time for coordinating our fires, but we'd all gone through the same training and we split the compartment in half. Vicky and I were on the left, Martz and Fargo on the right and for all Vicky's equivocation, she didn't hesitate. Twin bursts of laser fire took our guy in the torso, the stream of superheated blood gushing out of his back sending him tumbling forward head over heels across the compartment. The other suited figure went limp as a tungsten slug shattered his faceplate, making the spray of laser fire from Martz redundant.

"Go!" I snapped, cutting loose the magnets in my boots and pushing off across the compartment.

Adrenaline had dampened the sound of the brief and one-sided gunfight, but the sounds of a pulse laser discharging were unmistakable and if anyone had been listening, they'd know something was wrong. We had to get to the bridge before it was sealed off.

I sailed through a twisting cloud of crimson droplets, the globules floating through the air like bubbles until they splattered against the front of my vac suit. Stained with blood, I flew across the utility bay, grabbing the railing of the staircase heading up to the bridge to catch myself, swinging my legs around until I could boost upward.

Someone called down from an upper deck, but the suit's external mic seemed to be defective and the words were garbled, incomprehensible. They were probably calling down to the other cargo team, the ones we'd killed down in the utility bay, asking them why no one was answering their radio calls. Or maybe they'd heard the shots and were trying to figure out what was going on. Either way, we didn't have much time.

"Skip the other decks," I announced. "Go straight to the bridge!"

A head popped out from the next deck up, leaning over the railing, one hand attached to keep him in place. I just caught a flash of pale skin and fired, not thinking about it, trying hard not to focus on it because I knew what a head looked like after it had been hit by a laser blast. And I knew what it *smelled* like, and thanked God for the helmet and the internal air supply. The figure disappeared in a haze of red and then I was past, leaving any further resistance from that level to the others. I didn't hear any firing behind me, so I guessed no one else had stuck their head out.

The overhead loomed just meters above and I knew I'd reached the bridge level, so I grabbed at the center column supporting the staircase and slowed myself down, then loosened my grip and trailed my fingers along the metal surface until I reached the command deck. I'd never been aboard a freighter this large and had no idea which side of the staircase the bridge would be on, so I gripped the center column hard at the last second and pushed off from the railing, sending my legs swinging outward, rotating my whole body around the metal post.

Shouts rang out and I caught a glimpse of a blur of motion to one side, but I had to give it one more rotation before I let go. Something flashed past the visor of my helmet, crackling and sizzling and trailing a thundercrack, and I abruptly realized that someone was shooting at me with a laser weapon. I let go of the center column and cannonballed feet-first into the bridge, just as the security shield began to slide down out of the overhead.

One second the other way and I would have been chopped in half, but I slid through just beneath the heavy blast shield, right into the middle of four bridge crewmembers armed with bulky, awkward laser hand weapons. They tried to follow my course, not firing because they didn't want to fry their own bridge controls or each other. I didn't fire either, not because I was worried about damaging the ship but because I was frozen in shock for just the bare moment it took to soar across the bridge.

They were Tahni.

It all suddenly made perfect sense, yet I didn't have the time to consider it because I was about to hit the front display screen and when I did, the Tahni were going to kill me. I twisted in mid-air and jammed my finger against the firing stud. I was way too close to use the weapon's optical sights and didn't have any glasses or contact lens to sync them with, so I used what Top called "Kentucky windage," aiming by instinct and walking the rounds onto their targets.

Crackling cylinders of ionized air chopped across the bulkhead and the backs of acceleration couches and across two of the Tahni. They weren't wearing any body armor, just tunics and trousers of the same sort of woven strips of fabric that I'd seen on their technical troops during the war, and the cloth caught fire briefly but violently as the pressure pulses cut through them, sending sprays of blood heated near to steam out their backs.

Then I was turning, twisting in mid-air, the hail of fire following my passage and slicing through the two on the other side of the room just as my feet touched the display screen, disappearing into the holographic projection as if the ship's bulkhead were swallowing me up. I bounced off and activated my magnetic soles as I touched the ground, anchoring in place and watching the Tahni carefully, in case one was still alive. They turned and tumbled in mid-air, as if restless in death, their black eyes wide open, blood still beading out of their mouths, but not one of them showed a sign of life.

"Cam!" Vicky called into my 'link's ear bud. "Are you okay? Can you open the blast shield?"

It took a moment before I could answer her. My heart was beating out of my chest and I couldn't catch my breath. I knew what it was, knew the adrenaline dump and its aftermath like I knew my own name, but the knowledge didn't do anything to assuage the gut-level fear which accompanied the reaction.

"I'm all right," I told her once I could get the words out.

"Bridge is secure. Give me a second to find the control for the barrier."

I tried to look for it, but I couldn't seem to tear my eyes away from the dead Tahni, as if their motions in the air currents of the bridge ventilation were hypnotic. I was deathly afraid one of them was going to run into me, wrap itself around me.

"Did you find anything?" Vicky wondered. "Is there anything up there that could tell us who these people are?"

"Oh, yeah," I said, nodding even though she couldn't see it. "I found something."

———

"Jesus," Martz murmured, staring at the Tahni like he'd never seen one before. "What the fuck are they doing here?"

"It's pretty obvious, isn't it?" Vicky snapped, not looking up from the control panel, still hunting for the communications board. "Didn't you read any of the reports we wrote? I know Dukanovic made them available for all of you."

"I was gonna get around to them," he said, shrugging.

We'd all taken off our helmets, mostly because Vicky and Martz would have run out of air by now, but we'd left on the suits because the magnetic boots were handy and none of us was wearing any other shoes. I missed the helmet. The blood had been carried away by the ventilation system, but the stink remained, scorched flesh and burnt blood, a smell that would come back to me in my nightmares.

"It's Zan-Thint," I explained, too exhausted to even be impatient. "He's got plenty of troops and even battlesuits, but he doesn't have enough warships to take on the Commonwealth, or even the CSF. If he did, he'd have used them by now."

"You think this Tahni renegade general is building his own

fleet?" Martz sounded incredulous. "How the fuck could he *afford* that?"

"Nickel-iron is dirt cheap," Fargo pointed out. "Fusion drives aren't *that* expensive, particularly if you buy them used. Besides the rhenium for the weapons, the hardest thing to get would be the Teller-Fox generators for the Transition drives."

"And he might have access to pre-war Tahni equipment stores," I added. "That would get him the Transition drives."

"Yeah, but he'd have to build his own shipyards!" Martz said. "That would take years and he hasn't had that long."

I frowned, eyes narrowing. He was right about that. Shipyards weren't overly complicated, but they were large-scale operations. He'd have to have dozens of drydocks, construction frames, construction pods, worker bots...

"Unless," I said, the words cohering in my thoughts even as I said them, "he's using someone else's shipyard. One that's already built. You finding anything, Fargo?"

The woman had been trying to make sense of the navigation console, but she shook her head at my question.

"I'm finding lots of shit, sir," she said, "but it's all in Tahni. I couldn't tell you where this ship is now, much less where it came from."

"I think I've figured comms out, at least," Vicky said. "I just had to open a connection to my 'link and slave the ship's antenna to the frequencies already saved there. Hold on a sec." She scrolled through a menu on the display of her 'link, then touched her ear bud. "*Yantar*, this is Sandoval. Do you copy, *Yantar*?"

"Are we wide-beaming this?" I asked, worry nagging at the back of my mind. Extreme Measures had sent out their space assets against the *Yantar*, but that didn't mean they couldn't come back and take care of us if they heard the broadcast. Vicky waved the worry off.

"Yeah, but it'd take them a while to break the encryption and, without knowing what we're saying, they couldn't be sure who we were talking to. As far as they know, we're just the Tahni freighter." She keyed her mic again. "*Yantar*, this is Sandoval, please come in."

"They could still be trying to evade Extreme Measures," I reminded her. "They wouldn't be able to respond without giving away their position."

"Hey Vicky," Fargo said slowly, "do you know what that is?"

Vicky scowled at her, probably because Fargo always called me "sir," but the expression faded to worry as she followed the corporal's finger to what I thought was the ship's tactical display on the main screen. The curve of the planet was easy to make out, but rising above it were four red triangles. I didn't know for sure what they signified, but I didn't like the look of them.

"*Yantar*," Vicky said again instead of answering, "this is Sandoval! Mayday! Mayday! Mayday! We have assault shuttles heading our way and we need help ASAP! Please make for this location immediately!"

"Assault shuttles?" Martz exploded, looking around like he could see them through the bulkheads. "How the hell did they know we were here? I thought you said they couldn't decrypt your message!"

"They launched at least an hour ago," Vicky told him. "Someone sent off a signal, either from the shuttle or this freighter."

"Or it was one of those repair techs back on Portent!" Martz's words were an accusation levelled at me. "I fucking told you it was a mistake letting them live!"

"Can we get out on the cargo shuttle?" Fargo suggested, half inspiration, half desperation.

"They'd see it and blow us out of orbit in a heartbeat." I shook my head, searching the display, the console, searching anywhere for something. Weapons, the jump drive, anything. "Can we get the fusion drive going, Vicky?"

"Not without the proper ID codes. *Yantar*, please come in! Goddammit!"

"Those things look close," Martz said, taking a step closer to the screen, like he could make out more detail by moving another meter forward. "Do you think they'd just open fire? I mean, they do business with these...." He motioned at the bodies. "...people. They'd be risking killing their customers."

"They're probably hailing this freighter right now," I guessed. "We just can't hear it because we can't work their controls. We're just patching into the antenna, not the comm system directly. Does this thing have any gun turrets, Vicky? Can you tell?"

"I'm sure I don't know, Cam," she ground out, stopping in the middle of another call to Ruthie to clip off the answer. "As much as it may seem short-sighted at this late date, I still don't speak or read any Tahni and wouldn't know where to find a detailed layout of the ship's plans even if I did."

"You want me to go look for a gun?" Martz offered, waving toward the central hub behind us. It's not really possible to fidget properly in free fall, but he was making a good effort at it. "Maybe we should get to the escape pods?"

"Yeah, that's a brilliant idea," Vicky growled. "I'm sure those assault shuttles wouldn't notice us at all as long as we were in tiny, underpowered, unarmed escape pods."

"Fargo," I said, "use that cracking module and try to get the damned fusion drives online. Use the Tahni translation software in your 'link and I know that's going to be slow, but it's all we got. Martz, you're with me. If this thing has guns, we're going to find them."

"Cam, if the *Yantar* doesn't come for us," Vicky warned me, "none of that's going to do any good."

"Then keep trying to call them," I told her, brushing the back of my hand against her cheek as I passed by on the way out of the bridge. "And the rest of us will keep trying to fight."

It might be a waste of time, but what the hell else were we gonna do?

[15]

"Found it!"

Martz's voice came from a passageway off to the port side of the ship, calling me away from the storage compartment I'd stumbled onto while searching for the outside hull. Unless I wanted to throw containers of preserved Tahni food at the assault shuttles, though, nothing in the closet was going to help me.

I hated running in magnetic boots, but I hated slamming into bulkheads even more, so I dealt with the clacking and clomping and kept my eyes open. We hadn't found any more Tahni crew on the freighter, but that didn't mean one or two weren't hiding out, waiting for a chance to make a move. The passage was just as empty as it had been two minutes ago and across it, a hatchway in the bulkhead was thrown open and Simon Martz was halfway through it.

"What have we got?" I asked him, trying to see past the bulk of his suit.

"Looks like a coil-gun turret," he said. "I don't know why the hell they have a crewed turret instead of just slaving it to the ship's sensors and having it fire automatically."

"Because they're Tahni and they don't believe in automated weapons," I said, feeling like I was back in my platoon, explaining shit to a new private that they should have already known if they'd paid attention during the enemy familiarization classes we'd been given. "They do everything the hard way, which was one reason they lost the war." Martz settled down into the gunner's seat, and at least he seemed to know where the controls were, even if they were labelled in Tahni.

"This only covers half the ship's firing arc," he told me. "There's probably another one on the opposite side of this level."

Which was uncommonly good sense, particularly coming from Martz, but I didn't point that out.

"I'll go check." I touched my ear bud. "Vicky, are we making any progress with the drives?"

"Fargo is working on it." Vicky was trying not to sound stressed, and most people wouldn't have picked up on it, but I knew her better than that. "Those assault shuttles will be in firing range in less than ten minutes."

"You think they'll just open up on us," I asked, grinning when I saw that Martz was right, that there was an identical hatch on the exact opposite side of the ship on this level, "or try to board?"

"Extreme Measures, remember? Blowing things up is kind of their default."

"I was afraid you'd say that." I squeezed into the gunner's chair, which was tight quarters with a vac suit on. "Tell Fargo to get this thing moving."

"I'm sure my looking over her shoulder will do all sorts of good."

I found the controls easy enough. All coil-gun turrets were basically the same, whether they were anti-aircraft emplacements like the ones we'd been cross-trained on or a point defense turret on a spaceship. Fed from a magnetic chute, which the display told me held ten thousand rounds, and thank God they'd only changed the physical labels and not the digital display, because Tahni numbers looked something like a chart of the constellations.

The sensor displays lit up and I had a ringside seat to the four shuttles coming in thanks to the ship's lidar and radar. It wasn't quite up to the military-grade gear I was used to with the CSF, but the four red triangles were obvious enough. Coil-guns didn't have any range limit out here, unless I tried to fire at something beyond the curve of the planet, which was the main reason the military and law enforcement didn't use them, since the projectiles would keep going out there, orbiting the planet and putting big holes in whatever they happened to hit. I had ten thousand rounds to play with, so I opened fire.

The lead shuttle in the formation was the closest and the most convenient and I hosed it with five hundred rounds, spreading them out from top to bottom and left to right in case it was running an avoidance vector. And then I waited, crossing my fingers, because this was a mercenary shuttle, not a military one, and if it had been a military assault shuttle, it would have been outfitted with electromagnetic deflectors. And electromagnetic deflectors were the perfect defense again metal coil-gun rounds.

The thermal bloom from the assault shuttle's port wing told me that Extreme Measures, while well-funded and well-equipped, couldn't quite afford military-grade assault spacecraft. The shuttle wasn't destroyed because it hit its belly jets and evaded before the next salvo of tungsten slugs could reach it. The others in the flight did the same, splitting up and running avoidance courses, learning from the mistakes of their friend, which was good and bad. Good because it meant their course would take longer to get them to the freighter, bad because it would be much harder for me to hit one of them.

But it wasn't going to stop them from hitting us, though, and if they had coil-guns of their own, they were already in range and we couldn't do a damned thing to evade them unless....

Something kicked me in the ass, pushing me back into the chair with twice my normal weight and I grunted, about to curse with annoyance until my front brain caught up with my hind brain and I realized what that meant.

"Good job, Fargo!" I crowed. "Vicky, you think you can take this thing on a random avoidance course?"

"I pretty much guarantee that any course I take will be a random one," she shot back. "But I'll do my best."

"We really need to learn how to fly a spaceship," I murmured.

Maneuvering jets hammered at the hull, loud and close enough to vibrate my turret, and the view through my gun display shifted abruptly.

"They're gonna be in your firing arc, Martz," I called to him.

"I got it."

I scrolled through the display screen with a swipe of my finger, switching to Martz's side of the ship and catching sight of the mercenary shuttles again. They might have been firing, but I couldn't tell because coil-gun rounds, for all their limitations and vulnerability to deflectors, were almost impossible to detect. I could see the outgoing slugs, though, because Martz's gun simulated them for the display, a stuttering, red line reaching out towards the shuttles. He slewed the rounds from side to side, either trying to spread them out enough to out-think their avoidance pattern or just a sloppy shooter. Either way, it paid off with another hot vent of gas on thermal, a hole right through the fuselage but nothing fatal either to the shuttle's drive or its pilots. It deked sharply on flares of steering jets and the red lines followed it.

"Don't chase them," I advised Martz. "Stick with your firing arc."

"You suddenly a fucking expert on this too, Alvarez?" He kept his finger on the trigger and the red line kept running after the wounded bird until it went out of range.

"Asshole."

Something banged hard against the hull, and I thought for just the briefest moment that the maneuvering thrusters were firing again until I heard the alarm sounding. Air leak.

"We've been hulled!" Vicky told me. "Get your helmets on!"

"How much air do you have left in your suit?" I asked, biting back a curse as I grabbed my helmet off the bracket beside the backpack and slipping it on.

"Ten minutes. Maybe twelve, if I breathe shallow."

"Fuck!" I couldn't hold that curse back any longer.

"Don't worry about it," she said, infuriatingly phlegmatic. "This thing can't pull more than two G's, and we don't have fuel to do that for more than another five minutes. We aren't going to be around in another twelve minutes."

The shuttles arced around to my side of the screen and I fired, keeping the targeting reticle as close as I could to the aerospacecraft on the far left of the screen, then when the whole formation swept to the right to avoid the incoming rounds, I jerked the turret the same direction and skewed straight across the line of them. Vicky was right, we were dead, but I was determined to take one of those fucking assault shuttles with us.

I didn't see the round that did it, because it's not easy catching a glimpse of a non-reflective metal slug traveling at five thousand meters per second, but the effects were hard to miss. The holes appeared between one eyeblink and the next, as if they'd always been there, the sudden outrush of air the only clue that they hadn't. I twisted in my seat and saw the gaps in the bulkhead behind me. Four of them, only centimeters from my head.

The targeting display was still active, but the status lights were flashing red. I'd survived the hit, but the gun hadn't.

"My turret's down," I announced to the others.

"And they know it," Martz spat. "They're staying on your side of the freighter."

I should, I thought, climb out of the turret, go back to the bridge. Be with Vicky before the end. But all I could do was stare at the screen, at the shuttles coming in. I wouldn't have time to reach her.

Something flared on the screen, shining like a ring of fire on optical, thermal and spectroscopic, and I wondered if they'd hit our engines. But the glow faded, and where it had been was a starship, a massive, silver delta, twice the size of the shuttles, an eagle scattering crows away from a carcass. The rainbow ring of the Transition drive faded, taking with it the glimpse of utter nothingness that was T-space, but leaving the cutter behind, its fusion drive igniting.

The discharge of the proton cannon was a distant supernova on thermal, its beam invisible in the vacuum, but the hit obvious to every sensor I had. One of the shuttles disappeared, ceasing to be in a globe of radiant white, a new sun in Portent's sky, and then the starship was burning in at the others, a Gatling laser firing from a turret on its port wing.

Thermal blooming from the second assault shuttle's cockpit showed where the laser bursts had struck home, and that was more than enough for the remaining pair of aerospacecraft. They didn't try to decelerate; their pilots were too smart for that. They knew the cutter would be on them well before they could get any momentum heading back toward the planet, so instead, they ramped up their boost and hit their port bow maneuvering jets, steering for a lunar orbit, probably intending to slingshot around the moon for a return to Portent.

They hadn't made it more than a hundred kilometers before the proton cannon speared out again with a surge of raw nuclear energy and vaporized the trailer in the formation. The starship could have gone after the last one, hunted it down and caught it from behind, a predator on its prey, but instead, it maneuvered back around and boosted for us.

The voice in my ear bud was familiar, but I don't think I'd ever been quite so happy to hear it.

"Hey guys, you said you needed some help?"

"Dunstan," I told the pilot of Intercept One, the word a sigh of utter relief, "what the fuck took you so long?"

"Well, you know how it is, just livin' that outlaw life, hiding in the asteroid belt from mercenaries. How've you guys been?"

"Get your ass over here," I said, my impatience cutting through the man's usual banter and bullshit. I pulled open the hatch and maneuvered out of the battered turret, not bothering with my magnetic boots, just floating freely toward the stairs. "We're hulled and Vicky is running out of air."

"I'm coming. You just be ready to go, because those merc ships I was running from? Well, they're gonna be jumping in right on top of me once they figure out where I am. I hope this little adventure of yours was worth it."

"It was," I said, glancing aside at the headless body of the Tahni I'd shot earlier as it continued its macabre dance in the air currents, "very enlightening."

[16]

"Does anyone know where the hell we're going?" Simon Martz demanded, busting out of his cabin like a force of nature. He had, at least, had the brains to take advantage of our hop into Transition Space, and the temporary return of gravity, to shower and change clothes before he decided to complain about it.

"We're not going anywhere," I told him, rubbing at my eyes, slumped in one of the chairs in the galley and lacking the energy to even sit up. The shower had helped, but it wasn't an adequate substitute for sleep. "We took the *Yantar* into T-space so we could regroup without having to worry about the mercs tracking us down."

"I have the ship on a dead-end Transition Line to a brown dwarf a light-year out," Ruthie explained, hands cupped around a steaming mug of coffee. "We'll bounce back to Portent in about twelve hours. By that time, hopefully, they'll think we've vacated the system."

"Ruthie, you look like I feel," Vicky told the woman.

"It was rough," Dunstan answered for her. The pilot was unusually keyed up, and had been since he'd taken the four of us on board Intercept One and micro-Transitioned back to the asteroid belt just seconds ahead of the Extreme Measures lighter. We'd docked with the *Yantar* and jumped out of the system before any of us could get off the cutter. "We've been jumping from one end of this system to the other for two days straight, trying to stay ahead of those motherfuckers. Haven't gotten a minute's sleep." He shrugged diffidently. "Bastards are pretty good," he admitted. "Came close to boxing us in a couple times."

"For once, the doofus is right," Ruthie confirmed, ignoring Dunstan's aggrieved frown. "Even with Intercept One out trying to split up their forces, we just didn't have the firepower to take them on nose-to-nose."

"That was my first time getting shot at," Foster confided. He didn't look as wrung out as Dunstan or Ruthie, just very relieved to be out of the system, even if it was only temporary.

"Well, I hope you enjoyed it," I told him, "because it'll probably happen again."

"Let me get this shit straight," Gavin Lynn said, pacing back and forth in the galley. The rest of the squad had pulled up some spare folding chairs and were watching the conversation like it was a tennis match, a few munching on popcorn. "The Tahni are behind this? Seriously?"

"Zan-Thint is behind this," I corrected him around a mouthful of chicken and pasta...or, more accurately, around a mouthful of soy and spirulina masquerading as chicken and pasta. I was hungry enough to even make the faux food taste good. "The same renegade Tahni general we've been chasing since Hausos." I shook my head. "Didn't *any* of you read the briefs we sent out?"

"I did," Fargo said, raising her hand like we were back in elementary school. I felt bad that I didn't have a gold star to reward her.

"He's a Tahni general who didn't surrender after the war,"

Vicky explained. "He has at least a battalion worth of ground troops, maybe even a brigade. And now he's buying up rhenium to try to build a fleet to deliver them. Somewhere."

"Fuck me," Ruthie moaned, rubbing a hand on her neck as if trying to massage away an ache. "As if we didn't have enough problems."

"Wait a second," Foster said, leaning forward in his chair, staring at me like I'd grown an extra head. "There's a Tahni general who has his own rhenium mine? Where's he getting that kind of money?" I was about to repeat the discussion I'd had with Martz about how he could just be using someone else's shipyards, but he waved a hand like he knew it was coming and was already dismissing it. "I mean, think about how much he has to be paying the people down there, this Konigsberg guy, to make that worth his while. And you said you think the Tahni might be paying for the mercs, too? That's a lot of Tradenotes. Millions, maybe. So, he's a Tahni general...but that doesn't mean he's rich. He sure didn't get a pension."

"That's a good question," I admitted. One I'd been thinking about myself. "I just don't know. I guess it's possible their intelligence service managed to forge Commonwealth Tradenotes during the war."

"The weapons," Vicky said, pointing a finger at me as if she was accusing me of something. I frowned and she clucked with exasperation. "The weapons on Hausos! The ones the cartels were caching there. We assumed they were going *to* Zan-Thint, but that doesn't make any sense knowing what we know now, that he has access to old Tahni military caches. He wouldn't need our weapons. Maybe they came *from* Zan-Thint...maybe he was selling them to the cartels to finance his insurgency."

"Of course." I thumped the heel of my hand against my forehead. "How did we not think of that before?"

"This is all some high-level shit," Martz said, grabbing a pita sandwich out of the food station and stuffing about half of it in his mouth, swallowing it in one bite. "But what the fuck does it have to do with our mission? If some Tahni asshole is buying the rhenium, that makes it even more important for us to cut off his supply by doing our job and taking over that mine."

"Jesus Christ, Martz," Dunstan snapped, "I know you're a Marine, but do you have to eat like that? You remind of a fucking boa constrictor dislocating its jaw."

"Kiss my ass, you Fleet pansy." Martz shot him a bird.

One of the Marines chuckled, a compact, shaven-headed man with beady eyes. His file said he was Malcolm Petrovic, but everyone just called him Mal. Lynn wasn't laughing, though. The team leader was still restless, his jaw clenched, and if I had to guess, I would say he didn't like this any more than Martz, but was taking it more seriously. Fargo was taking it all in wide-eyed, like a kid seeing Mommy and Daddy arguing for the first time.

And how much I could believe that either of them was genuine was up to me.

"Martz is right," I said, and no one was more surprised than I was to hear me say it. Vicky tilted her head toward me, eyeing me like I'd gone nuts. "We have to shut down this operation. I still thought maybe we could work something out peacefully, something the CSF could live, without dragging a bunch of civilians into our fight, but there's no way we can let Zan-Thint get his own fleet of warships. God only knows what he'd do with it, but I think I can guarantee it's nothing good."

"Huh," Martz grunted. "Nice to know even an officer can admit that they were wrong."

"More importantly, though," I continued, not responding to the barb, "there's only one place we can find out where the Tahni were taking the rhenium, where their shipyards are located, and that's down on Portent."

"I thought you were convinced Konigsberg didn't know who he was selling to," Vicky reminded me.

"I think he doesn't *want* to know," I corrected her. "I think he especially doesn't want his people to know. But you've met the man. He's former special ops, with a reputation for ruthlessness. You really think he's going to make a deal like this without knowing his customer? Knowing where the stuff is going?"

"Probably not."

"This is bullshit!" Martz exploded, throwing his hands in the air as if appealing to God for help. "We've already been over this! The Tahni are *not* our job! Collecting intel is *not* our job! We have a fucking assignment, and it's to take down this mine!"

"And we're going to complete it," I said, too tired to even get angry with him. "Relax, Martz. It's two birds with one stone. We take out the mercs, occupy the mine, you get everything you want. And then we get to have a chat with Konigsberg and find out where Zan-Thint is taking the goods." I nodded toward Dunstan. "Look, we're going to be jumping in close, but I need Intercept One to take out the air cover."

He sneered. "You mean, you need *me* to take out the air cover, since Junior here...." He motioned at Foster. "...is going to be driving your bus."

"Exactly. Ruthie, you're going to be alone up here. You think you can hold off the mercs' space assets while we drop?"

"If I can't," she said, sniffing a humorless laugh, "you're going to have an awfully long walk home."

"Flight crew, draw me up an attack plan," I instructed, feeling as if I was back in command of Delta Company during the war. "Martz, go get the suits ready. Then everyone try to get some sleep. We've got less than twelve hours."

Neither Vicky nor I moved as they filed out...and Ruthie hung back as well, eyeing Dunstan and Foster as they headed for the cockpit. When she was sure they were gone, she turned back to us, leaning against the bulkhead.

"Do you think they knew?"

I was tired enough that I almost pretended I didn't know what she was talking about, just to make her keep talking so I wouldn't have to think.

"You mean Dukanovic and Wellesley?" I assumed. She nodded. "If they did already know, why wouldn't they tell us? They know our story; they have to figure Zan-Thint being involved in this would make us even more motivated to accomplish the mission."

"Unless they didn't *want* us to find out about Zan-Thint," Vicky mused. "We know they want the Predecessor tech, but that doesn't mean they actually care about getting rid of Zan-Thint."

"Maybe it's not in the Corporate Council's best interest to remove Zan-Thint or the Tahni as a threat," Ruthie suggested.

I squinted at her, uncomprehending.

"Why the hell would they want him around? Terrorism has to be bad for business."

"You two really don't follow politics much, do you?" she asked, with just the slightest hint of scorn in her voice. "You know why the Corporate Council exists in the first place, right?"

"I know what they told us in school," Vicky replied. "It was formed in concert with the Commonwealth government after the Sino-Russian War, right? To make the new global economy more efficient?"

She snorted.

"Yeah, that's what they tell you. It's only about a tenth of the story. The Corporate Council that was formed after the Sino-Russian War was just what it sounds like, a committee of the most important industries cooperating with the government in a sort of emergency situation when they were all trying to pull the world out of the Collapse. It didn't become what it is now until after the first war with the Tahni. When we found out we weren't alone, and that the aliens were hostile, well...as you can imagine, everyone panicked. We barely came out of that war with the colonies we had at the start of it, and it was a damned close thing. Everyone got to thinking it was because the Tahni had a unified government and economy and that we needed something similar to keep up with them."

I was running on little sleep and a lot of stress, but even a Marine can get a point when they're hammered with it right between the eyes.

"The Corporate Council only exists because of the threat of the Tahni," I summarized.

"Bingo. And since the Tahni aren't a threat anymore, who needs the Corporate Council?" She shrugged. "At least that's what the Commonwealth Senate is thinking lately. It may take a couple more years before the right people get elected to pull it off, but it's only a matter of time. Once it really sets in that there is no external threat anymore, well...." Ruthie shrugged. "There's an awful lot of scratch to be made and right now, the Council controls all of it, and the Council is top heavy as all hell. The Executive Director is old money, a guy named Andre Damiani, and his family has run the whole thing from the beginning. That makes them a lot of enemies, even from the inside. It's big house of cards, ready to tumble."

"Unless there's *another* external threat," Vicky interjected. "Like Zan-Thint and his army."

"Or," I said, my brain finally beginning to work now that I had some food in me, "the Skrela."

"Shit," Ruthie murmured, eyes clouding over. "That makes altogether too much sense."

"Oh, come on," Vicky protested. "Even the Corporate Council wouldn't be *that* reckless. They have to know the story, that those things killed off a whole civilization. They wouldn't just let them loose. They're not *that* crazy."

I eyed her sidelong.

"You never saw the rich people who'd come down to the Underground just to see how the other half lived? To score Kick and slap on a patch right there in the middle of all the chawners and gangbangers, because they wanted to experience the risk? Every once in a while, one of them would get rolled and then the cops would sweep through and pick up the usual suspects. But they never stopped coming." I shook my head. "People raised with that kind of wealth and power all around them think nothing can touch them. They think they're invulnerable, right up until the hammer falls."

"What the hell are we going to do about it?"

"We need to get a message to Hachette," Ruthie said. "I checked the public departure logs for Portent while we were in orbit. There was a private cargo ship making a delivery that was scheduled to break orbit in fourteen hours. I can send an anonymous upload to their relay list when we jump into the outer system to do a sensor check. Unless they're into breaking federal laws and doing serious time, they won't check the sender, just deliver them to the ComSat in their next system. That should get our message to the dead drop within a few days."

"That's taking a big chance," I warned her. I motioned at the cargo bay. "You know at least one of them has to be a mole for Wellesley and Dukanovic. If they've tapped into the ship's systems and figure out you sent a message, we're blown."

"And if we get killed doing this and no one tells Hachette what's going on?" she shot back. "You signed on for this, Alvarez. No one made any guarantees you'd survive it."

I looked to Vicky and she nodded.

"All right. I guess there's no other choice. The two of us had better get to the cargo bay before they start asking questions." I turned to head after the squad of Drop Troopers but paused and looked back over my shoulder at Ruthie. "Get some sleep, okay?"

She laughed harshly.

"Really? And you're telling me that you're going to be able to sleep now, with everything that's going on?"

"When we were back on the farm at Hausos," I told her, "everything was peaceful and safe, and the biggest threat I had to worry about was the harvester breaking down, and I woke up sweating every night, sometimes screaming, sometimes throwing myself on the floor because the enemy was shooting at me in my nightmares." I motioned around us. "Since all this, since people are actually shooting at me again, and the fate of the Commonwealth is on the line?" I grinned. "I'm going to sleep like a baby."

17

"Back in the saddle again."

Vicky whispered the words in my ear, as clear as if she'd been leaning on my shoulder, but she was across the cargo shuttle's drop bay, her Vigilante tucked into the gantry beside Corporal Lynn while I was beside Martz. They'd filed in like that and I had to think it wasn't an accident, that Martz wanted to keep an eye on us in combat, that he didn't trust us.

Well, it's mutual.

"Feels like it's been years instead of weeks," I replied, keeping our exchange innocuous. Theoretically, we were supposed to be on our private net, our conversation totally private, but the battlesuits had been provided by the CSF and if they did have a mole on the squad, they might have given them open access to everyone's net. "I wish we'd had more time for simulator training with these guys."

"It'll be fine," she assured me. "Dukanovic may be ruthless, but she's efficient. She wouldn't hire idiots."

Again, I disagreed but said nothing. I was trying to keep my mouth shut for fear my breakfast would make an encore appearance. Free-fall wasn't too bad normally, but stuffed inside my battlesuit, locked into a drop harness inside the cargo bay of a heavy-lift shuttle tucked into the hangar of a starship, the insult to my inner ears was harder to ignore.

I switched my helmet's HUD from the unchanging dull greyness of the cargo hold and the line of featureless golems across from me to the feed from the *Yantar's* sensor display, trying to distract myself from the endless sensation of falling. It was nearly as dim and colorless, though. The system primary was barely more than another star in the darkness, Portent only visible because the computer was projecting a red halo around it. Here and there were other red dots, symbolizing the position of spacecraft, some in the asteroid belt, some near the moon, others in high orbit around the planet.

"What are we doing out here?" Martz demanded on the general net, which would not only annoy me but travel all the way up to the bridge of the *Yantar,* and the cockpits of Intercept One and our own dropship, where it could also annoy Ruthie, Dunstan and Foster. "Let's jump in and get on with the drop!"

"You *would* like to live long enough for your drop, wouldn't you, Sgt. Martz?" Ruthie asked him, her tone acerbic. She'd totally abandoned the quiet, stern persona she'd adapted before Vicky and I had joined the crew, and I thought maybe it was because the only one around who'd notice was Dunstan. Whether she wasn't worried about him because she'd learned to trust him or because she just couldn't take him seriously as a threat, I wasn't sure. "If that lighter is in orbit where we plan to jump in and drop you, your operation will end pretty quick. Why don't you just let me do my job so you can do yours?"

Of course, the real reason she was delaying out here was to send the transmission. I wondered if I could help with that by engaging in some typical officer time-wasting chatter.

"You seeing the lighter, Ruthie?"

"I think so. We're pretty far away, but I think it's in lunar orbit. That's where it was when we Transitioned into the system, so I guess it's their normal anchorage while they're in-system."

"It's also a good spot to see us jump in, unfortunately," Dunstan commented. "They're going to be up our ass from minute one. You're barely going to have time to drop the shuttle before they come after you. And I don't see that cutter they had coming after me before."

"It might still be out in the belt." Ruthie said nothing for a moment, and I was about to cut in, but I had the sense she was considering the matter and decided not to interrupt. "We're going to do it."

"You're alone in this thing," Dunstan reminded her. "You're going to have to run the guns *and* the boat and you're not even a pilot!" She started to snap something, but he cut in before she could get through the second syllable. "You know what I mean! You know how to fly this thing, but you weren't trained as a pilot by the Fleet. You've got no experience flying a ship this size in combat!"

I thought she was going to yell at him, but instead, when she spoke, her voice was quiet, almost gentle.

"I know, Kyler," she told him, and I was shocked because I couldn't remember her ever calling him by his first name. "But what choice do we have? We can't form a stable wormhole out of T-space any closer than trans-lunar space. You can't argue with hyperdimensional physics."

"Well, that's not strictly true," he said, and it sounded like he strained the words out against his better judgement.

"What do you mean?" I asked him. "I don't know much about the Transition drive, but we were told pretty clearly that there was an absolute physical limit to how close you could come out to a planet."

"That's because they don't want idiots trying stupid shit like this. There's a spot, and it's different in every system depending on the relative masses of the bodies involved, where the gravitational pull of the planet is exactly matched by the pull from the moon. If you know that exact spot, you can jump in there... maybe. If you time it just right, you can jump into that spot, basically the Lagrangian point between the planet and the moon."

"Do we have that spot?" Vicky asked, sounding much more eager to try it than I was. "Can we figure it out?"

"It's in the Corporate database," Ruthie said. I couldn't see what she was doing, but I saw the results. A schematic overlay imposed itself on the sensor map, showing a gravitational chart of the system, focused on Portent. A moment later, a tiny section of space between Portent and her moon began flashing green. "Right there...I think."

"You think?" I asked her.

"She's right," Dunstan confirmed. "If we're gonna do it, we should just go ahead and do it."

"What happens if you did it wrong?" Martz asked. "Like, if it's not the right spot? Do we just keep going in T-space?"

"No." Dunstan's voice was flat, fatalistic. "We wind up as pure photons spread across two different universes. We'll be dead before we realize it."

"Oh, wonderful," I sighed. I wished there was gravity. I would like to have let my head sag backwards and I couldn't do it with no gravity.

"You're the mission commander, Cam," Dunstan told me, the slightest hint of hope in his voice, like he expected me to be sensible enough to not do something this insane. "You make the call."

What else could I say? We had a mission and I'd taken an oath.

"Do it."

"Transitioning in ten seconds."

She didn't count it down, for which I was grateful. One second, we were sitting as near to motionless as possible out past the asteroid belt. The next, Portent was exploding on the front screen in glares of green and blue and Ruthie was yelling at Foster and Dunstan.

"Launch! Launch! Launch!"

Acceleration pushed me into the left side of my suit and I suddenly remembered how inadequate the interior padding was for dealing with lateral G-forces. I maintained the link to the *Yantar*, knowing the mercs would jam it eventually but wanting to get a picture of the battle up in space before it was lost. Intercept One was boosting ahead of the drop ship on a starburst of fusion flame, only a few dozen kilometers away, running point for the dropship, but Ruthie wasn't waiting around to watch the show.

The view from the bow cameras swung around until the moon was visible in the corner of the screen, huge and craggy, pockmarked by ancient meteors. The mercenary lighter, a cargo ship they'd slapped weapons pods and extra armor on to turn it into an impromptu warship, was a star glowing off to the left of the curve of the moon, haloed in red by the ship's computer.

They wouldn't have missiles, that much I was pretty sure of. Missiles were only useful for combat between large ships if you had military guidance systems hardened against ECM and armored against point-defense turrets. And they couldn't just slap a jury-rigged fusion bomb on the end of a rocket and expect it to do anything. Fusion explosions in space were basically point-blank weapons since there was no atmosphere to conduct the shockwave. Military warheads channeled the fusion blast through a short-lived magnetic coil into the biggest plasma gun ever, which was damned cool but also damned expensive and restricted, not something even an outfit like Extreme Measures could get their hands on.

Railguns, maybe. Those were easy and cheap and, most importantly, unregulated. But there was a reason for that. Deflector screens made them just about useless against military spacecraft, and the *Yantar* was just as tough as a military ship, if a bit underpowered for her size.

But they couldn't have kept Ruthie on the run all that time with just railguns, and I had to assume they'd paid off the right people to get themselves a proton cannon or two. Or four. Proton accelerators were devastating but only at fairly short ranges. They'd want to duke it out, and she'd have to let them if she was going to get close enough to take them out.

As if they'd been reading my mind, the lighter leapt forward, though I knew it was an optical illusion caused by the high-G boost from both spacecraft. They were lions throwing themselves at each other, fighting for the right to lead the pride, but before I either of them got a chance to fire, the image faded to black with the bland accompaniment of an error message. Signal jamming.

I switched the feed to the bow camera of the dropship just as the atmosphere began to buffet at the aerospacecraft's lifting-body shape, grabbing us teasingly like children pushing each other on the playground. The blue glow of the atmosphere was swallowed up in the incandescent exhaust of Intercept One's main drive. Dunstan had switched from a pure fusion burn to running the metallic hydrogen as reaction mass, heating it to a vapor with the reactor and shooting it out the back. Wasteful but better than setting off a fusion reaction in an atmosphere. Lower still and we'd both be running air from the turbines through the reactor instead.

That's what the red triangle icons on the sensor display would be running as they soared up from the spaceport straight at us. Assault shuttles. Not as many as they'd had before, not since Dunstan had chewed through them to save our asses on the Tahni freighter. Only three left, which must have put a sizable dent in the Extreme Measures spacecraft budget. To give the pilots their due, they didn't shy away from the sleek brawn of the cutter, not even when their coil-gun rounds skewed away from the hazy plasma shield of his electromagnetic deflectors. Their lighter might have proton cannons, but they didn't have the juice to put them on every assault shuttle like the military.

Dunstan had no such issues, nor any compunction about using that advantage. The proton cannon firing in an atmosphere was a lightning bolt straight from the hand of Zeus, ripping apart the atmosphere, grinding the ragged edges of reality and sending a mass of heat and ionized gas rushing ahead of it like a wall. The assault shuttles were in a tight wedge and when the spear of charged particles turned the tip of that wedge into disassociated atoms, the turbulence sent the other two spiraling out of control. One managed to pull out, his belly jets flaring, but the other shed its wings and nosed in. I didn't see its inevitable impact because Foster jerked the dropship to port, throwing us into a barrel roll and one of the Drop Troopers in my squad let out a hapless squawk that ended in a liquid burp.

Rothman. I put the name together with a lean, angular face and dark, curly hair. Poor guy. Puking in a suit wasn't pretty. I was able to hold my jaws shut until Foster pulled us out of the maneuver, and once my eyes were able to focus again, I saw why he'd done it. Missiles curling upward from launchers on the ground, and Dunstan was already heading down to take care of them.

Below us were the mountains, snow-capped at the peaks, and were heading lower over them until the jagged edges seemed as if they could scrape the paint off our belly.

"Drop in five mikes," Foster said, his voice tight and strained. He had never done this before. I guess I'd known, but I'd managed not to think about it until now.

"You're doing great, Foster," I told him, thinking that it couldn't hurt to bolster his confidence.

He snorted, the sound like a burst of static in my helmet speakers.

"Thanks. I'm just driving the bus."

I would have argued that he was driving the bus while simultaneously keeping us alive, but he seemed busy and I had to say some meaningless shit that everyone already knew because I was an officer and that was my job.

"We drop in five. The merc compound we're hitting has coil-gun turrets, and armored vehicles, so use the terrain for cover and don't be stingy with your missiles. You're not paying for them and you don't get a bonus from the CSF for returning unfired munitions. Your grenade launchers should make effective suppressive fire weapons to keep the gunners' heads down until we get close enough for the plasma guns. Sgt. Martz, after we nail down the compound, you take Bravo team and run a sweep through town, make sure we flush out any of the merc units scattered at posts at the spaceport or anywhere else around Perfection. Lt. Sandoval and I will head straight for the refinery and shut down the operation there. We'll call you if we need support, but otherwise, secure the spaceport and make sure our dropship has a place to land. Everybody got that?"

"Copy five by five, sir," Fargo said smartly, though I only received grunts of affirmation from the others. Except Martz.

"We should stick together," he grumbled, repeating the same complaint he'd already made a half a dozen times during our planning sessions back in T-space on the *Yantar*. "I don't like splitting up the squad."

"So you've said," Vicky observed. "We're doing it anyway

because it's the only thing that makes sense. If we secure the port first, then the miners can hunker down behind the blast shield inside the reactor and wait us out, and I have better things to do with my time than to wait for them to starve to death. And if we send everybody to the refinery and the mercs at the port have anti-aircraft missiles, they could take down the dropship and we'd be stuck here."

"If we run into more than we can handle at the refinery," I assured Martz, "we'll bring you in. Same for you at the port. Good to go?"

"Yeah," he replied without enthusiasm.

The town was just off our starboard wing now, and Dunstan was rising above a road intersection to the west, leaving a cloud of smoke rising from his gun run.

"No more missiles from that emplacement," the pilot assured us.

"Get back topside," I told him. "Help Ruthie out against that lighter."

"Roger that. What if you need air support?"

"I could have sworn that people used to follow my orders in the war without arguing with me every single time."

"Not me. I outranked you back then, jarhead."

"Well, you don't know, so get the hell up there and make sure we don't all have to squeeze into your cutter to get back to Canaan."

"Yeah, yeah."

"Thirty seconds to drop," Foster reminded us.

I was about to tell everyone to check their drop harness, despite the fact that they were all combat vets and had done this a hundred times before when three neat, round holes punched through both sides of the drop bay, letting in spears of light and a deafening whoosh of outside air.

"Foster!"

"We're taking some ground fire." I had to hand it to Foster. For someone who'd never gotten shot at before, he was handling it well, with that same old classic pilot cool.

"Gee, you think?" Lynn blurted, fear leaking through his sarcasm. "What was your first fucking clue?"

I didn't blame him one bit for being afraid. Those slugs had come just centimeters from punching right through the chest of his suit.

"Gonna circle around to the east, try to come in low." Foster banked the dropship to the port and the tone of the engines climbed in pitch, the G-forces slamming me into the inside of my suit.

I checked our position and made a snap decision.

"Fuck all that," I told him. "Drop! Drop! Drop!"

I slapped the oversized lever fitted to my drop harness and a hatch retrofitted to the lower hull of the aerospacecraft fell away. I barely had time to switch off the feed from the dropship's cameras before I was falling from three hundred meters up. The ground rushed up to meet me and I waited a couple seconds longer than regulation height to hit my jump-jets, not wanting to catch a coil-gun round in the head to avoid undue metal fatigue.

Air ran through the isotope reactor in my Vigilante's backpack, superheated and accelerated out of the variable thrust nozzles protruding beneath the power pack, sending up billowing clouds of dust beneath it. Soft dirt gave way as the spiked soles of the battlesuit's feet slammed into the ground and I cut off the jets, taking half a heartbeat to check that nothing was broken, either in the suit or myself.

I'd landed below the rise from the compound where we'd been held earlier, the grey crenelations of the walls barely visible through the trees. Somewhere over that hill, over those walls, waited Dhoni, and I was pretty eager to return his hospitality.

"Squad," I said, kicking the suit forward, slow at first, barely a jog as the machine threw its energy up against its armored mass, but speeding into a long, loping run. "Follow me!"

18

The run was hypnotizing, just enough of my own effort going into it to make it seem real, but not enough to tire me out. I was in a dream, running for kilometers without tiring, without feeling it, and I could have done it in the suit, could have run all day. But running straight into the defenses on that wall wouldn't have been good tactics. That's why God and the Commonwealth Fleet Marine Corps gave us jump-jets.

"Up and over!" I yelled at the rest of the fire team rushing up behind me, and suddenly I felt as if I was a corporal again, the last time I was responsible for me and my team and no one else. It had been, upon reflection, my happiest experience as a Marine.

The jump-jets carried me over the rise and the wall above it in a single bound, and in the next three seconds, I found out why they don't let officers walk point. I didn't see the slugs, of course, not as fast as they were going, nor did the suit's sensors pick them up, but I sure as hell felt them. The only thing that saved me was some impatient private with his finger on the trigger, who fired before I cleared the wall. The rounds went through the wall first before they hit me, spent just enough energy that they couldn't penetrate my chest armor, though they gave it a damned good try. If I'd been standing flat-footed, the shock of the impact might have been enough to send me toppling over backwards, but I was leaning into the jump, the jets pushing me forward and upward and the only consequence was pain.

It was a dull ache, like being thumped in the chest with a baseball bat, since the armor plate spread the impact out, and the red flares in my vision were matched by the red warning lights in my damage display. It was letting me know if I did anything that stupid again, I'd be dead, which was helpful information to have but I could have figured it out myself. I launched a missile by instinct before I was all the way over the wall, sending it straight up and then looking the targeting system into a lock a half-second later when I saw the coil-gun turret projecting out of the top of the fortified compound.

The missile flashed downward out of the sky and touched the turret about the same time as my Vigilante touched down in the courtyard, the *crump* of its warhead detonating a chest-deep vibration even through the armor. Heat and concussion washed off of the explosion, a wave crashing on the rock of my suit, leaving me on my feet. The Extreme Measures soldiers who'd been rushing out of the FOB shelter to man the weapons weren't so well armored or so fortunate. Four or five of them were smashed to the ground by the blast and the two closest to it wouldn't be getting back up again if the flames licking off their clothing was any indication.

I had the space of two or three seconds to assess the situation in the wake of the blast, which was a luxury in combat, and I took advantage of it. I knew from my previous visit where the other coil-gun turrets were positioned on the wall and I marked them with my targeting laser, putting a pin in them to notify the others coming over the wall behind me. Inside the compound walls, a single cargo truck was parked across the entrance to the shelter, charred and smoking from the explosion but otherwise intact.

The front gate was partway open, and I had the sense they'd hit the control to open it when they'd figured out our dropship was heading straight for them. The armored assault vehicle was squeezing through, scraping the paint off its right side in a desperate attempt to get clear before it was caught inside. I spun towards the APC, lining up my plasma gun for a shot, but got distracted when something blew up in my face.

It wasn't anything that could penetrate my armor and I had to think the guy who fired it knew that. He had to be a combat vet because I was sure Dhoni wouldn't have trusted anyone else to wear one of the armored exoskeletons, and because he hadn't panicked. He'd seen me gunning for the vehicle and decided his shoulder-mounted grenade launcher would be just the thing to attract my attention. And it did, but not as much as the platoon of exoskeleton troopers who ran out of the shelter behind him, laying down fire with their Gauss rifles.

The rest of the team was coming in behind me, but they were taking care of their own targets. Missiles streaked out, turning the coil-gun turrets at the corner parapets of the perimeter wall into Roman candles, spouting gouts of flame into the morning air, the detonations peals of thunder echoing back and forth inside the compound. I flinched at the blasts, then flinched again at the rain of tungsten smacking like hailstones into my helmet and shoulder plastrons. They didn't penetrate, but enough of them could wear down my armor.

Well, they wanted my attention and they were going to get it. I touched the trigger inside my right glove and fired a plasma gun for the first time since I'd gotten out of the Marines. The backwash of heat was a caress from an old lover, familiar and comforting, though I doubted the Extreme Measures mercs felt that way. A blast of ionized hydrogen meant to rip through Tahni battlesuits three meters tall and armored with fifteen centimeters of honeycomb boron alloy blew two of the exoskeleton troopers in half and turned three more into melted slag. The rest scattered, trying to put space between them so I couldn't take out so many with one shot, either not remembering or never knowing that it took the plasma gun several seconds to recharge.

I didn't wait for it, just waded into the midst of them, swinging the Vigilante's left fist like a mace. The exoskeletons weren't the size and weight of a battlesuit, but the impact still shuddered through the suit and into my shoulder as the fist crushed the helmet and the head inside it. More Gauss gun slugs, these not so concentrated, just the ones who kept their spine, determined to bring one of us down no matter how unlikely.

I grabbed the headless trooper by a leg with the articulated claw of my left hand and threw him sidearm at the cluster of troopers, bowling them over, just a temporary solution, but I didn't need forever. The rest of the team was coming up behind me, and, most significantly to me, Vicky was standing beside me. Plasma fire cut a swathe through the mercenary troopers, then another shot from the other side, from Fargo, and finally, the mercs broke. The ones who were left tried to follow the APC out the gate, but a missile that my HUD told me was from Lynn's battlesuit speared into the rear of the vehicle, the blast from the warhead lifting it a meter off the ground and swallowing up the troops racing to catch up.

Then Martz was there, coming in at the rear of the formation, slamming his shoulder into the side of the cargo truck, sliding it across the gravel out of the way of the shelter entrance. Gunfire spanged off his armor from inside the doorway and he answered it with a plasma round, the starfire glow lighting up the hallway with a backwash of flame. The hallway was too narrow for a Vigilante to squeeze through and Martz didn't try, instead unlimbering the grenade launcher from over his shoulder and pouring a fusillade through the doorway. The detonations were a snare drum pounding deep within the shelter, with the shrill accompaniment of screams.

I shouldered past Martz, leaning into the entrance hall.

"Surrender and come out unarmed," I called over the suit's external speakers, "and we'll let you live. If you keep firing, we'll burn this place down around you."

"We should burn it down anyway," Martz snapped, and I had to double-check to make sure he wasn't doing it over his own speakers. "Fuck these assholes."

I was inclined to agree after they'd tried to kill Vicky and me, but the nagging voice of my conscience kept telling me to give them a chance to live. Or maybe that was Vicky's voice. They sounded a lot alike.

I waited ten seconds but got no response.

"Last chance," I warned. "We open fire in three, two, one...."

"Wait!" It was Dhoni's voice. I hadn't known him long, but there was no mistaking the nasal flatness of the man. "We're coming out!"

He was barely recognizable as the man I'd seen earlier, his uniform charred and stained by smoke, his face black with soot. He had his hands over his heads as he led a dozen of his people out the door, most of them wounded or burned. I wondered how many had died inside the building.

"You don't look quite so tough now, do you, Captain?" Vicky asked him. The mercenary officer frowned in obvious confusion.

"Who the hell are you people?" he demanded, somehow still determined to be an arrogant prick even in defeat. "You aren't the fucking Marines. The government wouldn't bother with a shithole like this."

"Forget who we are," she snapped, shoving him hard enough to send him tumbling two meters before he landed on his side. "We should talk about who *you* are, you piece of shit! You're a bloodthirsty, cowardly excuse for an officer who got his own people killed because you were too stupid to take a deal! We wanted to do this without having to break any heads, even though our bosses couldn't care less about you or the people who run the mines, wanted to make sure everyone walked away with a fair payout, but you got all these men and women killed." She motioned around us at the charred and burning bodies littering the ground. "If you don't want the rest of your force on Portent to wind up just like these poor fucks, you'll call them right now and tell them to surrender before we have to hunt them down."

"You're those two freighter tramps who tried to sell me that story about wanting to buy rhenium, aren't you?" Dhoni said, ignoring her demands. He pushed himself up to a crouch, his lip set in a scornful sneer. "I knew you were Corporate Council spies. I should have killed you myself instead of trusting that moron Reindl."

"Call your people," I repeated Vicky's demand. "The ones at the port, the ones at the mine. Tell them to lay down their arms and surrender. If they don't, their blood is on your hands."

"Extreme Measures doesn't surrender," he replied, scornful.

I was about to point out that he'd done just that, but I stopped myself in mid-word.

"Something's not right," I said, half to myself but over the net to Martz and Vicky as well. "This asshole wouldn't have given up."

"Incoming!"

I didn't know who'd said it, didn't take the time to check the comm screen. What was much more important was the flight of hoppers popping up over the northern wall, and the missiles streaking off hardpoints on their upper fuselage.

My reaction was instant and instinctive, training and experience and something older, a self-preservation from deep inside my subconscious.

"Jump!"

I don't remember the sensation of the jets driving me up to meet the ducted-fan hovercraft, don't remember the sound or the vibration or the pressure. I'd been on the ground and then between eyeblinks, I was transported thirty meters in the air, nose to nose with the matte-grey aircraft, the red circle of my targeting reticle hanging over the clear plastic of the canopy. I had just a microsecond's glimpse of the pilot's face, a mask of sheer terror as he saw the green-camouflaged mass of the Vigilante sailing towards him, and then I fired.

A sun-hot ball of fire erased the cockpit and the two mercenaries in it, and then I was heading down again, the momentum of the hopper carrying it past me even as it tumbled in. I'd barely touched down when I felt the tremor from the aircraft crashing only a few dozen meters away, somewhere inside the compound's walls. A chain-fire of warheads detonating was a muted rattling from behind me, contained by the walls of the compound, and I wanted more than anything to check the IFF and make sure Vicky was okay, but the enemy wasn't going to wait for me.

I had never hunted any sort of bird, not even on Hausos, where there was little else to do for entertainment than go out and shoot critters, as our old friend Dave would have put it. But I'd never done it, and had no experience leading a flying bird, though I knew the concept. Thankfully, the targeting software in my helmet was smart enough to figure things like that out. I trusted it to do the hard work and fired my grenade launcher, programming the rounds for proximity detonation. It wouldn't have worked for a shuttle or a battlesuit, or just about anything else, but hoppers didn't have the kind of lift that a shuttle did and couldn't carry much armor.

Puffs of smoke marked the detonation of the grenades, an inadequate advertisement for a wicked little piece of ordnance that used HpE to turn sintered metal into plasma and internal baffles to target it in a fan-shaped spray of ionized gas. They were great tools for antipersonnel work and, as it turned out, for taking down ducted-fan helicopters. Two of them spun out of control, their pilots injured or killed by spears of plasma, and the last few tried to bank away, get back to a nap-of-the-earth course and out of my firing arc. Missiles tracked them down, not from me but from Martz and a couple others from Bravo team.

I had a moment's space to breathe and I used it to check the IFF. Vicky's icon was shining bright only ten meters off to my right, and I let out the breath I'd been holding...then it caught in my throat when I saw Gavin Lynn's transponder flashing red, still inside the compound.

"We got a man down!" Kennedy, one of Lynn's team. There was a sob in his voice, and I thought I recalled him mentioning that he and Lynn had served together during the war.

"Shit," I murmured, kicking my suit into a lumbering run back to the compound.

Smoke was pouring out of the compound walls like they were an industrial chimney, and the main entrance was blocked by the wreckage of the APC, so I had to pop the jets again to hop over. Dark billows clogged the ground all around the shelter, trying to conceal the bodies. They couldn't quite manage it. The smoke eddied and swirled with every shift of the breeze, revealing the shattered and melted mercenaries in their powered exoskeletons, the shredded bodies of the dismounted troops...and the hunched form of a Vigilante battlesuit.

The suits were tough, but not tough enough to take a direct hit from a guided missile, and it had taken him right in the juncture of his chest and neck. I didn't need the suit's diagnostics to tell me he was dead.

I sagged against my suit's restraints, the air going out of me. I hadn't known Lynn very well, didn't know any of them that well, but he'd been under my command, and I hadn't lost anyone under my command in a long time. But Martz knew them all.

"Goddammit!" he yelled over the general net, loud enough for the word to disappear into static. The suits all looked the same, but the IFF told me he was standing across from me, his Vigilante staring down at Lynn's body with a blank, metal face. "Those fuckers! Those fucking assholes!"

"Hey, umm...we got a live one here," Kennedy said. He was over by the cargo truck, standing by the rear right wheel, his plasma gun trained on a prone figure.

I couldn't see the man's face at first, obscured as it was by the smoke, but then he rolled onto his side and rose into a crouch. He was battered and covered in blood and soot, but there was no mistaking Captain Dhoni.

"Little shit is a cockroach," Vicky ground out. "Lives through everything."

"He ain't living through this," Martz declared, stepping past us.

I made an instinctive move to block his way, but I was a second too late. His boot connected with the mercenary officer's chin, boosted by the suit, and everything that made Dhoni the man he was splattered across the side of the truck. I looked away from what was left of him, staring instead at Martz. I couldn't see his face, but I knew the scowl he'd be aiming my way—I'd seen it often enough.

"What?" he demanded, spreading the arms of his suit in a

mimic of the way he talked with his hands when he was out of the Vigilante. "You gonna lecture me on how I should have taken him alive so we could be all fucking humane?"

"No," I told him. "Honest to God, Martz, if you hadn't killed him, I might have broken his neck." I shrugged. "I probably wouldn't have crushed his head. You're headed for the port. If you want, one of your team can take Lynn's body back to the dropship while you check the town."

"No," he said, the word a harsh rasp. "We talked about shit like this. If any of us had anyone back home who'd want a memorial, we wouldn't be working as hired guns, would we?"

He knelt his suit down beside Lynn's and popped open a panel set in the side beneath the right arm.

"You're gonna toast him?" I blurted.

The technical term was field-expedient thermal disposal, but everyone called it getting toasted. I'd never actually seen it happen, though everyone had talked about it, talked about how they would rather get toasted than have the Tahni get their hands on them.

"Yeah, let the local shits clean up the burn spot." He yanked the lever inside the panel, then stepped back. "Everyone back up, back up now."

There wasn't a lot to see. Everything happened inside the armor, the control rods pulling out of his isotope reactor, the shielding between him and the power source cracking open. Steam and smoke poured from the cracks in the chest armor where the missile had torn through, and inside, Lynn's body was turned to ash while the electronic circuitry and computer hardware for the suit was charred useless.

He was gone, his remains merged with the suit, like they'd never been separate entities.

Was that going to happen to me? I'd thought I could live

without the suit, but it had drawn me back in. Maybe that was the only way out.

"Alpha team, with me," I said, walking to the gate and pushing the APC out of the way so I could squeeze through. "We're heading for the refinery. Martz, go clear the port and wait with the dropship for the call to pick us up."

"You're gonna fuck this up, Alvarez." He was on the general net this time, not even bothering to try to keep it private. "You might have been a stone killer back in the day, but civilian life has made you soft. You're going to get people killed, just like you got Gavin killed."

I would like to have handled it between us, would like to have had the chance to reason with him, to explain that even if I hadn't given the mercs inside the shelter the opportunity to surrender, the hoppers still would have come. They had to have been called before Dhoni and the others came out. But he'd made it public, and dealing with people like this, there was only one way to run at him and that was to go hard.

"Maybe I will, Martz," I told him, "but I'll tell you right now, if you ever question my orders again, I'll put a fucking plasma blast through your helmet. And if you don't think I can, you just try me. I've killed more Tahni High Guard than you've ever *seen*, and that was right at the beginning of the war, before they started losing their old, seasoned warriors and putting kids inside those suits. You're not half as good as they were. I doubt I'd break a sweat."

"And if he doesn't kill you," Vicky warned, sounding annoyed that Martz had forgotten her, "then I will."

"You wanna go, Martz?" I asked him, stepping closer to his suit, only centimeters separating us. "You wanna go right here and now and I'll leave you on the ground beside your friend? Or do you wanna act like a professional and finish this damned mission?"

I thought for a second that he'd take me up on it, that he'd finally worked himself up to it. But he took a step back, and when he spoke again, it was on the Bravo team net.

"Bravo, follow me. We're going for the port."

"Asshole," Vicky murmured as we watched him go.

"He is that," I agreed. "Fargo, are your people ready to run?"

"Umm...yes, sir." The woman sounded flustered, as if she hadn't expected the confrontation. "We'll follow you, sir."

I hoped they would. But watching Martz and Bravo head over the wall and back towards town, I was beginning to have my doubts.

[19]

Screams, shouts, people running in a panic, trying to get inside the double doors ahead of the massive metal monsters, ahead of us. The refinery complex could have been any of a dozen colony worlds we'd liberated during the war, except that the running and the screaming had been a reaction to Tahni troops back then, which gave me a sickening feeling in the pit of my stomach about which side I should have been on.

"We got fire coming in from the northeast entrance," Vicky reported.

She was a blue dot on my mapping overlay, advancing on the stairs to the personnel entrance on the northeast side of the refinery with Liao and Walsh while Fargo, Montgomery and I circled around to the west, to the cargo entrance. The run to the refinery had been short but nerve-wracking, with potential ambushes behind every rock, phantom squadrons of hopper gunships hiding behind every cloud bank. But there'd been nothing. The roads had been clear of everything but automated diggers plodding along in their preprogrammed courses, blissfully ignorant of the conflict going on around them. No trains running, no maintenance trucks, not so much as a remotely piloted drone out observing the mining operations. Everyone was hunkered down here at the refinery or maybe back in town, probably from the second the *Yantar* had jumped into orbit.

"You need support?" I asked Vicky, pausing at the bottom of ramp to the cargo entrance.

"Negative, we can handle it. It's a squad of merc dismounts. Get inside before they figure out they're outgunned and seal the radiation shields."

"Roger that. We're going to lose comms once we head inside. Meet you at the control room." I switched to the team net. "Montgomery, take point. Watch those trucks we saw at the top of the ramp. Someone might be using them for cover."

"You want me to try launching another drone?" Fargo asked, hesitating on the other side of the ramp.

"Yeah, go ahead. We're in line-of-sight now, they shouldn't be able to jam it."

A niche opened in the backpack of her Vigilante and a tiny, quad-copter drone popped out, rising straight up four or five meters before it zipped up the ramp ahead of Montgomery. I linked into the feed from the camera drone, the image an unsteady roller-coaster in a quadrant of my HUD. The ramp was huge in the view of the tiny camera, the cargo entrance a yawning cavern, and parked in front of it were the three cargo trucks we'd seen parked there on our run in from the mines. They were old and decades obsolete, their canvas covers ragged and worn, and behind them was something else, something I couldn't quite see yet except that it was dull grey and metallic, almost as big as the trucks.

And then nothing. The quadrant of the screen went grey.

"Jammed or shot down," Fargo said. "They're up there." I refrained from my instinctive reaction to tell her that yes, it was either jammed or shot down, thanks for that blinding flash of insight. I didn't say it because I had enough enemies in the squad without making new ones.

"You still want me to go up there?" Montgomery asked, not sounding so eager all of a sudden.

I sighed.

"I'll go." I stared up at the curve in the ramp, as if I could see around the retaining wall and into the cargo entrance if I just looked hard enough. "Launch smoke grenades," I ordered. "Rolling barrage across the ramp."

My grenade launcher unfolded from its shoulder mount into the left hand of my suit, and I scrolled through the warhead settings until I reached smoke screen. I only had five rounds left and I decided to use them all, reasoning that my life would likely not depend on having an anti-personnel grenade in the next few hours.

"Fire."

The grenades arced high, the trajectory designed to give whoever was up there plenty of time to see them coming and force them to duck. I couldn't see them hit, but I could see the black smoke billowing up from the top of the ramp, crackling as if it was the storm cloud around an erupting volcano, filled with electrostatically charged metal powder. It was designed to defeat radar, lidar, thermal and spectroscopic sensors, though the double-edged sword of it was, it would do the same for me.

"Give me a three count, then follow," I told the others.

I didn't use the jump-jets because that would have taken me on an arc that would have left me at the thinnest part of the smoke cloud. Instead, I lunged into a sprint, or as much of a sprint as a Vigilante could muster in just a couple dozen meters. The ramp was sheet metal over concrete and the footfalls of the Vigilante were drumbeats, painfully obvious but there was nothing I could do about it.

Someone heard. Coil-gun rounds ripped into the surface of

the ramp less than a meter to my right, peeling it like a banana and sending sprays of concrete dust blossoming like grey flowers, and my balls retreated into my stomach. One hit in the weak spot on my chest armor and that would be it. But them shooting at me did have one benefit. My sensors and cameras couldn't see them through the smoke screen, but my targeting computer took the impacts and projected the course back to their source, putting a flashing yellow circle around the point it wanted me to shoot at.

I obliged.

The packet of accelerated plasma burned a corridor through the smoke cloud and through that tunnel, I could see the coil-gun turret of an armored vehicle parked across the front of the cargo entrance, just behind the trucks. The shot from my main gun struck right in the emitter of the turret, doing nasty things to all that electromagnetic energy stored up in its coils, turning the weapon into a huge fragmentation grenade going off right in the middle of the enemy position.

I moved off my shot, because that whole business of tracing gunfire back to the shooter worked for the other side as well. Just three steps to the right, and just in time. Another burst of tungsten slugs cut through the air where I'd just been running and pounded the retaining wall on my left into pulverized dust and concrete fragments, and then I was inside the cargo entrance. I knew there was a second assault vehicle parked inside, though I still couldn't see it, but I knew for sure where the first one was. I ducked my right shoulder and slammed into it, giving a boost with my jets.

The APC was heavy, much heavier than the trucks we'd shoved aside earlier, but it moved under my push, the fat tires squealing against the cement flooring as the rear end swung around. There were bodies on the floor. Men and women in light armor, Extreme Measures mercenaries who'd taken up firing positions around the APC and paid the price for it. The smoke hid their features and I tried not to look at them, not needing to add more fuel to my nightmares, just kept pushing the APC until it banged into something and stopped short.

That would be the other vehicle. I jumped, not far and not high, cognizant of the roof of the cargo garage only ten meters up, and with one bound and a one-second burst from my jets, I was standing on top of the coil-gun turret of the second vehicle. The gunner was firing it wildly, slewing it left to right, as if he still thought I was out there shooting at them, but when I landed, he looked up through the open hatch in the roof, his eyes going wide under the rim of his open-faced helmet.

I didn't shoot him. Not out of any mercy, but because the plasma gun took time to recharge, and I didn't know if I'd need it. I yanked him out by the neck and flung him backwards across the garage, not particularly caring if the landing killed him. He wouldn't be in any condition to climb back on the gun and that was all I was concerned about.

"Sir!" Fargo yelled, a hysterical edge to her voice. "Montgomery is hit!"

"Shit."

I jumped down from the top of the assault vehicle and almost collided with an Extreme Measures soldier who was stumbling out of the assault vehicle. He might have been the driver, since his only weapon was a handgun, and if he'd had two brain cells to rub together, he would have just run away. Maybe he was panicking, maybe he just had more balls than brains, but he emptied the magazine of his pistol at me. I brushed him aside with a swipe of my plasma gun barrel and he went flying, screaming, his clothes smoking where the outer casing had touched them.

Fargo was just a couple meters inside the entrance and Montgomery was at her feet, unmoving. I whispered a prayer that he'd just taken suit damage, but God wasn't listening this time, or perhaps He just had other ideas. The Vigilante could take a single coil-gun round where its armor was the thickest, maybe two, but Montgomery had taken a burst of the tungsten slugs straight through the helmet. I couldn't see what was inside, and I didn't want to.

I remembered what Martz had said and bent down to trigger the thermal disposal system.

"Go," I told Fargo, motioning down the tunnel and into the garage. "Get moving."

"I can't believe Monty's dead," she said softly, following me through the rapidly dispersing smoke. "He made his way through three years of the war. I can't believe he died in a place like this."

"You roll sixes a thousand times in a row," I told her, "and it makes you think you're lucky, that you're invulnerable. But it's blind chance. You can be the best troop in the galaxy, but all it takes is a gunner on an obsolete APC shooting blind and hitting you in just the right place and all those other times where you didn't die don't count anymore."

"You saw that happen?"

"Over and over. And I was still stupid enough to put this suit back on."

I didn't have a map of the refinery's interior in my helmet systems, mostly because the CSF hadn't been able to get any intelligence on it, but I'd gotten the grand tour from Konigsberg himself. I didn't have an eidetic memory, but ten years in the Underground off the grid, sleeping in maintenance tunnels had given me a fair sense of direction. The garage ended in a storage area, the sort of place they kept spare parts, raw material for the industrial fabricators, and whatever else they needed to make this place work. And thank God, the corridors inside were all large enough to let two cargo jacks through abreast, which meant they were large enough for us.

"To the right," I told Fargo when we reached the T-juncture. "Then fifty meters."

There were no workers in those hallways as we made our way to the control room, none inside the rooms we passed, their doors hanging open revealing offices, workshops, and break rooms. I don't know why I expected there to be. They knew we were coming, had to have taken shelter. Hell, if Konigsberg was as smart as I thought, he'd have already sealed himself away. But I had sense he wouldn't. A man like him wouldn't trust a plan that left him locked away, counting on the whims of chance for survival. He was a Marine, a Special Ops Marine at that. He'd be proactive.

Maybe it was that thought that saved us. The hallway narrowed as it approached the control room, a function of the radiation shields that could dilate inward to seal off the corridor and turn the control room into a shelter. There were two of them there, unarmored, dressed in the normal work clothes of the miners, waiting for us where the tunnel narrowed. They were aiming weapons at us, and I thought for a brief instant that they were Gauss rifles, but there was a strange thermal signature to the weapons. I didn't remember where I'd seen it, but I knew I'd encountered it before, been cautioned to look out for it.

We didn't have time to try to shoot them first, didn't have time to charge into their position. What we did have was a small alcove off to the left, on Fargo's side of the hall. It might have been a waiting room, might have been a break room, I didn't know. What I knew was that it was barely big enough for both Fargo and I to squeeze into it and I hit the jets and crashed into her, pushing her inside ahead of me...and just ahead of twin gouts of superheated plasma. Hair seared away on my arm and leg closest to the opening and a wash of heat stole the breath from my chest, turning the interior of the Vigilante into a broiler for a few seconds, until cool air from the helmet vents swept the stifling heat away.

"What the hell?" Fargo squawked.

What the hell they'd been were plasma projectors. Single-shot, disposable, man-portable versions of the gun I carried on my Vigilante, they'd been developed for Force Recon as an anti-armor weapon, but few of them had ever been fielded. They were heavy, unwieldy and expensive, but they were one of the few weapons a dismounted troop could carry that would kill a battlesuit. We'd been given familiarization training with them on the off chance the Tahni might have developed something similar, and that half-remembered class had saved both of us.

Unless they had more of them. The corridor was on fire, awash with white smoke and fire suppression foam, but my helmet's thermal sensors could still pick out the heat signatures of the two miners who'd shot at us bolting back towards the control room. I pushed away from Fargo and loped down the hallway after them.

"Should we be doing this?" Fargo asked, scrambling after me, looking like a baby gorilla as she balanced on her left hand until she got her feet beneath her. "What if there's another ambush?"

"Just stay behind me."

I didn't tell her that if there *was* another ambush, I wanted to spring it myself instead of leaving it for Vicky. The doors to the control room were partially closed, and around the edges of the thick radiation shielding, someone was firing Gyroc rifles at us in an exercise in futility. Each of the impacts was the tap of a raindrop, nothing that could penetrate even the weakened armor on my chest plate. I paused, raising a hand.

"Hold your fire!" The echo from my Vigilante's external speakers was painful. I'd set them to maximum output to make sure they heard me over the gunfire. "Hold your fire! I want to speak to Konigsberg."

Someone was yelling orders inside the control room, out of my line of sight, and the shooters clustered in the doorway slacked off their barrage and withdrew behind the partially closed doors.

"You're talking to him," a familiar voice yelled up the hallway. "But if you're working for the Corporates, you're wasting your breath. I'd rather burn this place down around my ears than give it to them!"

"Mr. Konigsberg, this is Cam Alvarez. We met a few days ago."

That seemed to give him pause, because it took a moment before he replied.

"I feel somehow you weren't being completely honest with me, Mr. Alvarez."

"I'm coming inside," I told him.

"I wouldn't recommend that. These people are feeling pretty trigger happy."

"Doesn't matter. If I wanted to, I could kill every single one of you and there wouldn't be a damned thing you could do about it. And if I was what you think I am, I would have done it already. But things aren't like you think, Pavel. You need to listen to what I have to say."

"What are you *doing?*" Fargo asked over our private net, disbelief dripping off each word. "Are you nuts?"

"Stay out here," I told her. "If they kill me, feel free to kill them back."

"Cam." My first thought was that it was still Fargo nagging at me, but then I saw on the IFF that it was Vicky...and if she was able to reach me, she had to be close. "Are you there?"

"Yeah. I'm okay. We lost Montgomery but we're through."

"Us too. Ran into another platoon of the powered armor

troops, but they didn't last long. We're at the south entrance corridor to the control room. I heard some shooting up there... that you?"

"Yeah, but things are under control now. Stay put unless you hear me call for help."

Which was not an unlikely event.

I couldn't even count the number of gun barrels being pointed my way as I stepped inside the control room. It looked significantly different from the last time I'd been there, with cargo pods hauled in and placed at key points, sand spilling out onto the floor to show what they'd filled them with. Konigsberg also looked different, no longer dressed in his casual work clothes. Instead, he wore full combat armor dating back to the Pirate Wars, a Gauss rifle cradled in the crook of one arm, his helmet in the other. There was something subtly different about his face, too, a hardness I'd seen in the eyes of the coldest killers I'd ever known. He was the only one standing. The others were huddled behind the sand-filled pods, guns aimed at me. Except for Oscar Wendt. He was still in his chair, staring at me with a look of casual contempt, one hand hovering over a control pad.

"You know," I said, motioning at the cargo pods, "those are good bullet-stoppers, but they'd be worse than useless against this." I raised my plasma gun upward demonstratively, ignoring the tension it caused among the armed miners packed into the room. "One blast would turn that whole thing into a giant fire-bomb. Kill everyone in the room."

"Not before I touch this button," Oscar warned me. "You wanna know what it does?"

"Not particularly," I admitted.

"It deactivates every safeguard the reactor has, that's what," he declared, apparently determined to finish the threat despite my feelings on the matter. "And then it pushes the output to overload. Plasma will spill out everywhere and turn everything to radioactive slag. Your Corporate Council bosses won't get any use out of *our* refinery, and it'll cost them more to clean up the site than it would have to just find their fucking rhenium someplace else."

"Good."

Oscar blinked, frowning at me, and Konigsberg's expressions was a funhouse mirror of his.

"I don't want your fucking rhenium," I told them. "I sure as hell don't want the Corporate Council to have it." I sighed, feeling like I was talking to myself. "Oh, the hell with this."

I yanked the quick release on my chest plastron and the stale stink of sweat filtered in along with the chill of the overtaxed air conditioning. I pulled the interface cables free of my implant jacks and climbed out of the suit. The rifle barrels were a little harder to ignore now, but I did my best to stare Konigsberg straight in the eye...though I carefully kept my hand away from my holstered handgun. His expression didn't change, but I thought perhaps I saw a hint of appreciation for the gesture.

"The Corporate Council wants your rhenium...well, they *say* they want it. I don't give a shit who you sell it to as long as you stop selling it to your current buyer."

"And why would I do that?" Konigsberg asked, though the words were more curious than challenging.

"Because your buyer is a rogue Tahni general named Zan-Thint. He and a whole brigade of his troops didn't surrender at the end of the war, just took off and holed up somewhere, getting ready to fight a guerilla campaign to avenge their loss. They have ground troops but not enough warships...which is why they need your rhenium."

"Why should we believe anything you say?" Oscar demanded, rotating his chair around to face me, hand off the demolition control now that I was out of my armor. "You work for the Corporate Council."

"The CSF *thinks* I work for them," I corrected. I felt weak in the knees, like I was about to stumble, and I chalked it up to not really caring for being outside my suit in situations like this. I really wanted to lean against something.

"And who *do* you work for?" Konigsberg wondered.

"Fleet Intelligence. Me and Vicky both. I'm probably breaking all sorts of regulations and protocols and shit by telling you, but to hell with it. The mission comes before the rules."

"Why the fuck should we care if you're a spook?" one of the others demanded, standing from where she'd been ducked behind cover, the muzzle of her Gyroc carbine still trained on my chest. "You've been killing our people!"

"I'm not a fucking spook," I snapped at her. "I'm a Marine. And we've been killing Extreme Measures mercenaries, not your people. When we came down here, I was trying to even avoid doing that. The idea was to get you to agree to sell rhenium at a reasonable price to the Corporates so I could get out of this nightmare and still maintain my cover. But that Captain Dhoni was a bloodthirsty little fuck and didn't give me any choice."

"Was?" Konigsberg asked, eyebrow arching.

"Yeah. I hope the Tahni were paying him, not you, because if you approved that piece of shit, my opinion of you would go down a few notches."

"The buyer was paying for the mercs. It was part of the contract."

"Anyway, once I found out about Zan-Thint, I couldn't let things just go on, and after Dhoni snatched Vicky and I and our people had to rescue us, I couldn't put off taking the mercs out any longer without giving ourselves away. But we can still salvage this. I can negotiate a deal for you with the Corporate Council where you retain control and sell to them at a fair price." I shrugged. "Or, I can go to my superiors and see if they can arrange some better mercenaries for you. But you're going to have to do two things for me. One, stop selling rhenium to the Tahni, and two, tell me where they've been shipping the stuff."

"And if I refuse? If I tell you to go fuck yourself and do whatever the hell I want with my ore and my mine?"

The words were harsh, the tone challenging, but the look in his eyes was calculating, as if he was testing me. I went with honesty.

"Right now, I sent half my squad to clear the mercs out of the city. But if you turn me down, then those CSF assholes are going to come in here with their battlesuits and you're not going to be able to stop them." I shook my head. "And I won't help you, because as much as I don't like the Corporate Council coming in here and taking over, I'd like Zan-Thint building his own private fleet of warships even less."

"Hey Boss," Oscar said, voice going up an octave. "We got some more activity coming up through the cargo entrance."

"What is it?"

"Just movement. Something's jamming our sensors."

I looked at him sharply, moving around beside him to look over his shoulder. The pattern of interference was very familiar to me, the signature of the ECM equipment built into a Vigilante.

"Goddammit, Martz," I muttered.

"Sir," Fargo said into my ear bud, "didn't you send Sgt. Martz to the spaceport?"

I shot Konigsberg a helpless look.

"We got a problem."

[20]

The Vigilante was a mother, her arms spread wide, offering safety and comfort, but I couldn't accept her embrace. The clomp of heavy footfalls just down the hallway were too close and the muzzles of the miner's guns even closer.

"Vicky, Martz is coming in," I blurted, but stopped when Konigsberg's pistol rose level with my head.

"You said you sent the others to the spaceport," he reminded me.

"Cam?" Vicky said, but I couldn't answer her. "Cam?"

"He doesn't trust me," I told him, hoping Vicky was still listening. "He's coming here to kill you and everyone else. You'd better let me get into my armor if you want to have any hope of keeping him out of here."

But it was already too late. The hulking form of a Vigilante burst into the room and the only reason all four of them didn't push through at once was that there just wasn't room. I didn't need my IFF to know who was in the lead suit. Martz had a certain way of moving in the suit, as distinctive as a fingerprint, something I'd noticed even in the simulator. He didn't fire immediately, his plasma gun scanning around the control room.

No one else fired at him, either, perhaps realizing the futility of it, and for that I was truly thankful, since I likely would have been caught in the crossfire.

"What the hell are you doing out of your suit, Alvarez?" Martz bellowed through his external speakers and I winced as I realized just how loud the damned things were. "What happened to the mission?"

"I was trying to negotiate a surrender," I told him, not caring how stupid it sounded, just trying to buy time. "I thought we might be able to get out of this without killing any innocent civilians."

"Or maybe you never gave a shit about the mission," he growled, and his plasma gun swung my way, the interior of the muzzle an inside-out nautilus shell, the electromagnets that propelled the ionized gas twisting and coiled. "Maybe you're exactly what Chief Investigator Wellesley *thought* you were: a plant. A spy. Maybe it's time I took care of you just the way she said I should."

"Sergeant, no!"

I hadn't seen Fargo moving, hadn't noticed her squeezing through the other three Drop Troopers, but I did now. The whine of her jets was a banshee screeching inside my head, the collision between her shoulder and Martz's chest a vibration I could feel in my sinuses. Miners went flying like bowling pins as the massive battlesuits slid across the floor and even Konigsberg's attention was pulled away at the spectacle.

I used the distraction, jumping up and balancing precariously on the edge of my open chest plastron, then twisting around to plop straight into the suit. It hurt. I'd seen hotshots try the move during Armor School, seen more than one of them break an ankle or bust their head open, which was why any training NCO who saw a student attempting it would give them about a million pushups. I didn't break my ankle or slam my head into the side of the suit, but I did twist my knee and back and I knew I'd pay for it later.

For now, I yanked the chest plastron closed and jammed home the ends of the interface cable. The helmet display blinked to life, and I saw that in the scant seconds I'd missed, things had changed. Fargo's suit was on the ground, with Martz standing over her, about to fire his plasma gun at her head at point-blank range, while the other members of Bravo team were squeezing into the room behind the two of them. Bradley was in the lead, a lance corporal who'd had a cup of coffee on Tahn-Skyyiah at the very end of the war. If he'd had half the brains and balls he thought he did, he'd have pulled up his grenade launcher, but he was aiming his plasma gun into the miners instead, ignoring the fact he could hit his own squad leader with the blast.

I had no such worry, since the only people behind Bradley were the other two members of Bravo team, and I knew they wouldn't hesitate to shoot me once Martz got around to giving the order. I was still hoping I could avoid killing any of them, as unrealistic as that might have been, so I blasted a plasmoid into his main gun. Not that he enjoyed the experience. The right arm of his suit was engulfed in a white-hot glow and his screams decohered into static in my helmet comms.

The plasma gun would take precious seconds to recharge and there wasn't time to wait. I backhanded Martz across his helmet and he staggered backwards just as he fired his main weapon. I'd deflected him from his target, from turning Fargo's helmet into a mass of molten metal, and the burst of ionized hydrogen splashed against the ceiling, bringing down a shower of flaming plaster and, on its heels, a curtain of flame-retardant foam.

Miners ran and I didn't blame them. This was a battle of the titans, not a fight for mere mortals. Martz swung a clawed fist at my head and I blocked the blow with my plasma gun, the impact still ringing through my suit like a bell. I had seconds to live. Fargo was trying to push off the floor and once Bradley's suit injected him with painkillers, he'd have the presence of mind to move his flailing, screaming ass out of the way and let Toussaint and Yeltsin through. Then there'd be no reason for either of them not to blow me to cinders.

Unless I could keep all of them occupied, of course.

Martz tried to take another wild swing and I ducked under it, putting the shoulder of my Vigilante under his armpit then hitting the jets. He dragged his heels, sending sparks off the floor, but he moved, crashing backwards into Bradley and knocking them both into a heap, blocking the doorway. I barely kept my feet, stumbling backwards and nearly colliding with Vicky.

I'd hesitated to kill, but she didn't. Her plasma shot spared Bradley a long and painful recovery from the burns to his right arm by spearing a hole through his chest. I winced at his death, but we'd crossed the Rubicon now and there was no going back. I tried to target Martz, but he'd gotten back to his feet and was scrambling back out through the door, taking the other two with him, and my shot splashed molten metal across the back of his leg but did no real damage.

"Seal that fucking door!" I yelled at Konigsberg, not caring if it hurt his ears.

The man looked stunned—physically, not psychologically, because I didn't figure him for someone who was prone to psychological shock—but he lunged for a switch on the wall and smacked his gloved hand against it. The doors dilated shut, the radiation shield a good fifteen centimeters of solid lead.

"The other doors too," Vicky insisted. "I took out Liao, but Walsh ran."

I winced at the casual way she spoke of killing the man, but

Konigsberg didn't question either her morals or who Liao and Walsh were. He found another control and the opposite entrance to the control room slid shut, the clang of thick metal chilling and final. I hissed out a breath and scanned the room for casualties. A few of the defenders were grimacing or moaning in pain from flash burns, but their friends were tending to them and no one looked as if they'd received any major wounds. That left our only other ally, and an unlikely one at that.

"Fargo, are you all right?" I forgot and said it over the external speakers because I hadn't switched back over to the comms, but didn't realize it until I saw Konigsberg's eyes go to the third suit in the room.

The woman's Vigilante was standing stock-still, which usually meant that the person inside the suit was off-balance and the gyros were doing their best just to keep her on her feet.

"Yeah," she murmured, responding in like manner, aloud. "What...what you told him about being with Fleet Intelligence. Is that true?"

"It is. From almost the beginning."

"That's what Martz thought."

I blinked, sure I'd heard her wrong.

"Martz *knew*?"

"He didn't *know*," she corrected me, sounding a bit steadier. "He said that Chief Investigator Wellesley told him she suspected you two were working with the military. He told me on the flight over. I think he thought it would make me more likely to be loyal to him if things went bad. But I'm a Marine, sir. I took an oath."

"And so did I," Konigsberg said, so softly I wasn't sure if he was speaking to me or himself. "I didn't know who I was selling the rhenium to, but I was...." He shrugged. "...curious. I bought a skip tracer module. You know what those are?" I was about to say no, but he went on, rightly assuming I'd have no idea. "It's a tracker you can plant on a cargo pod, programmed to separate from the cargo when the freighter arrives in-system and transmit a message to any ship heading for a wormhole jump-gate. It was a risk. If the freighter crew had detected it, I could have kissed the contract goodbye. But I had to know, you know?"

I waited impatiently for him to finish, wanting to make a go-ahead motion but knowing it would be hard to do inside the suit.

"Khepera," he finally said. "They dropped out of T-space in the Khepera system."

"Thank you," I told him. "You've saved us a lot of hours beating our heads against a wall. And we may need those hours if we're going to stop this guy before he can set his plans in motion."

"What are you gonna do about those other assholes?" Oscar interjected. He'd thrown himself out of his chair when Martz had burst through the door and was only now getting back to his feet, using the chair as an anchor. His work-casual shirt was torn and singed and part of his beard was burned off, but he other-wise seemed unhurt. "Your buddies who you chased out?"

"I need to call in our dropship," I said, "get them to pick us up and get us back to the get them to pick us up and get us back to the *Yantar*. You think you could switch off the jamming?"

"It's off," he told me. "We shut it off to try to reach the Extreme Measures troops earlier, when you guys showed up in the hallway."

"Foster, this is Alvarez," I transmitted. "We need a dust-off at the refinery."

I waited a few seconds but heard no reply. Cursing softly, I checked the automated response system, hoping for a ping back showing me the system was receiving my transmission. And there it was. They were receiving.

"Foster," I repeated, "this is Alvarez, please respond. I need a dust-off at the refinery ASAP."

"Oh, do you now?" The reply finally came, but the voice wasn't Foster's. It was Martz. "Isn't that just so sweet that you think Foster is loyal to you and not to the people who pay us all?"

"Foster," I ground out through clenched teeth, "Martz is off the reservation. He tried to kill us and if you listen to him, you'll wind up either dead or in a military prison. Do *not* let this prick drag you down with him."

"Nice try, Alvarez," Martz answered, "but the only ones who are gonna end up dead are down there. You and your new friends are gonna find out exactly how bad it sucks to be on the wrong end of an airstrike."

"Hey boss," Oscar said, hand cupped to his ear like he was listening to someone on an ear bud, almost on top of Martz's words since he couldn't hear the conversation, "we got a report from one of the spotters we left outside. He says that big cargo shuttle that dropped these guys off is circling around the refinery. Looks like it's about to head in."

I switched on my external speakers and wished I had time to get out of the suit again, because this felt like something I should say eye-to-eye.

"Mr. Konigsberg, is there any way you can get a transmission from here to orbit? Because I think we may be fucked."

———

"You want me to do *what*?" Kyler Dunstan demanded, disbelief strong in his voice, even over the tinny external speaker of the control room's comm panel.

I would have preferred if Oscar could have synched the transmission with my 'link so I could have the conversation in private, but this was no military command center, nor was it a Corporate Council operations web and I was lucky they even had the equipment at all.

"Dunstan," I repeated with strained patience, "Martz is going to kill us, and he's got Foster believing it's the right thing to do. If you don't take down the dropship, Vicky and Fargo and I are all dead."

"That fucking thing is coming in again!" Oscar warned.

He had the feed from the observation post up on the room's main screen, showing the massive lifting-body shape coming in from the west, the noonday sun glinting off its fuselage. Its first pass had been just two minutes before, a gun run that had taken out the two anti-aircraft missile launchers Extreme Measures had emplaced around the refinery control building with burst of coil-gun fire. We'd barely heard it buried at the center of the building, just watched it on the screen like it was a news broadcast.

I had a feeling we were going to feel this one.

"It'll be missiles this time," Vicky warned, staring at the walls around us as if judging whether or not they'd stand up to the attack. "The dropship is carrying GV-760 Shrikes. Air-to-Ground, hypersonic, plasma spear ahead of a tungsten penetrator."

"Dunstan, Goddammit," I growled, really wanting to smash my fist into something but not sure what I could hit in the control room without breaking the reactor, "you need to make a decision!"

Nothing.

"Let's open the shields and get the hell out of here!" Fargo suggested, taking a step toward the door. "We can't do anything in here!"

"The shields will hold," Konigsberg insisted.

"We're about to find out," Oscar said, calmer than I was. He pointed at the screen, at the twin trails of smoke coming from either side of the dropship's fuselage.

I didn't even have time to brace for the impact.

I was inside my suit, inside a heavily shielded control room at the center of hundreds of thousands of tons of reinforced cement, but the thunder of the missiles striking the roof of the building was the loudest sound I'd ever heard. Dust and fragments of concrete showered down from the ceiling, sending the miners scrambling under desks and tables, some of them screaming in terror, though not Konigsberg. The only concession he made to the carnage was to put his helmet on, completing the set of Pirate-War era combat armor.

I was sure the ceiling was going to come down and bury us beneath it, and I had brief nightmare fantasies of being trapped alive in my armor until my on-board air supply ran out, a lonely and claustrophobic death. But the vibration died down and the ceiling was still in place, if cracked and splintered. Oscar kept a careful eye on it as he struggled from beneath his desk, staring at the flickering screen on the wall. The fact that it was still operational was a miracle, but I suppose Konigsberg had bought gear he knew would last.

"Holy shit, we're alive," Oscar blurted. He motioned at the view on the screen from the watchers outside, showing the wreckage of the eastern side of the building, smoke and dust rising from what looked like fallen building blocks. "We're gonna need a renovation, but we're alive."

"How many more of those missiles are they carrying?" Konigsberg asked.

"Six." Vicky's tone was bleak. "Fargo's right. We should get out of here. We can draw their fire away."

"They'll cut you to pieces," Konigsberg warned us. "There's nowhere you can hide from that bird."

"Yeah," I agreed, "but you and your people can get to safety." Which wasn't really my greatest priority in life, if I was being completely honest, but I decided I'd rather die outside, trying to fight back than get buried alive. "Raise the shields before they come around again. Let us out."

The circuit was still open to the transmitter and the missiles hadn't taken down the antenna since it was a kilometer away, connected to the control center via a wireless relay. I leaned my armor over the audio pickup and delivered one last message.

"Ruthie, if you can read me, Zan-Thint is in the Khepera system. Get the info to Hachette, make sure someone cleans them out." I smiled thinly. "It's been nice working with you."

"Oh, for Christ's sake," Dunstan's replied, "don't be so fucking dramatic."

"Hey!" Oscar exclaimed. "What the hell's that?"

That was a delta shape, gleaming in the sunlight, its surface polished silver, streaking down out of the glare of the system's primary. The dropship had been on an arcing return course, set to circle around for another firing run, but they seemed to notice the incoming starship and tried to bank away. But the dropship wasn't an assault shuttle, and its moves were slow and ponderous.

The spear of coherent protons whited out the cameras for just a fraction of a second, and when it flickered back to coherence, the dropship was gone. In its place was a cascade of white fire, pieces of the ship tumbling down on trails of smoke, impacting the ground in giant sprays of dirt and debris.

I tried to feel bad for Foster, for the vets who'd been taken in by Martz, by the Corporate Security Force, but they'd had the same choice as Fargo, and they'd made the wrong one. All I could feel as a profound sense of relief, of disbelief that I was still alive.

"Thanks." The word was half to Dunstan, half to God.

"Find an LZ as close to the refinery as you can and we'll be right out."

"Roger that." His tone sobered briefly. "Cam, you'd better fucking be right about this. 'Cause if you aren't, I just tossed my life down the shitter."

"You did the right thing, Kyler."

I turned back to Konigsberg, who still had his helmet on, the visor up, regarding me with cold, calculating eyes.

"I don't know this fella Dunstan," he said, "but I agree with the sentiment."

I swallowed hard, realizing the responsibility I'd shouldered by talking him into helping us.

"You did the right thing, too. And we'll do right by you. You have my word."

The door to the cargo entrance ground open slowly, partially blocked by wreckage from the missiles, and as it did, I caught a flicker out of my IFF display. It had been dead since the radiation shields had come down, blocking out all external signals except through the hardwired comm panel, but now, it was beginning to pick something up.

My first thought as I stepped toward the opening radiation shield was that my receiver was picking up Bradley's suit where they'd left it outside the door. The man was dead, but his transponder might still be active, and I wasn't concerned...until my helmet detected motion down the corridor, motion right at the spot where the IFF transponder signal was coming from.

"Get down!" I yelled over my loudspeakers. Acting on instinct, I fired.

It could have gone badly. If it had been just others from the mining crew coming in from outside, if they'd just happened to be walking by what was left of Bradley's Vigilante, I could have wound up killing innocent people. But part of me that I trusted implicitly, the part that had gotten me through the war alive, knew I was right, knew the target was the enemy.

The plasma splashed away from the battlesuit in a shower of sparks, but the important part of it had already burned through the bare curve of the helmet, just as the man inside the suit pulled the trigger. It was, I noted with abstract indifference, Kennedy. I'd kind of liked Kennedy. I didn't like the wash of breathtaking heat that came off the coherent packet of ionized gas when it passed only centimeters from my left arm. I bit down on a cry of agony as the skin on my left bicep blistered and baked, the pain enough to make the roar of the steam explosion from the plasma hitting the concrete wall beside me fade into the background.

Bits of debris pitter-pattered against my armor and I skittered backwards, going against my first impulse to charge headfirst into the threat. The IFF signals were clear now...and Martz had suckered me. He'd given me the idea that all of the squad was on board the dropship, that they'd died with it, but they had never boarded it at all. He'd been relaying his transmissions through Foster and I had to think he'd intended this from the beginning, that he'd talked to Foster before we'd even dropped in the first place.

There were just two of them left. Martz and Aboya. I didn't know Aboya at all, except that Vicky had mentioned she was from Cameroon, though I had no idea where that was. She was quiet and did her job and, apparently, she was more loyal to Martz and the CSF than she was to me or the Commonwealth, because she smashed into Kennedy's propped-up Vigilante, knocking it off its feet to get a clear shot at me.

She didn't get the chance. Fargo had made it through the door ahead of Vicky and the lance of sun-hot gas accelerating from her plasma gun took Aboya's arm off at the right shoulder. Losing an arm would have been survivable. The suit had medical systems that could seal off the stump, stop the blood loss and stabilize the Marine inside for further treatment. But I'd seen wounds like this before and even though it was contained inside the armor, invisible to us, I knew the heat from the plasma was enough to cook the woman's brain inside her skull.

Martz was a lot of things, but he wasn't suicidal. In the space of three seconds, he'd gone from even odds to three-to-one, and he had to know he wasn't getting down that corridor alive.

He ran. And I ran after him.

I could blame it on the pain, the anger at being forced to kill other vets affecting my judgement, but honestly, it was just my normal stubborn insistence on walking point. And probably the conviction I couldn't shake even after all these years that I was the best Drop Trooper to ever put on the suit and no one else would have a better chance of living through a fight than me.

Yes, it was egotistical and full of enough hubris to fuel a Greek tragedy, but nobody's perfect.

"Cam, wait!" Vicky called after me, but I kept going. She was going to tell me that it was too dangerous, that I should let Dunstan take care of it.

But Dunstan was in the process of landing, and if he opened up the ramp of his ship, Martz could get on board and then we'd be truly fucked, without a way back to the *Yantar*. I smashed into Aboya's suit and toppled her sideways, tasting blood in my mouth from where I'd bitten my tongue in the collision but not caring. Martz was already turning the corner and I couldn't give him time to take up a defensive position and set up an ambush for me. I had to stay on his heels, not give him a second to think.

I was going too fast, unable to come to a halt, my spiked soles scritching against the concrete floor, and I thumped hard against the wall at the turn, then hit the jets for a fraction of a second to get myself going again, to build up the momentum I'd lost. Martz was thirty meters ahead but targeting him would have meant slowing down, and slowing down was death.

Daylight loomed ahead, the end of the hallway, the cargo entrance. The smoke had cleared, the wreckage still smoldering, the bodies scattered in pools of crimson, their battle lost.

"You've got nowhere to run, Martz!" I tried to yell the words, but my throat was dry, my mouth filled with cotton from the heat of the blast that had burned my arm, and it came out as a rasp. "Just give up. Get out of your armor and surrender and I swear, I'll drop you off on a Periphery colony, somewhere you can get a ride home." Wherever home was for the man. I'd neglected to ask and certainly didn't care now.

His only response was a remarkably agile turn and spin and twist in mid-air with an assist from his jump-jets, a move I'd seen maybe a half a dozen Drop Troopers accomplish in my career. It brought his plasma gun in line with me for a half a second and he fired. I wasn't there anymore, of course, because one of those half dozen people who could pull off that move was me.

The plasma splashed against the rear wheel of one of the Extreme Measures APC's, but I was already on top of the vehicle, stepping over ground I'd tread just a few minutes before. And I finally had a vantage point to take a shot. The downside to that wonderful maneuver Martz had pulled off was that once he touched back down from the burst of the jets, he'd lost all his forward momentum and was standing flat-footed, nothing but a target.

If I'd had a second to think, I might have shot him in the leg. He still would have been in bad shape, would have required days in an auto-doc and then days or weeks, depending on how quickly we could get him to the proper medical facilities, to clone and assemble a new leg for him.

But I had no time and every bit of training I'd gone through in the Marines put my shot center mass.

I dropped down from atop the APC and only the artificial muscle of the suit kept me from staggering, from falling over. Pain and shock were hitting me in waves of fatigue, and it took me a few seconds to register the roar of Intercept One's landing jets as it descended to the parking lot at the foot of the cargo ramp, only twenty or thirty meters from where Martz's metal tomb stood smoldering.

"Cameron Alvarez," Vicky scolded, planting a fist into the center of my chest with enough force that it almost knocked the battered Vigilante over, "you are one reckless, thoughtless son of a bitch and when I get you out of that armor, I'm going to kick your ass."

I didn't know why she was so mad...because I hadn't noticed the red flashing in my HUD damage display over my left arm, hadn't had the presence of mind to read the medical warning streaming above it. My arm wasn't just singed and blistered, and the shot hadn't just been a near miss. The plasma had burned away the top layer of armor over my left bicep and taken a good chunk of my arm with it. I'd been running on adrenaline and the painkillers my suit was hitting me with, and it hadn't hit me until now.

The smell of burnt flesh reached my nostrils and when I figured out it was my own, I passed out.

[21]

"You two," Ruthie declared, arms crossed over her chest, "are the worst fucking spies I've ever met."

"If your Colonel Hachette wanted spies," I countered, rubbing at my left bicep out of habit, as if I couldn't believe it was whole again, "then he shouldn't have sent a couple of Marines."

I'd spent two days in the auto-doc once we'd reached the *Yantar*, and Ruthie Amendola seemed to have saved up all her outrage and vitriol until I was out. I'd emerged starving, the way I had the last time I'd been in one of the damned coffin-shaped things, all my stomach contents and a lot of my fat reserves scavenged by the nanite-infused biotic fluid to repair the damage to my arm, and I'd headed straight from the shower to the galley after Vicky had pulled me out of the machine. Ruthie had been waiting for me there, along with Dunstan and Fargo and I'd known the second I'd seen the look on Ruthie's face that I was in for a dressing down.

"I can understand you having to tell Dunstan," she said grudgingly while I retrieved my imitation cheeseburger and fries from the processor. "I mean, you might as well post on the

InStell bulletin boards, but I guess you didn't have any other choice." She plopped down in a seat across from Vicky and I, thumping it with her ass like it owed her money. "I can even, maybe, understand you telling Fargo here, since you needed her help to survive. But why the hell did you have to tell Konigsberg and all his people? Does operational security mean *nothing* to you?"

"The cat was out of the bag already," I said around a mouthful of soy and spirulina doing a bad impression of a burger. "Wellesley already suspected we were working for the military, and if the enemy knows, who the hell else are we keeping it from?"

"Let me get this straight," Dunstan cut in, still looking in a bit of a daze even two days later. "Back on Bathala, I crashed, and these Marines you're talking about came in and saved us all?"

"Sgt.-Major Campbell," Vicky supplied, regarding him with clear amusement.

"And I wasn't the big hero who beat the alien monsters?" His expression was so forlorn, I couldn't help but feel sorry for him.

"You did the best you could, Kyler," I assured him. "Those things killed the Predecessors. You weren't going to beat them with one cutter, no matter how much of a hotshot pilot you are."

Dunstan stared askance at Ruthie.

"And Amendola was a spy all along? I mean, you're a spy, Ruthie? I never would have guessed that!"

She eyed him sidelong, as if she didn't want to reward the comment with as much as a glare.

"Never mind all that," I said. "What have you found out about the system Konigsberg gave us? This Khepera place where the Tahni were taking the rhenium?"

"I never heard of it before you asked me to look it up," she admitted, pulling a small tablet out of the thigh pocket of her fatigues and reading off its display, "but it's out on the very edge of the Periphery, as in next stop, the Pirate Worlds. And it's home to one of the few shipyards in the Commonwealth not under Corporate Council control." She shrugged. "They mostly manufacture freighters and transports for independent cargo services, but from what I read, they're getting squeezed out of a lot of business by new regulations passed since the war ended. There've been a couple investigations into the firms who've rented out space there, allegations they've been selling ships to the Pirate World cartels, but nothing that's ever stuck."

"That's genius," Vicky said, shaking her head between sips of a squeeze bulb of fruit juice. "Zan-Thint is hiding in plain sight, constructing his fleet right in the middle of a commercial shipyard."

"But he's gotta arm them all," Dunstan objected. "Won't anyone notice?"

"Not in a place like this," Ruthie pointed out, waving the tablet demonstratively. "Like I said, they take their money wherever they can get it, and no one pays too much attention to where the ships go or what goes into them."

"What about the Patrol?" I wondered. "If this place is under investigation, wouldn't they be keeping an eye on it?"

"The Patrol is responsible for protecting the Core worlds." She scowled at me as if I'd said something stupid. "They don't give a shit about the Periphery. This is military jurisdiction and we've been spread too thin to keep people on a nowhere place like this."

"And look where that got us," Vicky murmured.

"It's not an accident." Ruthie cocked an eyebrow at her. "It's been by design, to get most of the systems reliant on the CSF for security and law enforcement. And the CSF doesn't give a shit about Khepera because it's got nothing for them to exploit. They don't even care enough to try to get them shut down."

"At least we got a message off about Khepera before we jumped out," Vicky sighed. "I just hope it gets there in time to do some good."

She was grim and fatalistic and so was Ruthie. I was still fuzzy and lethargic from my time in the auto-doc, and Fargo was silent, staring at the bulkhead like she was still in shock over the deaths of people she considered friends.

But Dunstan was grinning broadly.

"What," I asked him, "is so damned funny?"

"Does this all mean I'm like a secret agent now?"

I snorted a laugh and Vicky buried her head in her hands.

"No," Ruthie Amendola assured him, "you're still just an asshole."

***

"Maybe we should wait."

I stopped what I was doing and sat up in bed, a little surprised. Teased with shadow from the dim glow of the chemical strip lighting, her face was thoughtful, which hadn't been the reaction I'd been hoping for.

"Is it my arm?" I asked flexing the limb in question demonstratively. "Because it's totally good. No issues at all."

She rolled her eyes, which for her, was more of a full-body motion.

"No, you dunce, I meant, maybe we should wait to go into the shipyards at Khepera. Until Hachette and Top and the rest get here to back us up. After all, we only have three ground troops left."

"I don't know," I admitted. "I guess we'll figure that out when we get there, get a chance to look around."

I leaned back against the bulkhead of the cabin, hands cushioning my head. The air conditioning was cold against my skin and I considered putting my T-shirt back on since it was clear we weren't going to be doing anything that required nudity.

"That's not what's really bothering you," I told her. It wasn't a question. I knew her better than that.

"No, it's not," she admitted. She sighed and rubbed a hand over her face. "I think this is changing us, Cam." She frowned. "I think it's changing *me*."

"How?" I thought I knew, but I didn't want to assume.

"It's the killing."

"We've killed before. Between the two of us, we've killed more Tahni than any ten other Marines."

"They aren't human," she insisted, though the denial was rote, no feeling behind it. "It's not the same."

"They're people. Sentient beings, the only others in the whole galaxy as far as we know. And we killed them because there was no other choice, because they'd kill us if we didn't. And it's no different now. We didn't ask for this to fall into our lap, but it did."

"This isn't a war, Cam." She was staring straight ahead, not looking at me. "It's not the same."

"It feels the same. We're fighting the Tahni again."

"We're killing humans this time. And it's not the same. We're killing other vets, and I know it bothers you, too."

"It does," I admitted. "It has for a while now. Not so much with the smugglers back on Hausos, but the mercs and Martz and his squad, yeah. I didn't want to kill any of them. But I once they'd made their choice, they made ours for us. And I don't know what else we could have done except stay on Hausos and tried to ignore all of this."

"Maybe we should have." She turned and finally met my

gaze. "Maybe we shouldn't have given up on the idea of being normal people again."

"Again?" I repeated, chuckling. "When was I ever normal before?"

She looked hurt and I knew I'd screwed up by being flippant.

"Sorry," I said. "I know you had a normal family and everything. But this is all new to me. The first place I felt like I had a home, a purpose, was with the Marines, with you and Scotty and Top and the Skipper. After...." I shrugged. "After, I had a home with you, but I never felt like I had a purpose on Hausos. I was just marking time. Maybe I shouldn't have let that drive me into taking Wade's offer to join the CSF, but if we hadn't...well, what would have happened on Bathala? If we hadn't been there, would those things have gotten loose on the Commonwealth? Maybe all this happened for a reason. Maybe we weren't meant to not be Marines yet."

"You mean maybe *you* weren't meant to not be a Marine," she corrected me. "I know I said I was good with all this, but there's something I have to know. When it's over, when we've taken out Zan-Thint and got his last Skrela pod, what then? Will you be ready to get on with your life doing something else? Something where we can build a home that doesn't involve getting into that suit? Or will you keep climbing back into it because it's the only thing that can protect you from the nightmares?"

That hit like a punch in the gut, and not just because it was Vicky and I didn't expect it from her, but because it was way too close to being true.

"I don't know." I wanted to say something else, wanted to reassure her that this was temporary, but I couldn't lie to her. "It feels right. It feels like the place I belong."

"It's not something we can do and be together," she said,

nothing angry in the words, just a flat declaration, a doctor diagnosing a fatal illness. "Not in the long run. Wars end and we move on, we put them behind us and become something else. If you can't do that, if you're going to keep chasing the comfort of certainty, of meaning, that's not going to leave room for the life I want to live someday."

My stomach was a lump of neutronium, sinking, searching for the center of the nearest planet. When I tried to speak, nothing came out on the first attempt. I closed my mouth and swallowed a lump, tried again.

"Do you want...are you saying you want to...?"

She smiled and I don't think I'd ever seen a sadder expression.

"I don't want a divorce. I don't want to leave you. This isn't a threat, Cam. It's a prediction. It's me telling you what I see happening if that's the way this plays out." She caressed my cheek lightly, her hand burning hot against my cold skin. "I don't want us to end. I'll stay with you as long as I can do it and still be me. Right now, yes, this is important enough that I can put on the suit again, be a killer again for the same reasons I did it during the war, because no one else is going to step up and do what has to be done, because otherwise, a lot of innocent people are going to die."

Her hand fell away limp, as if she'd lost the strength to keep it there.

"But after...if we live through the after...that won't work anymore. I know myself. I'll try, but it's not life I want to live, and, eventually, I'll resent you for keeping me in it. And as much as I love you, I won't let even you make me into something I don't want to be."

"That's the last thing I want to do," I said, feeling very helpless. I wrapped her in my arms, holding her tight, unwilling to let her go. She didn't pull away, but I didn't sense that the gesture gave her any comfort. "We can both leave once we get Zan-Thint," I promised. "I don't have to stay. We can find another colony and maybe start a business this time. Maybe I'd feel more of a purpose if I was making something...."

She let her head rest against my chest.

"I would never tell you to abandon something that made you whole. I'm not trying to talk you out of staying in the military. I'm not threatening to leave you if you do it. I just don't want you to feel like it's a blindside attack if it turns out I can't live that life with you." She smiled, a glint in her eye. "There's no use worrying about it now. Maybe the horse will learn to sing."

"Horse?" I repeated, frowning. "What horse?"

She laughed softly.

"I thought you were the kid who read anything he could get his hands on. You've never heard of this story?" At the shake of my head, she settled in more comfortably against me and went on.

"It's supposed to be a story that happened a long, long time ago, like when there were kings and queens, and they could have people put to death."

"That sounds a lot like now," I murmured, remembering how I came to be a Marine in the first place.

"Shut up," she warned me, twisting my chest hair until I yelped. "Do you want me to tell this story or not?"

"Go ahead," I said, raising my hands in surrender.

"Anyway, there was like a king and he had this pretty white horse he was really proud of. And there was this thief who had tried to steal the horse, but he got caught and he was sentenced to be executed. As he was taken away, he made a bargain with the king: in one year he would teach the king's favorite horse to sing hymns. The other prisoners watched the thief singing to the horse and they laughed and told him he was crazy, that no one could teach a horse how to sing. And the thief told them that he wasn't crazy. He had a year, and who knows what might happen in that time. The king might die. The horse might die. The thief might die. And maybe the horse would learn to sing."

She kissed me, a kiss hot with passion, as if she'd talked herself into hope. I returned it and the ardor behind it, because hey, I might be a lot of other things, but I was still a guy. But even with her in my arms, sailing into possible death, I couldn't shake the nagging thought that the fate of my marriage hinged a singing farm animal.

[22]

"Damn," I murmured, hanging over Dunstan's shoulder, looking at the display on the main view screen. "Two habitables in one system."

"Yeah," Ruthie agreed from the copilot's seat. Unlike me, she was strapped in, secured against the free fall. "Not unheard of, but not exactly common."

"How come I haven't heard of this place before, then?" I wondered. "Two habitables, you'd think the Corporate Council would be all over this place."

"Habitable," she informed me, "doesn't necessarily mean hospitable. Remember Inferno?"

I eyed her sidelong, not bothering to answer the question. No one who'd served in the military could ever forget training at the Fleet base on Inferno. It was aptly named, the ugly sister of the earthlike Eden, just a bit too close to 82 Eridani for comfort, habitable in the far northern hemisphere and even there a tangled mass of ever-humid jungle, ranging into baking deserts farther south until it reached the latitude where a human couldn't survive without protective gear.

"Yeah, so imagine one world like that and the other one is a refrigerator that's only livable on a few islands at the equator. No one *wants* to live in either place, but they're better than breathing canned air twenty-four-seven without anyplace to take a walk with real gravity and growing soy and algae for food. Which is why the Corporate Council, and the Commonwealth government, don't give two shits about this system. And *that*...." She jabbed a finger at the broad swathe of asteroids stretching between the two worlds, thicker than most I'd seen, floating black dots on the screen, the computer simulation much more visible than the actual rocks would have been from our vantage point. "...is why the Chandrasekhar Brothers LLC *is* interested in it. It's the biggest and richest field not under direct Corporate Council control, the perfect place for a shipyard."

"Can we see the shipyard from here?" Fargo asked. I glanced at her, not mocking because she'd been a corporal in the Marines and not any sort of pilot. Dunstan wasn't so gentle.

"Oh, yeah, it's as plain as the nose on your face," he assured her with thinly disguised sarcasm. "Don't you see it right there on the screen?"

Ruthie shot him a glare.

"We're too far away and the sensors haven't picked it up yet. We have the coordinates of the shipyards from their commercial advertisements, though, and we have the exact coordinates of the Tahni construction from Konigsberg's skip tracer."

"And what do we do when we get there?" Dunstan asked, spreading his hands. "We got Intercept One and this boat and you three hard-shells and that's it. If they have any kind of solid defenses, we're fucked."

"This ship isn't *actually* a freighter," she reminded him. "We're equipped to fight Zan-Thint and his Tahni, and we're equipped to fool them, too."

I raised an eyebrow, floating almost upside down in relation to her, anchored by one hand to Dunstan's acceleration couch.

"What'd you have in mind, Ms. Amendola?"

———

"That's pretty damned impressive," Fargo said, and I couldn't help but agree.

Up close, the Khepera Shipyards were a marvel, massive and yet intricate, a web woven by a spider the size of a world. Or rather, dozens of webs, since the yards weren't one, continuous construct but many separate, skeletal structures, each anchored to an asteroid, each of the asteroids fitted with a refinery to churn out nickel-iron and other ores for use in the construction process.

Construction pods and orbital transfer vehicles swarmed around each of the glittering, metallic webs like a cloud of flies infesting a cow, and here and there, a newly completed ship would amble out of its corral and pick up speed, maneuvering jets taking it to a safe distance before the fusion drives lit up and galloped the vessel out to the Transition point. As we watched, another ship popped out of T-space and began to cruise inward to a reserved slot.

"Have they challenged us yet?" Vicky asked.

She, Fargo and I were all strapped into the unclaimed seats on the ship's bridge and I felt utterly useless, the controls on the panel in front of me as cryptic as some ancient tome.

"Challenged us?" Dunstan shot her an amused look. "This is a construction site. They sent an automated traffic control signal and we said 'hi, we're heading to check out berth 23K for a future rental.' These guys get paid to not look at things too closely. I doubt they'll even notice when we divert course toward the Tahni work skeleton."

"Glad you're so confident," Vicky snapped. "Guess that's what comes from ignorance, huh?"

"Jeez, you're grouchy now that you're an Intelligence spook," he grumbled. "I think I liked you better when you were just an ex-Marine working for the CSF."

"There are no *ex*-Marines," I reminded him.

He snorted a sharp laugh and slid a finger through the haptic control hologram. The fusion drive boosted us forward at a half a gravity, pushing me down in my seat. The *Yantar* crawled forward, the spider-webs passing by on all sides of us, the pods and transfer vehicles and shuttles so thick I could have gotten out and walked across their hulls. Okay, not *quite* that thick, but that's how it seemed in the sensor display.

"You never did tell me," he went on, guiding us through the clutter with an expert hand. "I mean, I asked, but Ruthie won't answer. Do I have a job? I can't go back to the CSF, obviously." He shrugged. "Well, technically, maybe I could if they don't know what happened on Portent, but it'd be weird, and they'd ask all kinds of questions and I suck at keeping secrets."

"You saved our asses," I told him, intercepting any corrosive retort Ruthie might have had ready. "I don't know if I have any kind of authority...hell, I'm not even a hundred percent sure what my rank is. But when we report back in, I'm going to ask Hachette to bring you back in, with us if he's willing, but back in the Fleet either way. I owe you that much."

"Cool." He twisted around and grinned at me. "Huh, me back in the military. I guess I'm gonna have to start being a little more careful. My mouth was always getting me into trouble back in Fleet."

"I'm impressed at your level of self-awareness," Ruthie said, and I wasn't sure if she was being sarcastic or not. "But I think I've spotted the Tahni drydock. Better start our braking burn."

"Hold on, performing a turnaround."

The *Yantar* was no cutter, certainly no assault shuttle, but Dunstan handled her like one, spinning her end for end and then cutting in the fusion drives again within only a few seconds, slowing us down relative to the approaching asteroid.

"Oh, yeah, that's definitely a warship," Dunstan said, staring at the display.

I looked at the feed from the sensors and saw just another drydock structure around another starship. It was massive, maybe a half a kilometer long, and wedge-shaped like a half a dozen others I'd seen in the shipyards, the usual shape for a larger starship.

"How can you tell?" I wondered. "They all look the same to me."

"Form follows function." He sounded happy to be an expert at something that the rest of us weren't. "Any starship that uses a single Teller-Fox warp generator is going to be generally streamlined, because every part of the ship has to be inside the field when it jumps, and the field is basically spherical. The big Commonwealth cruisers and carriers get away with breaking those rules because they carry multiple generators, but that's expensive and it eats reactor output. But look right here." He pointed at the spectroscopic readout beside the computer-enhanced optical image in the screen. "That's the signature for BiPhase Carbide. No one would waste that much BPC on a civilian hull. And those power routings...." He traced the same finger down the thermal analyzer. "...those are running to weapons pods. You can't see 'em, the way the ship is oriented in the dock, but I'd guaran-damn-tee you that they're proton cannons."

"How many of those fucking things are they building?" Ruthie wondered, and I nodded in agreement.

Now that I knew what to look for, the tell-tales were obvious...and they were obvious in one cluster of drydocks after another.

"Ten corvettes," Dunstan estimated. "And one destroyer."

He nodded off to our right, to the center of the cluster, to a drydock a good three times the size of the others. The corvettes cloaked it from outside view, but I'd seen its like before in the tactical feed from the *Iwo Jima* troop ship as we burned insystem toward our target.

"Jesus," Fargo hissed, a quaver in her voice. "That thing's huge."

"Yeah, I've heard that before," Dunstan said, no intention in the joke, just an automatic response.

"We're being hailed," Ruthie announced, not even bothering to glare at Dunstan. "Voice only." She manipulated a menu, and a male voice came over the bridge speakers, stern and flat and very obviously simulated.

"Attention unidentified vessel, you are approaching a restricted construction site. Change course now or you will be intercepted."

"Ooh, scary," Dunstan murmured.

"Here's where we find out if those codes Intelligence gave us were correct," Ruthie said, crossing her fingers before she touched a control.

"This is the Tahni vessel *Trin-Van*," she said, and on a tiny sub-screen in the display, an image appeared of the *Yantar*'s bridge, except reconfigured to look like a Tahni ship. "We are inbound from Portent."

And on that bridge, we were reengineered as well, transformed by Intelligence spoofing programs into a Tahni crew.

"I should be taller," I whispered to Vicky, but she shushed me with a nudge.

The screen beside our little deception video had been blank, grey and disused since the Tahni traffic control had been transmitting audio-only. But it flickered to life and the image coalesced into the face of a Tahni male in what I recognized as a military uniform.

"Trin-Van," the male said, and by the delay between the movements of his mouth and the sound coming out of the speakers, I assumed the computer was translating for us. "We did not expect you for several hours. Is there a reason for breaking schedule with this shipment?"

"We bring no shipment," Ruthie replied, and the ugly-looking Tahni taking her place in the simulation relayed the words. "There will be no more shipments of rhenium from Portent. The mine was attacked by the Corporate Security Force and the mercenaries General Zan-Thint hired are dead or scattered. The human Konigsberg has been captured by the Corporate troops and we barely managed to escape ahead of their ships. We must speak with the general immediately."

Tahni facial expressions were as opaque to me as hyperdimensional physics, but it didn't take a linguist to see that the officer in the video image wasn't happy.

"How is this possible? Extreme Measures assured us that they could handle the Corporate soldiers."

"They are humans," Ruthie reminded the male. "They lie. It is in their nature. We must speak to General Zan-Thint. There are things he must know before decisions can be made."

I tensed up, wishing I was in my suit. This was where it could all fall apart. If they suspected anything, this would be the time when they turned those proton cannons on the *Yantar* and blasted us to vapors.

"The general has left the facility. He traveled ahead to the operations base to prepare for the final push." Relief warred with sudden interest at the answer. *The final push* didn't sound good, but the way they talked about the operations base meant it was an established location and they would know where it was. "But we must have the rhenium to complete the destroyer *Jun-Tin Wan.* The general requires it."

Ruthie glanced back at me, touching a control to mute the audio pickup.

"What should I tell them?"

"Let me," I said, motioning at her to un-mute. When I spoke, the computer put the words in the mouth of the simulated Tahni its software had put at my bridge station. "We may be able to secure another load of the rhenium ore." I don't know where the words were coming from. I didn't think about them, just let them flow, and it felt the same as when I'd run street cons back in Trans-Angeles. "Before we left orbit, we received a distress signal from one of the freighters. The CSF had disabled its drives, but it was concealing itself in the asteroid belt. If we can return with this freighter and armed escort, we may be able to retrieve the ore. Are any of our ships ready for launch?"

Ruthie was goggling at me, but Vicky was nodding encouragement.

"We do. The corvette *Ganfa-Mor* is docked with the construction shack."

"We should come aboard," I suggested, "and plan the operation face to face."

Now Fargo was staring at me, too, and I hoped her wide-eyed horror didn't translate through the computer simulation.

"Agreed. Dock at the shack, airlock Seven Alpha."

The screen went dark, and as if it had been a cue, Dunstan and Ruthie erupted like a volcano.

"Are you nuts?" Dunstan wondered.

"For once I agree with Dunstan," Ruthie chimed in. "We have no idea how many of them there are, but I can tell you that just one corvette could blow the shit out of us and Intercept One, especially if it's equipped with anti-ship missiles!"

"I assume you want to climb into those metal pajamas of yours," Dunstan said, "but have you forgotten the fact that we don't have a dropship anymore because I blew it up?"

"Intercept One will do," I assured him. "You and Ruthie get in your vac suits and depressurize, and we can jump out the belly ramp. Ruthie can clip in on my back."

"I can what?" Ruthie blurted. "We can do *what*? Why would I be on Intercept One? What about the *Yantar*? Who's gonna fly her?"

"She can run on computer control, can't she?"

"Yeah, but she can't *fight* under computer control! What do you want her to do, run and get help?"

"You were right about the cutter," I told her, the plan coming together in my head like the pieces of a jigsaw puzzle. "It's the biggest weapon they have, and it could take us out before we got close...." I grinned. "You aren't particularly emotionally attached to this ship, are you?"

[23]

"This is," Dunstan declared, "a battle plan that only a Marine could come up with."

"No shit," Ruthie agreed, hanging off my back. "Is there any reason we couldn't wait for backup?"

"Because they could be days away, if they're coming at all." I put out a hand instinctively to steady my Vigilante against the hammer of the maneuvering thrusters, despite the fact that I was anchored to the deck of Intercept One's utility bay with the magnetic locks in my soles. "And we had to let the Tahni know we were here to get them to talk to us. If we hopped into T-space and left, they'd shut everything down and evacuate what they could, and we'd be left with nothing. They know where Zan-Thint is and they probably know where the Skrela pod is, too."

"And why do *I* have to come along?" Ruthie demanded. "Couldn't I stay here and listen to Dunstan bitch?"

"Someone has to use the cracking module," I reminded her. "And the free hand on this suit isn't exactly designed for delicate operations."

"We're ten seconds from separation," Dunstan informed me.

I linked into the feed from the *Yantar*'s external cameras and sensor array, and the blank grey metal of the utility bay was replaced by the gleaming wedge of silver metal that was the corvette, attached by a long docking umbilical to the glassy smooth cylinder of the construction shack. Like a chain of children's building blocks, the shack was connected to the shipyard web, which was, in turn, anchored in the nickel-iron core of a moderate-sized asteroid. Unlike the other ships in this section of the yard, there were no construction pods zipping around the corvette, probably because it was ready to launch, but I did notice larger sensor signatures out at the limits of the instrument range, blinking in and out as they passed behind thicker sections of the web.

"Launching."

At Dunstan's announcement, I switched to the feed from Intercept One as she slid out from dorsal docking niche in the *Yantar*'s hull, the gleaming mass of the converted freighter swelling to take up the whole screen. Then it dropped beneath us and shrank to half that size in conjunction with the kick in the pants of Intercept One's drive igniting. I knew what was going to happen next and I slitted my eyes in anticipation, despite the fact that the ship's cameras and my helmet's display would filter the image.

The screen lit up solid white with the fusion drive of the *Yantar*, washing out the details of the corvette and the construction shack for a few seconds. When the image cleared, the *Yantar* was kilometers away, accelerating at twenty gravities, a much harder boost than she ever would have attempted with us fragile humans on board. Arranging the computer-controlled flight had been tricky, requiring a half a dozen override codes and Ruthie and Dunstan's biometric IDs to accomplish. It was a lot of work for only three minutes of flight-time.

The corvette had enough warning for the ship to power up and just begin to move away from the docking umbilical, but not enough to get away. There was no sound, of course, no vibration or concussion, not even what could accurately have been called an explosion. The fusion drive kept running even after the nose of the *Yantar* plowed through the bow of the corvette, after the metal had shattered and shredded, until the reactor flushed and dumped in a spray of sun-bright plasma, and the cloud of ionized hydrogen ate through the hulls of both ships, turning their mangled remains into charred debris spinning in random orbits through space.

I had no sentimental attachment to the *Yantar*, had only been aboard her a few months, but seeing her destroyed in the blink of an eye was unsettling and the whole thing took on an air of unreality. I was watching the action on a screen from after the fact, the danger happening to someone else, and I shook off the disconnect, trying to bring myself back to the present.

Intercept One hurtled through the metal storm, shedding the debris from its deflector shields, coming in at a more sedate pace, not because we weren't in a hurry, but because even one gravity of boost wasn't very comfortable when we were standing at a right angle to the direction of the thrust. I didn't want to think how awkward it was for Ruthie, but it got even more awkward when Dunstan flipped the cutter end for end and applied the same boost in the opposite direction. At least it didn't last as long, because he didn't want to shed all of his momentum, only most of it.

"Pop the top," Dunstan told us. "Drop in ten."

I pulled out of the feed from the cutter and started paying attention to the tiny space around me, to the belly ramp as it ground open with glacial slowness. No air escaped because we'd dumped the air already, and thank God we'd had the spare parts and repair kit on board the *Yantar* to fix the arm and chest armor of my Vigilante, because otherwise I doubt it would have maintained its airtight integrity.

"Five."

"You ready?" I asked Vicky.

"Now's a hell of a time to ask me that."

"Go!"

I really, really, really didn't like spacewalks, and every single one I did proved that to me all over again. The jagged remains of the docking umbilical were our target and it took every single bit of self-control I had not to punch the jets to get there faster. That was the thing about the space close enough to a gravitational mass—we weren't just floating free, we were technically in orbit around the thing, and boosting forward would also mean climbing to a higher orbit. So, we just rode the momentum we carried with us from Intercept One, carefully calculated by Dunstan and the ship's computer, and I hoped I wouldn't grind my teeth right down to their nubs.

The umbilical had seemed a hundred klicks away, yet suddenly we were right on top of it, the charred and shredded ends of the flexible, metal cylinder still bobbing back and forth like a pendulum from the momentum the corvette yanking away had given it. The computer had accounted even for that, and we sailed inside, the interior walls rushing at us with threatening speed. I finally got to use my jets, just a brief, prescribed burst that made the impact of my feet on the metal a slight twinge in my knees rather than a debilitating agony.

"That sucked," Ruthie commented, strain in her voice. "Let's not do that again."

"Get the lock open," I instructed. Our three Vigilantes were anchored to the metal by our boot magnets, which left the lock-picking duties to Ruthie.

She didn't seem thrilled about it and wasn't shy about letting me know, unless the stream of curses on the operational net as she unhooked from the back of my armor and picked her way to the lock controls might just have been an accident.

"Dunstan," I transmitted as Ruthie made her way to the lock. "You copy?"

"I do," he told me. "But I won't for long. We have multiple bogies headed this way. Assault shuttles maybe, or maybe even Tahni space fighters. If they have ECM, they're going to be jamming our shit. I'll come back and dust you guys off after I take care of them."

"Or we'll be stuck here after they take care of you," Ruthie murmured, her voice distracted as she applied the cracking module Fargo had brought with her from the Corporate station at Canaan.

"Love you, too, Ruthie," Dunstan said. "Good luck."

The sudden silence on the line as he signed off sent a chill up my back. Because Ruthie had been right. If anything happened to him, we were dead. The corvette might be the only starship they had ready to roll here, but Zan-Thint wouldn't have left a place this unimportant unguarded.

"Got it," Ruthie announced, just a half-second ahead of both airlock doors sliding aside at once.

Red warning lights flashed and a gush of air frosted the edges of the tunnel, dust and debris fleeing the construction shack along with the air. I half-expected to see bodies flushing out with them, but I supposed the personnel inside had received at least enough warning to put their suits on. Ruthie wasn't experienced at this sort of thing and she didn't find a handhold quickly enough.

Her alarmed squawk was static on my radio as she began to float away from the lock on the current of air, but my suit and my reflexes were fast enough to catch her.

"Should I latch back on?" she asked, the fear in her voice telling me she really wanted to.

"Just anchor to the deck once we're inside," I told her. "People will probably be shooting at us, and it'd be better for you if you weren't plastered across my back when they did."

"I'm taking point," Vicky said in a tone that would brook no argument.

I said nothing, just fell in behind her, Fargo bringing up the rear.

The airlock was compact, confining, built to hold nothing larger than a crew of workers in suits, but it opened up into a larger utility area, crammed with spacesuit lockers and racks of the sort of smaller tools that the workers could bring back on their persons for maintenance in the comfort of an atmosphere. The rocket motor of an orbital transfer vehicle tugged at the strands of a restraint web in one corner, partially disassembled, waiting for a tech to finish repairing it.

The total silence of a hard vacuum was as oppressive and haunting as the utter stillness of the place, even my own footsteps a dull thump barely reaching up the surface of the suit. There was no weight behind them, of course, just the click of the magnets grabbing their electromagnetic purchase on the metal deck plates, then the scrape of them letting go, over and over. When Ruthie broke the silence with her transmission, it was obscenely loud in my earphones and my heart skipped a beat.

"The operations center should be near the middle of the shack." She sounded as if she'd calmed down a bit after her brush with the void. "There's a storm cellar at the core, but the operations room will be somewhere in the same area."

"Storm cellar?" Fargo asked, and if she hadn't, I would have.

"A place like this doesn't have energy shields. There's no way they could make it affordable. Instead, they have a storm cellar, a small, heavily-shielded compartment they can run to in case of solar flares and increased radiation. That's probably where they'll be right now, most of them."

"Except the ones they send out to try to kill us," Vicky corrected her.

"Yes, except those."

"What do you think?" I asked. "Will they spread out and try to attrit us or bunch up right in front of the entrance to the storm shelter and try to keep us out?"

It wasn't just an academic question. If they concentrated on protecting their people, we might not have to fight them at all. We didn't *want* their people; we wanted their computer systems. That would be the ideal situation. Which was why it was the least likely, because nothing ever worked out that easy.

"They'll spread out," Vicky declared without a hint of doubt, "try to ambush us. Since when do the Tahni go on the defensive?"

She didn't slow down, though. The workroom that connected with the airlock took up a large chunk of the construction shack, lined with lockers and toolboxes from floor to ceiling, and it looked like a great place for the ambush she'd spoken of, so I didn't blame her for wanting to get out of there as quickly as possible. She was on point so I didn't complain, just kept up a scan on thermal and watched my sector of the compartment. It might have been an ideal place to hit us, but the Tahni had other ideas, because they weren't anywhere to be found.

"Left, or right?" she asked, pausing about halfway through the compartment, framed between a pair of spacesuits. They were each anchored to the deck by their magnetic boots and I would have thought they were Tahni troopers waiting for us if they both weren't missing their helmets.

She wasn't asking about the suits. There were two exits from the utility compartment, ovoid, four meters in diameter, tight for a battlesuit, and perfect chokepoints.

"Anything, Ruthie?" I asked, hoping she had a suggestion because I was ready to flip a coin, but the microgravity made it impractical.

"They both lead around to the same place," she said. "The corridors lead in a circle, but I couldn't tell you which way is closer."

"The Tahni will be covering the closer route," Vicky declared. "We'll know if we're going the right way if they shoot at us."

"Instant feedback," I murmured. "Wonderful. Go left."

"What about the Tahni?" Fargo asked.

She hadn't panicked so far, which I appreciated. She hadn't whined or complained or asked why we weren't waiting for reinforcements, hadn't asked dumb questions. I appreciated that, too. So, I didn't say anything sarcastic or snap at her for asking such an obvious question. I just answered it.

"We all re-armed with missiles on the *Yantar*," I said. "Corporal Fargo, I want you to set your warhead for minimum detonation distance, baffles to 180-degree front dispersion, and launch one down that hallway. Then, you and Ms. Amendola keep walking while Lt. Sandoval and I break anchor and jet in just as fast as we can. How does that sound?"

"What if the Tahni are down the other hallway? And what if they come up behind us while we're walking?"

"Yeah, what if?" Ruthie agreed.

"Then you grab Ms. Amendola and jet on after us just as fast as you can. Now launch me a missile, Corporal Fargo."

It was my best platoon-leader voice. I'd been working on my company-commander voice back at the end of the war, but I never would have matched Captain Covington in that department. But I had developed a good platoon-leader voice, the kind that sounded all confident and self-assured and calming. The kind that could get nervous enlisted Marines to move towards gunfire instead of running away from it.

It still worked.

The missile popped free of the launcher on Fargo's back on a hiss of inert, cold-gas propellant before the rocket motor ignited. The glow was subdued, so unlike the violent blast of a launch in an atmosphere, the weapon streaking down the corridor in eerie silence. It was in flight less than a second, and if there had been air to conduct the blast, it would have sent a concussion wave back at us, but fighting in an airless environment took some adjustment. The warhead's detonation was a flash of actinic white lighting up the corridor, just a hint of the heat energy washing out to the front of the weapon. Metallic hydrogen powder sprayed ahead of a shaped charge of Hyper-Explosives, spears of plasma in a flower blossom.

Vicky and I were already free of our magnetic anchors and jetting forward on bursts of our jets, the engines fed by a small supply of the same sort of metallic hydrogen powder. We had no worries of cruising into our own detonation due to the lack of air and we were hard on the heels of the blast, close enough to see the plastic peeling off the walls, the metal beneath it eaten through by the heat of a star.

Close enough to see a Tahni High Guard battlesuit floating free just centimeters off the deck, and I knew by the proximity that it had been anchored down by electromagnets a moment before. He'd seen the missile and tried to run, but not fast enough, as evidenced by the blackened hole burned through his shoulder. It might not have been fatal under other circumstances, but it was far too close to his head for the armor to be able to seal properly against the vacuum.

Even if it hadn't been, the gunfire from behind him would have killed him in any case. His brothers in arms probably hadn't meant to shoot through him, but he'd drifted into their line of fire, and killing us was more important to them than saving him. If Zan-Thint had managed to equip them with the electron beamers they'd used during the war, even the attenuation by the floating enemy battlesuit wouldn't have been enough to save us, but thankfully, he'd run into more supply issues than the CSF had, and his battlesuits were only armed with coilguns.

The heavy, metal slugs were invisible, nearly undetectable, but their effect was plain. Metal shavings sprayed off the walls around us and off the High Guard suit tumbling between us, and, eventually, they would still have hit us. We were not, however, waiting for that to happen. Vicky fired first, but my shot came a half a heartbeat later, the plasma bursts not quite as spectacular as they would have been if we hadn't trashed the airlock, but impressive enough for all that.

Both packets of plasma struck the same suit, the leader in the offset file formation arrayed in the hall, one blowing off his arm at the shoulder, the other melting clean through his helmet, and that was enough for the rest of the formation. They were Tahni, so they weren't about to run away, but even the Tahni understood the value of a tactical withdrawal to a more defensible position. The hallway was straight and narrow, which they had thought made it a good chokepoint, but chokepoints worked both ways and no more than two or three of them could fire at once, which made the odds even. The fact that Vicky and I were two of the best Drop Troopers to ever climb into a Vigilante tilted those odds heavily toward us.

They were running and we couldn't afford to let them turn around and fight, not least because I had no idea how many of them there were. Their thermal signatures blurred into one another in sprays of exhaust from their backpack jets, further distorted by the heat still pouring off the walls and the two High

Guard suits we'd taken out. I wanted to fire off a missile at the fleeing Tahni, but the same distortion of their heat signatures and my difficulty in telling one from the other made it impossible. If I couldn't get a target lock, I couldn't fire, particularly not in these close confines.

It was hard to keep track of anything, as fast as we were jetting through the corridor and I began to worry about how, exactly, we were going to stop without running headlong into the proverbial wall. Then we hit the first curve and that worry solidified into a real wall, not a proverbial one. And we were heading right for it.

[24]

It rains, my father once told me, on the just and the unjust.

At the time, I'd been six years old and to my childhood self, rain had been a killjoy, the producer of the mud that made streets impassable and drowned soccer and baseball fields, and I'd taken the proverb to mean that bad things happened to everyone, good or bad. I had, of course, had it exactly backwards. Rain was the salvation of farmers everywhere, from Bronze-Age Palestine to post-Collapse Tijuana, and the Biblical saying meant that the blessings of God came down on everyone, helping us all no matter whether they were good people or bad. Both were equally unfair, of course, but somehow, I'd always taken some comfort in the former interpretation, the one little six-year-old Cameron Alvarez had believed, that no matter how shitty things were for good people, shitty things happened to bad people, too.

Something really shitty happened to the first Tahni High Guard trooper who tried to navigate that curve at full speed without decelerating. The flare of the suit's jump-jets slewed off to the side, making his passage obvious even among the packed-together clump of Tahni battlesuits, just as obvious as his plan.

He was trying to use the jets to slow just enough to coast around the curve without stopping, without losing too much momentum. It would have required expert timing, the instincts of a fighter pilot and probably, a flight computer.

The Tahni trooper had none of those. He crashed into the far wall hard enough to put a three-meter-tall dent in it, tumbled, then shot back into the wall on the other side before his jets cut off. The impact wasn't enough to kill him, at least not if their armor was as well-padded as ours, but he was out of the fight for a few seconds and, worse for them, he'd crashed through the Tahni formation like a bowling ball, scattering them to either side, slowing them down.

This time, Vicky and I selected different targets, though I couldn't honestly say it was by design. The plasma blast from my weapon lanced through the swell of the reactor blister on the upper back of the Tahni High Guard suit, and although there was no spray of sparks or gush of black smoke, I could tell from the thermal readings that the shot had taken out his power pack. He floated free, making no attempt to correct his course or raise his weapons and I let him go, taking the risk I was wrong because taking the time to try to finish him off would have meant ignoring the others.

A second Tahni battlesuit was still tumbling from the collision with the bad driver, but added to his problems was the fact that his left arm had been burned off at the shoulder, taking with it his primary weapon. I caught a half-second glimpse of him and then I was forced to deal with the unrelenting demands of Sir Isaac Newton. The maneuver was as natural for me as if the suit was my own body, and just as difficult, since I was no sort of gymnast or tumbler. I swung my arms to set myself into a roll, then gave the jets a hard, steady burn for three agonizing seconds that felt as if my spine was trying to tunnel downward out of my asshole.

I didn't know if the burn was long enough, but it was all I could take and I cut the boost, absorbing the rest of the hit in my ankles, knees, and hips. The suit helped, of course, allowing me to hit with force that would have broken bones and come out of it with nothing more than the promise of future aches and pains. I bounced off the wall the way the Tahni had tried to, and then I was on top of my less-coordinated enemy counterpart.

My plasma gun had a few more seconds before it recharged and I was way too close for missiles, but I did have an advantage. The Tahni was still stunned by the collision and I just needed to make sure the condition was permanent. The foot of his battle-suit was passing by my face as he tumbled out of control and I locked onto it with the claw of the Vigilante's left hand, simultaneously anchoring to the wall with the magnetic sole of one boot. The enemy trooper came to an abrupt halt, nearly ripping my boot magnet off the wall, and I would have gone flying if I hadn't reinforced my position with the other boot a fraction of a second later. A fraction of the momentum transferred from the suit to my puny, flesh-and-blood body, the brief flash of pain escaping in an involuntary grunt.

The Tahni suit might not have had weight, but it had a shit-load of mass and it took a mighty swing to get it moving...and once it got moving, there was no way I could have stopped it. Only the wall could do that, and it was happy to help. He bounced off the wall and I used the momentum to swing him back the other way, into one of the other Tahni troopers who was trying to get turned around in the microgravity, trying to get his coil-gun aimed at Vicky and me. This time, I let go of the leg when the suits collided because my plasma gun had recharged.

I hadn't had much time to think, but I'd been doing this long enough that I didn't need to. There were eight Tahni troopers in all, their version of a squad. We'd killed four, one with Fargo's missile, the rest with our guns, and now two more of them were distracted if not disabled, leaving two in the fight, one at each end of the shambolic formation. And both of these guys had time to aim.

I hit the jets out of instinct, just a half-second burst, but I was oriented straight up and down and smacked my helmet into the overhead hard enough to send my ears ringing. That pain was preferable to the pain I avoided with the maneuver, because a stream of tungsten penetrators sliced through the wall where I'd been an eyeblink before. He was walking the rounds upward, not letting off the trigger, so I fired even though stars were still floating across my vision, hoping I was close enough that I couldn't miss.

I was, but only just. The plasma lance came centimeters from missing entirely, but it was just close enough to slice through the side of the suit's neck. If I'd been firing a slug-shooter and he'd been in normal armor, the shot wouldn't have even been fatal, just a graze across his neck. But the plasma was as hot as the inside of a star and there was no such thing as just a graze. The armor stiffened and the coil-gun ceased fire and I turned my attention to the other active enemy.

Vicky had taken care of him, though, a charred hole burned through his chest. The other two, the ones I'd slammed into each other, were still floating, unmoving. On thermal, the one who had hit the wall, then been slammed into it again and into his compatriot, was cold, the isotope reactor shut down, probably from damage to the interior shielding. He was no danger anymore, and he'd probably be dead soon if he wasn't already. The other suit of armor was still active and still a danger, and I was about to grab him and play pinata again when a scintillating spear of plasma took him in the side. The armor jerked and then was still again.

"Is that all of them?" Fargo asked.

She was anchored to the deck, her plasma gun still glowing red, Ruthie hanging off her back like a remora.

"Yeah, I think...."

"Cam."

The note in Vicky's voice snapped my eyes around. Vicky was anchored to the deck, stalwart and upright, but the damage was obvious. Red globules of blood were freezing solid even as I watched, dancing away from her, but no new ones were joining them. The slug had taken her high in the right side, slicing a divot through her armor, and, I guessed, through the skin beneath it. Not a bad wound, certainly survivable...except for the whole part about there being no air.

"Is your suit sealing?" I asked her, knowing she wouldn't sound this concerned just over a near miss.

"It tried. But there's still a slow air leak. I've got maybe ten minutes before the tanks are drained and if there's no air, there's nothing to reprocess."

I turned on Fargo, staring past her at the opaque visor of the spacesuit.

"Get us to that fucking control room, Ruthie."

———

The operations center was sealed tighter than a drum. I couldn't tell how thick the metal door was that had slid into place across the hatchway, but I was pretty damn sure I couldn't shoot my way through it. I checked the stopwatch I'd set at the corner of my HUD readout. We had eight minutes.

"Ruthie, get that door open."

She didn't bother to respond, unclipping herself from Fargo's back and kicking across the hallway to the security plate beside the hatch. It was pretty standard, not enhanced by Zan-Thint's people because why should they? It wasn't as if anyone else would be coming in here. Their biggest worry had probably been the thought of an inspector from the shipyards getting nosy and stopping by to ask questions. It certainly wasn't built to deal with state-of-the-art software penetration and the cracking module took less than ten seconds to work its magic.

I was at the door when it opened, charging through without a thought in the world in my head except getting Vicky inside. I barely noticed the air rushing out of the room, didn't register until later the realization that the compartment hadn't been in a vacuum until we opened the hatch. But I did notice the Tahni in the pressure suit working frantically at a computer console, saw the Tahni writing floating across the screen in front of him. And I knew deep in my gut that whatever he was trying to do would be bad for us.

I didn't want to risk firing my plasma gun inside the compartment, fearing I'd wind up frying the controls I'd shortly need, so I jetted right at him. I must, I realized later, have looked like something from a nightmare to the Tahni, a hulking monster in mottled camouflage, a green golem lurching toward him in utter silence. He lunged forward, trying to reach one final control, enter one final command, but the metallic talon that was the Vigilante's left hand closed over his wrist and squeezed.

I couldn't hear his scream, but I could see it in the spastic jerk of his body. I hadn't ripped his suit, but his wrist was bent at what was an unnatural angle whether it was a human or a Tahni. I had to give him credit. He didn't give up even with his arm shattered, even confronted with a faceless monster. He tried to pull his sidearm out of its chest holster. The other arm broke just as ugly as the first had, and then I tossed him back at Fargo.

"Get him in restraints."

I didn't have to tell Ruthie to get to work because she was

already moving past me, the cracking module held in front of her like a magical totem that would solve all our problems. Vicky didn't take one extra step, didn't say one unnecessary word, and I felt a swell of pride in her. She was maximizing the air she had left, fighting for a few extra seconds, a minute.

We had six minutes left.

"This'll take a second," Ruthie said, as if reading my mind. "I have to translate with my 'link while the module does its job."

I wanted to snap at her, to tell her we didn't have time to wait, but I knew how useless that would be. Some people could perform well under stress, but very few performed better that way. I said nothing, just let her and the module do their work.

"How's the wound?" I asked Vicky, trying to distract her and myself.

"Hurts," she admitted. "It's not bad, though. I stopped the suit from giving me a painkiller 'cause I figured I'd need my shit together for this."

I wished I could hold her. Not just in general, but right now. She would probably deny needing it, but I did.

"This guy's in shock, I think," Fargo commented.

She was attached to the deck by her magnetic soles, her articulated hand grasping the captive by the back of his space suit, his arms and shoulders wrapped in an adhesive restraint web. They weren't standard equipment on Marine battlesuits, but the CSF had included them in case we ran into any prisoners worth taking. Far-sighted of them, I thought.

"Well, he's probably better off that way," I allowed. "It can't be too pleasant with two broken arms."

"I broke both my arms once," Fargo said, reminiscence in her tone, as if the whole thing was a fond recollection. "It was the first time I rode a horse back home on Hermes. My great-grandfather owns a ranch there and he used to have my whole family, grandparents, parents, us, everyone, all over there to go riding, shooting, fishing…it was awesome. Except that one time when the horse threw me. I tried to stop myself with my hands and broke the radius and ulna in both arms. I spent a week in regen casts."

I pressed my lips together, pinning down the sharp retort that threatened to explode out on its own. She was scared. *I* was scared. Yelling at her wouldn't make either of us less scared.

"Do you ever get back there?" I asked, instead. I wasn't watching her, though, and honestly, wasn't paying much attention to her answer. I was scanning up and down the back wall of the operations center, away from the banks of displays and data terminals, searching for the door to the storm cellar, the radiation shelter Ruthie had told us about. I didn't want to ask her where it was because I didn't want to distract her.

Four minutes.

"No," she told me. "Mom and Dad didn't think I should sign up. We had a big blow-up, and I haven't talked to them since."

"That's sad," I told her. "I'd give anything to be able to talk to my parents again."

There. There was a door. It was difficult to make out even with the enhanced vision of the suit, a seam so tight and slim it could have been mistaken for part of the structure of the wall, but there was the slightest thermal leak from inside. No control panel, no lock, no security plate, so I had to assume it could only be opened from the inside.

"If you get the chance," Vicky said, her voice quiet, contemplative, "you should send a message to your parents. I sent a message to my mother every single week during the war, and once a month since. She misses me."

The air went out of me at the hopelessness behind her words. She'd accepted she was going to die. I wanted to argue with her, wanted to yell at her, but I just didn't have the energy. And I didn't want it to be the last thing she heard me say.

"I love you," I said.

"Love you, too."

One minute.

"Ruthie," I finally ground out, "please tell me...."

"Got it!" Ruthie yelled, loud and sudden enough that I nearly jumped. "I got it!"

The door slid shut like a guillotine chopping down and the faint whine of fans cut through the silence as air rushed into the compartment. I pulled up the external atmospheric monitors and watched the percentages climb, infuriatingly slow.

"Now!" I told Vicky, but she didn't need me to tell her. She was already breaking the seals on her chest plastron, the armor plate pulling outward.

She gasped for breath and so did I. Her face was pale and drawn, drenched with sweat, and blood spotted her neck and cheek where a floating globule had made its way up from her wound, but she was alive and that was enough.

"Thanks, Ruthie," I told her, hoping it sounded as heartfelt as it was intended. "Get on that location for us. And see if you can pull up the exterior cameras so we can get a look at what's happening with Dunstan. Fargo, watch that wall over there." I pointed at the spot where I'd noticed the seam of the hatchway. "That's the emergency shelter and I don't want anyone jumping out and trying to surprise us. If that door starts to open, fire your plasma gun through it without asking any questions."

"Will do. What about him, though?" She shook the captive Tahni demonstratively, sending his head bobbling back and forth inside his helmet.

"I don't think he's going to cause you any trouble," I told her, "unless he can pull a trigger with his toes."

I yanked my interface cables, popped my chest plastron and slithered out of the suit, hurrying to Vicky's side. She was hanging half out of her suit, just taking deep breaths, hand pressed to her side,

"Are you okay?" It was inane, vapid, but I was too emotionally wiped to come up with anything more intelligent.

"It hurts," she confessed. Her fatigue top was ripped and stained with blood, but the wound itself was covered by a smart bandage, applied by the suit. The nanites suspended in its biotic gel would be busy repairing the damage, but they couldn't do anything about the blood loss. "I'll live. But the suit ain't going anywhere...which means we're screwed."

I didn't argue. We either had to find her a space suit or she'd be stuck in the sealed operations center behind the airtight door.

"What about *that* suit?" I asked, nodding toward our captive.

She rolled her eyes, aggravation at me overwhelming her pain.

"Besides the fact that I'd be swimming inside that thing, look at the way the shoulders and neck joint meet. I don't know that I could even seal the helmet right. Not to mention the labels are all in Tahni and I'd be just as likely to kill myself." I opened my mouth to protest, but she held up a hand. "If it's that or die, I'll try it. But for now, let's see what happens."

"External cameras are up," Ruthie announced.

I knew I should get back into my suit, but I wanted to breathe air that, if still canned, was a bit less confined, so I left it off for the moment and moved over to the position at the control panel Ruthie occupied. They didn't have chairs, since there was no gravity to make them a requirement for comfort, but each position did have an open frame with a net you could fasten around to hold yourself in place. Ruthie wasn't using it, having anchored on with her boot magnets, so I grabbed onto it while I looked over her shoulder.

The screens were crude and tiny compared to what I was

used to, nothing at all compared to the displays on a starship, and I had to lean in close to get a sense of what was going on.

"There he is," she said, tapping the hard, flat-screen display.

The construction shack had no long-range sensors, so everything we were seeing was thermal, infrared and visible light, and not well-rendered by a tactical computer but just slapped together with all the technical expertise of a child playing with his first graphics pad. Still, there was no mistaking the gleaming silver delta of Intercept One, lit up with the glow of its own, miniature sun, the fusion drive boosting hard. The reason for the boost was also unmistakable, four smaller drive flares, the aerospacecraft sharpened daggers against the rounded, bulbous lines of the cutter.

Assault shuttles, real ones and not converted commercial craft, built by Zan-Thint or bought on the black market. They weren't pre-war Tahni because the Tahni didn't use this design, which spoke to the general's willingness to adapt.

I scowled. The last thing we needed was a mentally flexible Tahni commander.

I couldn't see the incoming fire from the shuttles, but whether it existed or not, Dunstan was piloting the cutter on an avoidance course like he believed in it.

"He's in a bad spot," Ruthie said grimly. "He can't turn and fight. This close to their own construction, they're probably using lasers instead of coil-guns, but if he loses thrust even for a few seconds, they'll fry him."

"Do you have that location yet?" I asked her, hoping she wasn't letting the dogfight distract her.

"No, and I don't think I'm going to be able to find it."

I glared at her, not at all liking the answer. She shrugged, the motion exaggerated to make its way through the filter of the spacesuit.

"Our friend here...." She motioned at the Tahni captive. He

was conscious again, but seemed to be trying not to move, either out of fear or agony. "...was in the middle of trying to wipe the system when we came in. He didn't get the chance to run the final delete function, but he *did* sweep everything into the cleaner subroutine, which means the file structures are fucked. Even if I didn't have to translate everything from Tahni to English, it could take months to sort through it all and find what we need." She paused, and I thought she smiled, though it was hard to see through her visor. "I do have an idea, though. I can use this thing...." She gestured at the cracking module, plugged into a dataspike port in the side of the control console. "...to just download their whole database. If we can get it to Hachette and his people, they can figure it out." She motioned at the prisoner. "We'll bring him along, too, if we can."

"Do it," I told her, my eyes on Intercept One. She banked away with a boost from her belly jets, and the shuttles maneuvered to match the course. "And hurry. I don't know how much longer Dunstan has out there."

She went to work and I cast a worried glance at Vicky. I didn't, I confessed to myself what I hadn't told Ruthie, have any idea how we were getting out of here. Or if.

[25]

"What's happening out there?"

I nearly started, so wrapped up in the scene playing out in the display that I hadn't noticed Vicky coming up behind me. She was pale, pain cutting lines into the corner of her eyes and mouth, but she still seemed sharp and alert.

"Harder to see it now," I explained, tracing a line across the screen for her. "That's Dunstan's course, and he has four assault shuttles trying to pin him down."

I blinked at the sudden rainbow ring of light from the corner of the field of view of the external cameras.

"What the hell?" I blurted. "Did he just Transition?"

"Smart." Ruthie commented, not looking up from her effort to download the database. "They were closing in on him. He's going to micro-Transition out a few AU, then hop back in."

"You hope," Vicky added, eyeing the camera view with obvious skepticism.

Ruthie shook her head.

"Dunstan's a lot of things, but he's no coward. He won't leave us here."

"They seem to think he will," I pointed out.

The assault shuttles had all performed a turnover and were burning off their momentum away from the web, heading back toward the construction shack.

"And if the crew inside the shelter has comms, the shuttles know we're inside," Vicky pointed out. "Their people are all buttoned up, so they can just burn right through and take us out."

"Dunstan's coming back." Ruthie sounded so confident, I spared her a sidelong look. She'd never been the pilot's biggest fan, and I wondered if this newfound faith was more wishful thinking.

Wishful thinking or not, she was right. Intercept One flashed back into existence on the opposite side of the construction web, her previous momentum vanished into another dimension, her nose and the proton cannon within it lined up with the lead shuttle in the formation. The blast of protons was a white glow in the thermal camera, a giant flashlight, but when it struck the shuttle, the results were a bit more spectacular. The bird was sliced straight down the middle lengthwise, the fusion reactor venting plasma out as the shielding fragmented, consuming the rear of the aerospacecraft in sunfire.

The Gatling laser in Intercept One's wing was a tiny spark by comparison, even on thermal and infrared, the fist-sized pockmarks it made in the armor over the next shuttle's wing unimpressive, but it was enough to make the enemy ship bank away from Dunstan's firing arc. Dunstan had pushed his luck and a thermal bloom on his starboard wing gave the evidence, as a Tahni laser struck home. He broke off, goosing his course change with the ship's belly jets and I nodded appreciation.

For all his faults, Dunstan was one hell of a pilot.

"He's got them," Ruthie said, providing a running commentary. "They can't jump out, but he can. They'll overcommit themselves, get too much boost going and he can just bleed off his with another micro-Transition."

"Thank God for small favors," I sighed. "Now, maybe we can figure out a way to get a spacesuit from Intercept One to this chamber for Vicky and...."

"Oh, shit. What's that?"

I didn't have to ask her what she meant. The white wedge shape shone like a waning moon in the light from its drive flame, dwarfing Dunstan's cutter. I knew what it was and where it had come from. We'd destroyed one just like it a few minutes ago, run the *Yantar* right into it, thinking it was the only operational Tahni corvette in the shipyard.

Didn't I feel like an idiot.

"Get the fuck out of there, Dunstan!" Ruthie blurted.

As if he'd heard her, Intercept One spun on its axis lengthwise and burned upward—well, upward as compared to our orientation. I suppose the correct astrogational term was *north of the ecliptic*, but the thing that it had going for it was that it was away from the corvette's firing arc.

He Transitioned, the burst of polychromatic light reaching out, splashing against the nose of the closest assault shuttle. I'd never seen a jump that close, and I had the irrational hope that it might act as a sort of weapon, a laser formed by the jump into the neighboring reality, but it was just incoherent light waves and the shuttle sailed right through it. Heading for us.

"How long till the download is complete?" I asked Ruthie, staring at the suddenly overwhelming line of enemy ships arrayed against us.

She checked her 'link, and I had to assume she'd synched it to the cracking module.

"We're about halfway there. Maybe another four or five minutes."

Vicky was already clambering back into her suit and I frowned as her chest plastron sealed.

"What are you doing?" I demanded.

"They're going to come in here," she told me as if it was the most obvious thing in the world.

"And they're going to let the air out when they do," I pointed out, squeezing into my own armor. "You're going to have about five minutes on your internal air before it leaks out and you're dead. You need to get into that Tahni suit, and we'll figure out how to seal it up."

"What good is it going to do if we're dead, anyway?" She was infuriatingly calm and infuriatingly right as well. "We'll hold them off as long as we can, give Dunstan a chance. The priority is to get the data to Colonel Hachette."

"Is that our priority?" I demanded, closed in the armor now, transmitting on our private net. "Because it's not *my* priority! My priority is to get you out of here alive!"

"Cam, you knew it might come to this." She wasn't angry. I think that's what I found the most maddening. She didn't seem angry either at me or her circumstances, didn't seem desperate. But I was. I was furious and desperate. "When we were in the Corps, we both knew either or both of us could buy it on any operation. Well, we both decided to join back up."

"It wasn't supposed to be you!" I exploded, the words escaping before I could bite down on them.

Silence. I wanted to pretend I hadn't said it, but she wasn't going to let me get away with that.

"So, that's what all this has been about."

"No, I...." I couldn't finish the sentence. I couldn't lie to her. "I didn't know."

And I was telling the truth. I hadn't been lying to her, I'd been lying to myself. This wasn't about duty, wasn't about wanting to feel like I belonged, like I had a purpose. Those had all been excuses. This was about Lt. Ackley, Scotty, the Skipper, Delp. This was about all the friends and mentors and people who'd depended on me who hadn't made it back, who'd died while I lived. What right did I have to go on living? To sit on my ass on the porch of our farm and pump out kids and walk through the town with my thumbs tucked in my overalls and pretend that this was all normal?

It was gutting, the realization. I'd never been one to do much soul-searching before. There hadn't been much call for it living on the streets. But I thought I'd moved past the point of bottling everything inside and pretending it didn't exist.

"How long have you been feeling this way?" She was gentle, not judging, as if I was the victim here, as if it wasn't likely she'd be dead in another half an hour.

"I've known something was wrong since we left Brigantia. I thought it was just doubt, wondering if we'd made the right choice not settling down on the land Dak had offered us there. Then, I thought it was the fact we were so isolated, stuck out on the other side of Tahni space." The words tumbled out, nothing to stop them since it was just us. I idly wondered what Fargo would think if she could hear me. "But I guess it's always been this way. Probably since Delp."

His face was still part of my nightmares, although I didn't remember having them as much since this whole thing had started. Since I'd stepped into a situation where I was likely to get myself killed.

"Give me your suit." I broke open my chest plastron, the air cold compared to the stale warmth inside. "You can take mine."

"No."

"Goddammit!" I slammed my fist against the side of the Vigilante and would have gone flying if I hadn't been partially wedged inside the suit. "Why not? I'm the one who's ready to die! You don't deserve this!"

Ruthie turned, her eyes wide, and warmth filled my face as I realized I'd said it out loud.

"Cameron Alvarez," Vicky snapped, using my full name like she only did when I'd said something stupid, "you want to die because you feel guilty for having survived. What do you think I'm going to feel if I switch suits and let you die in my place? Are you that fucking selfish?"

"Guys, those shuttles are decelerating," Ruthie warned. "Maybe we should save the personal drama for later and get ready to repel boarders."

Something was squeezing my chest, making it hard to breathe, but I forced myself to think. I had to get Vicky somewhere with air, somewhere those Tahni couldn't get to her...

"Ruthie, can you get that fucking storm cellar open?"

"I can try." She began tapping instructions into her 'link, but my gaze was fixed on the screen, on the shuttles braking as they came nearer and nearer to the shack's ruined airlock, at the massive corvette hanging in space like a whale watching a school of smaller fish feeding.

Come back, Dunstan. Come on, man, we need you.

It was half a wish, half a prayer, but I had no expectations it would happen. Dunstan wasn't in the service anymore, had no reason to rush back into what was likely certain death by taking on that corvette. If he was smart, he'd have taken off already, looking for a black-market shop where he could sell off the cutter for parts and buy himself a ticket somewhere the CSF wouldn't look for him.

I guess he wasn't that smart.

Intercept One jumped back out of T-space only a hundred klicks behind the corvette, practically spitting distance in open space, a ballsy, reckless move. The slightest miscalculation and he could have opened the exit wormhole right into the structure of the construction shack, which would have killed all of us and him, too. He'd timed it just right, though, and there was no way the corvette could maneuver out of his firing arc before he got off a shot with the proton cannon.

A white sphere erupted from the corvette's flank, large enough that I thought the blast had to have ignited one of her maneuvering thruster fuel tanks, powerful enough to send the spacecraft lurching to the side from the expulsion of burning gas. Tiny eruptions across the belly of the giant craft marked hits from Intercept One's wing-mounted turret, though God alone knew if the laser bursts were penetrating the ship's armor deeply enough to do any real damage.

The corvette's port thrusters burned bright as she turned, trying to bring her main guns to bear on Dunstan, but our pilot was too smart for that. He Transitioned again and the corvette never got a shot off. The Tahni ship's main drive ignited for just a moment, enough to push her out from the shack and give it some breathing room, but she didn't jump, didn't try to guess where Dunstan had gone and follow him out there.

"Her Transition drive isn't installed yet," I murmured. She couldn't chase after him.

It was good and bad. Good in that Dunstan could keep hitting and running, bad in that it would encourage the Tahni to stay right here and guard those damned assault shuttles. And they were almost here.

"Ruthie," I snapped, the patience I'd had earlier totally abandoning me. "The shelter."

"Yeah, I got it," she said.

The hiss of the seal releasing was loud and abrupt, a warning that sent me inside the confines of my suit, closing the chest plastron behind me. My fingers trembled as I plugged in the interface jacks. I was scared shitless, but not at the thought of what I'd find behind those doors, not at the thought of more troops coming in from the assault shuttles, and not even at the thought of Vicky's air running out if the Tahni got through the vacuum seal.

I was scared shitless of what I'd told her, of what I'd been forced to admit to myself.

That's not me. I can deal. I'm not a burnout.

But it *was* me, and I *couldn't* deal.

The storm-cellar door ground open with a painful squealing I could hear even through my sealed suit, one centimeter at a time.

"You still want me to fire through the door?" Fargo asked, her plasma gun pointed at the widening gap. She'd shoved the injured Tahni aside and he was floating head over heels, destined to bounce off the far wall if no one interrupted his flight.

"Wait," I instructed her. "Let's see what they do."

What they did was shoot at us. The first Tahni through the door was outfitted with a vacuum suit identical to the prisoner's, and a handgun to go with it. The rounds ricocheted off of Fargo's helmet, ringing like a gong, and I would have sat there and watched him waste his ammo if I hadn't had to worry about Ruthie catching a round.

"Grenade launcher," I told her.

"Yes, sir."

The weapon unfolded from her left shoulder and she fired less than two seconds after I'd given my order. The round ignited inside the chamber, its blast partially contained by the door, which had only opened a half a meter. The interior was dimly lit, but the eruption of the plasma grenade flashed like a floodlight, sending shadows pouring out of Tahni workers and technicians caught in alarmed poses, their arms raised against an attack they couldn't stop. The one with the handgun took the brunt of the blast, a spear of ionized gas burning a hole in his chest. He was locked to the floor and I could only tell he'd been hit when the pistol floated out of his limp fingers.

"If you want to live," I yelled through the suit speakers, "come out with your hands in the air, fingers interlaced. You have five seconds." I didn't have time to translate the words into Tahni, and I hoped for their sake they'd bothered to learn English. "Four. Three. Two...."

"We're coming out. Don't shoot."

The accent was ungodly, like no inflection I'd heard from even the remotest colony world, the product of a set of vocal cords barely able to speak English at all. There were six Tahni left alive inside the shelter and they shuffled forward, hands raising, and I thought we might get out of this without any more bloodshed. I should have known better. These weren't just Tahni, they were the biggest fanatics in the Tahni military, people who'd refused to surrender after their Emperor had been killed and their government toppled. All it took was one and there was always one.

He'd been near the back of the group and he surged forward, magnetic boots click-clacking against the floor as he swung the weapon up to his shoulder. It wasn't a rifle, wasn't a plasma projector, but it was big, its muzzle yawning and dark and I had a sense that he wouldn't have tried to shoot at our armor with it unless he thought it would kill us. And I couldn't fire because she was in the way.

"Fargo!" I yelled. "Gun!"

She fired a fraction of a second before the Tahni, but she was shooting a grenade launcher, aimed not directly at the Tahni but over their heads to get an area-effect blast. That gave the Tahni the time to pull the trigger on his weapon, and we all discovered very quickly what he was shooting. I'd never seen one in combat, mostly because the Tahni mounted their heavy weapons on their powered exoskeletons and this thing was probably one war obsolete by the time I'd joined the Marines. It was a single-shot coil-gun, but the round it fired wasn't just a solid tungsten penetrator. Instead, it worked akin to our grenades, accelerating a disintegrating sabot that contained a load of powdered metallic hydrogen, then detonated it with an explosive charge.

The shockwave it produced was enough to knock the lights off in the compartment, but between the burning metal plasma from the weapon and Fargo's grenades, there was plenty of illumination. The HUD in my helmet flickered for a second, but then settled down and the aftermath of the twin discharges became plain.

Fargo had hit with her shots, the grenades dismembering the shooter and slicing apart the other Tahni as well as collateral damage, and I wouldn't cry for them. But the Tahni had missed Fargo.

He'd hit Ruthie.

I didn't realize it at first. I hadn't seen the actual detonation, just the instant before and after, like one of those concentration tests they used to give us in school. *What's different between the first picture and the second?* Sparks and smoke, for one thing. The control panel was blackened and broken, and I thought for a moment that the bits of debris floating across my vision were just metal and plastic from the console. Until the orbiting stream of red globules came into focus, along with the deep blue fabric that was the exact same color as the space suit Ruthie had been wearing.

Chunks of her were swirling up toward the air vents, and when I looked up, my gaze drawn in horrified disbelief, I saw her helmet tumbling with it, and I just knew her head was still inside.

"Fuck!" The word expelled itself from my throat like the vomit that wanted to follow it, and I barely kept that from clawing its way up.

"Oh, Jesus God," Vicky moaned.

Fargo said nothing, frozen in place. I couldn't see her face, couldn't tell whether she was stunned into silence or just unmoved because she hadn't known Ruthie as well as we did. I looked away from the carnage of Ruthie's remains, toward the screen. It was still intact, miraculously, though there were spider-web cracks across it. And a rainbow ring.

Dunstan was back. He jumped through dangerously close to the corvette, maybe twenty klicks away, almost touching her, and fired his proton cannon at point blank range through the stern of the ship, just fore of its drive bell. Plasma spewed from the gaping wound in her hull, a feed line to the main drive cut and bleeding like an artery. She was bleeding to death, but she wasn't dead yet. Maneuvering thrusters flared and she spun on her axis, just enough for main gun to almost line up with Intercept One.

Dunstan tried. His drive erupted in fusion fire and he tried to run, tried to get out of the Tahni's firing arc, but the corvette fired before she was completely lined up. The length of the laser beam wasn't visible, but the thermal cameras picked up the bloom from the emitter...and the larger bloom where it struck the drive compartment of Intercept One.

She wasn't destroyed, didn't explode. She might have if the shot had pierced her fuel stores, but instead, the beam had cut through the reactor shielding and plasma dumped out of it, ejected in a failsafe measure. Dunstan didn't give up, even with his reactor and main drive down, maybe because he knew the Tahni wouldn't either. He still had the Gatling laser turret, and he poured fire from it into the gap in the corvette's hull, the wound he'd given her on his last pass.

Heat and light gushed out from the rent in her hull, a brief flash of flame as escaping atmosphere caught fire just for a half-second before the vacuum dispersed it. I cursed, knowing that losing their atmosphere wouldn't do anything. They'd be in suits and the loss of air would be a mild inconvenience if....

The thought hadn't had time to bounce from one side of my head to the other before the laser bursts finally found something vital. I wasn't sure what it was, maybe the metallic hydrogen fuel stores, maybe missile launch tubes, but something ignited, a hemisphere of white fire that expanded to swallow up the whole ship.

Dunstan's Gatling laser fell silent, and I figured it had to be out of ammunition. He was defanged, his drive inactive, only his maneuvering thrusters to keep him from simply floating off into nothingness.

And there were still those two assault shuttles docking with the construction shack. I took a stiff-legged step toward the storm cellar, intent on getting us inside and sealing it up, but something caught my eye, a small, oblong shape tumbling through the space where Ruthie had been. It was her 'link. It had been in her hand when she'd been hit, and it seemed intact. I grabbed it, careful not to press too hard with the powerful talons on my gripping hand and cracked the chest plastron long enough to dump it inside with me.

"They're coming in," Fargo said. "We should get ready to fight."

"I'd rather seal ourselves inside the shelter," I told her, walking past her position, past the wavering statues that were the corpses of the Tahni crew.

The inside of the shelter was reminiscent of a squad bay back in the Corps, except set up for microgravity, with net hammocks rather than cots, lockers set into the walls probably containing food and water. The controls for the door were set in the wall just inside the door. Or at least, I assumed that was what they'd once been. The grenade blast had blown it to scrap.

The Tahni were coming, and we couldn't seal the door.

[26]

I was frozen.

It had never happened before. Inside a suit was where I was at home. War was my formative experience; combat was where I'd come of age. I'd seen death on a scale most people couldn't even imagine and never once faltered. I had fucked up my personal life over and over, but never once fucked up in combat.

But the enemy was coming, and I couldn't think, couldn't come up with any sort of plan of attack, because I couldn't pry my mind away from trying to figure out how to keep Vicky alive. I had nothing. Nothing but the Tahni spacesuit, and she'd already rejected the idea.

"What do we do, sir?" Fargo asked me again, and her question kicked my brain out of the feedback loop it had fallen into.

"The storm cellar," I said. "We can't close the door, but it's a good firing position. Vicky, check the lockers in there. There might be some sort of patch kit for space suits. You could use it to seal the leak."

"I'll look," she said, but didn't sound too convinced.

One thing at a time.

The Tahni with the broken arms was still alive, though his

291

suit had taken some charring in the shot from the anti-armor weapon. I pushed him ahead of us into the shelter and he bounced off one of the walls, spinning and tumbling. His mouth was open inside his faceplate, though I couldn't hear what he was saying. I assumed it was some vile Tahni curse. I don't know why I bothered with him, why I'd bothered to retrieve Ruthie's 'link. Even if we didn't all die in the next few minutes when the Tahni troops reached this compartment, our ship was toast, and we had no way off this shack.

"Did Ruthie have a family?" Fargo asked. I turned and stared at her, as if I could see her face through the bare metal of her suit's helmet. "It's just that...well, she didn't talk to any of us much. I mean, the squad, before Portent. And after, I didn't get the idea she trusted me. I didn't know her that well."

"She did," Vicky answered for me, which was a good thing, because I'd never thought to ask. "Her mother and sister live back on Earth, in Nuevo Rio. I guess Colonel Hachette will notify them."

And who's going to notify your family?

I didn't say it. It wouldn't be me. I wouldn't survive her, and I think she knew it. I wouldn't want to....

Shit. I was doing it again, thinking of myself. It had made perfect sense when I was growing up, because if I hadn't thought of myself, no one was going to. I'd thought I'd grown past it in the Corps, when I'd been forced to think of the mission and my troops first, had allowed other people to get close to me, but that had all been in the context of the military.

"What do you think they're doing out there?" Fargo asked.

"I never got inside a Tahni's head enough to guess what they were going to do," I admitted. "But I figure they're either refilling the station with air to make retaking it easier, or they're already on their way to the blast shield and they'll try to crack the security seal."

"They'll want the shack, right?" She sounded as if she was trying to talk herself into it. "I mean, they still want to use it. So, they might repressurize it. Before they come in."

"They might," Vicky agreed, the way a mother would agree with her child's foolish meanderings just to get them to shut up. She was pulling open the storage lockers inside the shelter, as best she could using the suit's articulated hand. Zero-grav meal packets floated out before she could close the door again and she left it open, letting them all drift out into the air around us.

I wanted to go help her, but there was no room for two of us abreast in the suits, barely room for all three of us to fit single file in the shelter. I stayed by the open door, leaning around the side, lining up my plasma gun experimentally.

"Wish we could get more than one solid, covered firing position out of this doorway," I grumbled.

Fargo laughed and before I could ask her what was so funny, she marched her Vigilante straight up the side of the interior wall using her magnetic boots until she was directly over me, boots anchored to the ceiling, her weapon trained at the entrance to the operations room.

"Not used to fighting in microgravity, sir?" she teased.

"Out of practice," I admitted. It was hard to go back to thinking three-dimensionally, and it gave me a new appreciation for the ability of pilots like Dunstan.

"I think I found something," Vicky said, drawing my attention back inside the shelter.

She'd pulled open every locker in the back wall and food packets, squeeze bulbs of water and spare clothing was scattered around like some sort of anti-laser defense shield. She stood at the center of the storm of debris, her suit's hand wrapped around what looked like an oversized handgun, an orange, plastic cylinder inserted in the back of it.

"I think this is some sort of leak-sealer for the hull," she told me. "The only writing on it is in Tahni, but it *looks* a lot like the ones I saw the Fleet maintenance crews carrying."

I didn't argue about the item's provenance, just un-assed my suit and grabbed it from her. The crack in the armor over her side was splintered and irregular and I wasn't sure where to start so I worked my way in from the edges. The gun had a thumb trigger, awkward and built for Tahni hands, but I managed to depress it and was rewarded with a thin spray of grey foam. It solidified as it touched the metal, filling the gaps with something that at least *looked* helpful, whether it was or not, and I skewed it back and forth along the wound in the metal, holding myself in place by grabbing onto the hand of her suit. It was cold metal, yet I found some comfort in it, a certain solidity.

By the time the tube went empty, a section of her suit the size of a dinner plate was completely covered by the stuff, hardening before my eyes. It was lumpy and uneven, but I hadn't the time to try for neatness.

"Is there another tube in there?" I asked, trying to figure out which locker it had come from.

"Cam! Vicky! The door's opening!"

I would have known that without being told in another second, because the air began to rush out of the operations center, a hurricane blasting the floating debris and food packets out through the entrance to the shelter. I dropped the sealant gun and threw myself at my Vigilante, worming back through the chest plastron and plugging in before I closed up again.

By the time my helmet HUD flickered to life, the door had edged open another few centimeters and debris was still swirling along with the escaping air, heading out through the gap.

"Missiles," I barked. "Arming distance fifteen meters." Which would make the detonation just outside the door.

I launched first, with Fargo right on my heels and Vicky a

second behind us. The three weapons barely squeezed through the slowly broadening gap where the door was opening. If there'd been a vacuum on both sides, it would have slid aside in one, smooth motion, but the atmospheric pressure on the inside of the door was grinding the metal door against the track, the friction taxing the motors.

There wasn't much air left when the warheads detonated, just enough for what should have been a massive concussion to be reduced to a kettle drum cacophony on the other side of the door. The flash of sun-bright light from the plasma threw long, humanoid shadows through the doorway, lingering long enough for one of them to jerk and yaw sideways, and then the rest of them made a break for the door.

Tungsten slugs ripped out of the doorway ahead of them, one of them smacking into the overhead and sending insulation billowing outward, and Fargo and I returned fire, pouring gouts of plasma back through the doorway. It was nearly wide open, but there was still enough of the door sticking out from the edge to block part of the rain of ionized gas, splashing it into a fireworks spray. Another of the High Guard battlesuits skewed off to the side, propelled by a jet of vaporized metal, converted to gas by the lance of plasma from one of us, though I couldn't tell which.

These were veterans, troopers who'd fought humans before, and they must have known exactly how long it took one of our plasma guns to recharge, because they jetted in immediately, trying to get to us between shots. Vicky had waited, though, because we were vets too, and knew about that recharge gap. The first trooper through barreled headlong into her shot, careening out of control into the wall, a blackened gouge through the center of his helmet, but then the others were inside and firing.

"Get back!" I yelled at the others, and then ignored my own advice and jetted straight into the middle of them.

I don't know what I was thinking, or if I was. A red haze had fallen across my vision and if I had any sort of strategy at all, it was to get inside their firing arc, get in the midst of them before they could hit any of us. I was too late. The only reason I didn't catch a burst of tungsten slugs in the chest was my plasma gun. I'd stuck it out in front of me on instinct, on the chance the capacitors would recharge before they had time to kill me and I'd get off another shot. But the gun was never going to take another shot because it took the rounds meant for me and blew apart in a shower of sparks, what charge had been stored in the capacitors ripping the electromagnetic coils apart and showering me with a rain of fragments.

Damage indicators flashed yellow, but nothing penetrated because the air inside my suit stayed inside and then I was surrounded by the enemy...and had them right where I wanted them. There was a weak point in the construction of Tahni High Guard armor, one that was taught to us in Armor School and yet one that was nearly useless because it was tucked away in a spot that was almost impossible to target. The power cable from their blister reactor ran through a groove between the pack and the suit's neck, feeding into a joint in the shoulder, just barely ten centimeters exposed if their shoulders moved the wrong way.

I grabbed at the shoulder of the suit closest to me, one whose back was turned, facing the storm cellar and Vicky and Fargo, and dug my metal claws into that niche in between his shoulder and neck. There was no tactile feedback, so I wasn't sure if I'd snagged the cable until I saw the sparks, felt the tug against the forward momentum of the suit. Severing the cable didn't incapacitate the Tahni suit, but it did cut the power to his coil-gun, and that would do for now.

A yank on the cable pulled him toward me, then a two-footed kick to his helmet sent him tumbling one way and me heading the other, into the two troopers behind him. My shoulder smashed into the chest of one of them, taking us both back to the opposite wall. I'd been counting on them holding their fire, on the remaining three Tahni being too worried about shooting each other to try shooting at me, but I had, once again, overestimated the concern the average Tahni soldier had for his brothers in arms. The slug from the coil-gun nicked my shoulder on the way into the chest of the High Guard trooper, and I hit my jets.

Didn't you want to die?

It was a whisper in my ear, a devil on my shoulder, and it had a point. If I wanted to die so badly, if I wanted the guilt to go away no matter what the cost, then why was I fighting so hard to survive?

For her, you moron. For Vicky.

And there was the angel, though he sounded a bit snarky for an angel, reminding me of what was really important, pointing out the paradox my life had become. I threw myself into one suicidally dangerous situation after another because I didn't believe I deserved to survive the war, but I'd dragged Vicky along with me, and I couldn't leave her alone.

And I couldn't lose this fucking fight.

The blast on the jets took me straight into the Blue Falcon who'd shot his buddy, and I pushed his coil-gun away from his suit's body as we both crashed into what was left of the control console and then over it into the main screen. Plastic shattered and lights flickered in polychromatic confusion all around us before the screen went dark, but the lack of an external view was the least of my worries. I anchored a foot against the wall and used the leverage to strike an overhand blow with the shattered remains of my plasma gun, smashing the nearly indestructible iridium receiver against the mount for his coil-gun.

The weapon came away in my suit's relentless grip, the power cable separating with a flare of severed electrical leads. The gun was useless as anything but a club, so that was exactly how I used it. The Tahni tried to raise his suit's arm to block the blow, but the arm had been exactly what I was aiming at. The shoulder was protected by a heavy pauldron, but the elbow...not so much. The metal there had to be thinner out of necessity, if they wanted the arm to move, and it cracked under the impact from the cooling jacket of the coil-gun, the joint frozen...and air hissing out from the break, coating the metal and plastic with a white frost.

Plasma flashed at the corner of my suit's visual pickups, white hot, but I couldn't turn to check who'd shot or what they were shooting at. The Tahni was desperate, but not dead yet, and his suit had jets of its own. He caught me raising the coil-gun again for another blow, plowed into me, his suit's arms wrapping around me, clawing for purchase, for anything he could tear or rip away as we flew across the compartment into the wall of the shelter.

My suit's padding absorbed *some* of the impact, but not enough. My head swam, bright lights clouding my vision, and the coppery taste of blood filled my mouth, but the pain in my head was nothing compared to the pain in my chest. I'd had cracked ribs before and now I had them again and it sucked just as bad. I tried to get my feet anchored against the wall, tried to get some leverage, an angle to use my jets against his and push him away, but the nascent concussion had me dizzy, disoriented. The Tahni bashed a fist into my helmet and the metal rang with the impact, smacking my head against the back of it, sending more flashes of pain through my brain, nebulae of blinking lights across my eyes.

I had the presence of mind to consider the fact that I might die, and I was surprisingly disturbed by the notion. This wasn't how I wanted to go.

How do you want to go then?

Was that the angel or the devil? Did it matter?

I want to go out on my own terms.

Who gets to do that? The tone was mocking. The devil, then? But that damned angel had been a real bitch, too.

The Skipper. My answer was defiant, righteously indignant.

Oh, and you're saying you're anywhere near the man Captain Covington was?

I wanted to shrug free of this half-delirious mental debate. Another punch slammed into my helmet, futile in that his fist would never break the BiPhase Carbide, but sufficient to rattle my head again. I had to move, had to get myself planted for leverage, but I couldn't reach the floor and if I hit the jets, all I'd accomplish was to bang my head into the ceiling and do more damage to myself. I grabbed at him instead, caught his fist with my articulated hand and pulled him into a blow with the stub of my plasma gun, but I lacked any real sort of leverage and only managed to push us apart a few meters.

It was enough. A wave of plasma smashed him sideways on a burst of burning metal and he was gone as if he'd never been. I pushed off the wall and spun around. Fargo's plasma gun was still extended, as if she wasn't sure she'd actually killed the Tahni soldier. I scanned the compartment, searching for threats, but there were none. The two Tahni I'd left alive were no longer so encumbered by mortality. From the looks of their charred and broken armor, they'd taken plasma shots as well.

They were dead, Fargo and I were alive...but where was Vicky?

"Are you all right?" It was her voice and I made the same mistake as before, thinking in groundpounder terms, looking around for a full three seconds before I finally looked up. She was hanging from what was the ceiling by my orientation, her boots attached by their magnets, main gun still trained at the open doorway. The sealant around the crack in her side was partially flaked away where I'd caked it thick, but seemed intact.

"I'm sore as shit," I told her, "and I think I have a concussion. What about you? What about your air?"

"The suit's tight. But the tanks are still empty. Once the oxygen in the suit is used up, that's it." She paused, not moving, just standing on the ceiling, a statue. "Maybe an hour."

"We'll figure something out," I insisted. An idea penetrated the fog over my brain and I would have snapped my fingers if there'd been room inside the glove. "Their assault shuttles! If we can get on board one of them...." I tuned the comms to the net for Intercept One. "Dunstan, do you read me? Are you still out there?"

Nothing.

"Even if their assault shuttles are still out there," Fargo said quietly, "they'll see us coming through the lock. They can blast us with their point-defense turrets before we get anywhere near them. And even if they don't kill us immediately, what would we do then? None of us knows how to fly a Tahni shuttle."

"You do one thing," I told her, remembering something Lt. Ackley had said to me. "You don't try to do everything. You do one thing, concentrate on that. Live another second, live another minute, and then you do the next thing. So, we get out there and if we can get on the shuttles, we do. And then we do the next thing. You get me?"

"Yes, sir."

"Dunstan!" I tried again. "Do you copy?"

He could be dead. Or, he could have simply lost his antenna, or the bulk of the shack could be blocking the signal. Either way, we had no choice.

"Let's go." Movement caught my eye from the storm cellar. It was the Tahni with the broken arms, our EPW. "Bring him." I don't know why I bothered, but it didn't seem right to leave him behind.

Going out seemed so much shorter than coming in, but then it always did. We stayed alert, because there was always the possibility that they'd left troops along the egress route, but all we'd left behind were dead soldiers. The lock was wide open, left that way by the Tahni, and coming up on it, all I could make out was blackness and the occasional flash of light reflecting off metal. The shuttles, maybe. Maybe Intercept One. I'd find out in seconds.

More flashes. Something close. Something big.

"What the hell *is* that?" Vicky wondered.

I emerged from the end of the lock and found out.

My first thought was that another Tahni corvette had arrived, and we were totally fucked...but the shape of the vessel wasn't quite right, its lines less regular, and the markings on the side were human, English letters, Arabic numerals.

It was the *Orion*.

"Alvarez," Colonel Hachette said in my helmet speakers. "Is that you?"

I couldn't speak immediately. I'd been ready to step into another fight, ready to rip victory from the grasp of our enemies, ready to die if I had to in order to keep Vicky rom dying for my sins. The feeling was like stepping off a cliff expecting a twenty-meter drop and instead, touching ground off-balance ten centimeters down.

"It is, sir," I finally replied. "And Sandoval, and one other. Our pilot, Dunstan, is on the cutter, if you can send someone to pick him up. But I'm afraid Captain Amendola didn't make it."

"Damn." There was what sounded to me like honest regret

in his voice. Well, he'd known her longer than I had. "I'm very sorry to hear that. I wish we could have gotten here sooner."

I let out a long and weary sigh, and if there'd been anything near normal gravity, I would have collapsed.

"No, sir," I assured him, "I think you arrived just in time."

Vicky's fingers teased at the skin over my ribs, and I flinched in remembered pain.

"They're all healed now, aren't they?" she asked, eyebrow rising. "Because if not, what we just did probably gave you internal bleeding."

I laughed softly and tried to pull her into a kiss, but she shrugged out of my embrace, her skin slick with sweat despite the ever-present chill of the ship's air conditioning.

"Not yet," she said, raising a finger. "That was the carrot. This is the stick."

I was listening to the words, I swear, but I was having trouble tearing my eyes away from her. Her skin gleamed in the dim glow of the chemical light strips at the base of the bulkhead. She put the same finger she'd raised up under my chin and tilted it upward.

"Eyes are over here, Marine."

"Sorry," I said, with a grin that was anything but contrite.

"We've been on the *Orion* three days," she said, her expression growing more serious. "And I wanted to give you some time to heal up...both from the injuries and from what happened to Ruthie."

I hissed out a breath and closed my eyes for a moment. The woman hadn't been a close friend, but she'd been the only ally we'd had, and she hadn't let us down. At least Dunstan had made it, though he hadn't been too happy about getting yet another cutter shot out from under him.

"But now," Vicky went on, "it's time to talk."

I'd known it was coming. I'd been hoping to avoid it, hoping to forget what I'd said, forget what I'd admitted to, but that was fool's gold.

"Yeah, I figured."

"I'm not going to watch you kill yourself," she told me. "If that's where this is going, you doing this until you finally run into a situation you can't handle, I won't stick around just to be the one to cry for you at the memorial."

I grunted like someone had punched me in the stomach. I wasn't surprised, but it hurt to hear it.

"But." She put a hand on my chest, her palm hot against my damp, cold skin. "We got out too soon, I think. Too quick afterward. We didn't have time to deal with what we'd gone through."

I nodded. I'd thought the same thing more than once. We'd both been so anxious to get away from what we'd seen, what we'd lost and start a new life somewhere else.

"And even before that, you never dealt with what happened to your family. You've got a double-handful of survivor's guilt and no one's ever tried to help you cope with it."

"There wasn't a lot of time," I said, shrugging. "There was a war on."

"And now you've found another war, so you wouldn't have to deal with it. But you have to, Cam. You have to, or you'll lose me and I'll lose you. And you'll lose your last chance at a fresh start."

"What do you want me to do?"

"We're back in the military." She rolled her eyes. "And with all the baggage that entails, including the chance to get yourself killed, it also gives you the opportunity to speak to a qualified military psychological counselor. And you are *going* to speak to one."

"I actually saw one when I was in," I admitted. "A long time ago."

"You did?" Her eyes went wide. "How come you never told me?"

"You'd just gone off to OCS. I...at the time, I felt really alone. And I didn't want to distract you from what you were trying to do. But she gave me some good advice." I snorted. "I didn't take it, but she gave it."

"So, you wouldn't be opposed to doing it again? And maybe this time doing what the counselor suggests?"

"Lt. Alvarez? Lt. Sandoval?"

My head snapped around and I half-expected to see one of the *Orion's* crewmembers standing in the hatchway of our compartment, but it was just the intercom system, which was a lot more elaborate and high quality than what I'd been used to during the war on beat-up old troop ships.

"Yeah?" I said, not knowing whether I was talking to someone higher or lower rank than me.

"Apologies if this is your sleep cycle, sir," the woman said, confirming she had to be enlisted or an NCO, because no officer would be calling a first lieutenant "sir." "Colonel Hachette would like to see you in the Ops Center in twenty minutes, if you please."

"We'll be there," Vicky said. She nudged me and eyed the head. At least we had one in our compartment, which was also a lot better than what I remembered from the *Iwo Jima*. "Time to hit the showers. But this isn't over."

"I'll see a counselor," I promised. "As soon as we're somewhere they have one available." I didn't know if it would do any good, but I was willing to waste a few hours if it proved to her I was trying.

"All right then." She stood and offered me a hand and the breath caught in my throat. She tugged me toward the shower, grinning. "I guess there might be time for a little more carrot then."

———

"You're late," Hachette observed.

As always, I felt he was towering over me, which I suppose I could blame on the lack of genetic pre-selection available in prenatal care in Tijuana. His dark hair was cut shorter than mine, though he lacked the interface jacks that might have made it a necessity rather than an affectation. He wore Fleet Intelligence blacks and had a sidearm belted around his waist, which was another affectation but one common to all Intelligence officers. I'd heard it was a regulation that they always go armed while on duty, though it seemed stupid to me while on board a starship in Transition space.

"Well, they were both civilians until a couple months ago," Sgt.-Major Ellen Campbell observed, amusement in the set of her eyes, though someone who didn't know her might not have noticed it. "I suppose we have to make allowances."

It was good to see Top again, and no, I couldn't bring myself to stop calling her that even though she was a sergeant-major now instead of a first sergeant. She'd gone out with her Marines to take down the remaining Tahni troopers on board the partially constructed corvettes and I hadn't had the chance to talk to her before I'd headed into the auto-doc to repair my ribs and concussion.

"I'm sorry about Captain Amendola," Top said, the humor going out of her eyes and her voice. "She was a good officer."

I glanced back at the hatchway to the Ops Center, expecting someone else to enter, but it was just the four of us.

"Is Wade coming?" I wondered. I hadn't seen Wade Cunningham since we'd boarded, either and I was getting a little worried. He'd been badly wounded when we'd left him on the *Orion* and headed for Canaan with Ruthie and Dunstan and I had a roiling in my gut at the thought there'd been a problem and he'd died of his injuries

"He and Major Kyari are still interrogating the prisoner you brought us," Hachette said. He waved at the chairs clustered around the curved table stretching across the rear half of the compartment. "Have a seat. We need to talk."

The chairs swiveled out from the table, attached by gimbals, another extravagance compared to the cheap, plastic versions that simply got folded up and stowed away when the ship was in free fall. Intelligence, I supposed, didn't skimp.

"Before we get to the primary reason for our meeting," Hachette said, hands flat on the table as if he was prepared to spring up and engage us in hand-to-hand combat, "we have to discuss Corporal Karen Fargo and Captain Kyler Dunstan."

"You told them about the operation," Top said, her tone not judgmental but questioning, as if she was begging with us to have a good explanation for it.

"You must have read the report," I told her. They'd made me record mine before they even stuck me in the auto-doc. "We needed their help, and I didn't have the time or the training to make up anything more plausible than the truth."

"You also promised them they'd be reinstated in the military if they cooperated with you," Hachette reminded me. "Did anything I did or said give you the impression you had the authority to do that?"

"Yes, sir," I told him, sensing the disapproval in his voice and not liking it. He might think he could intimidate me, but he was just pissing me off. "When you said you wanted the job done and asked me if I could do it."

I thought he was going to bristle at the near insubordination, but if he did, he was damned good at controlling his poker face.

"Couldn't you just find them a nice job on some remote outpost?" Vicky put in. "We never told them they'd be part of your task force."

"They know we exist," Hachette answered, his dark eyes emotionless. "And that's too much. We can either bring them on board or we'll have to have them both disappeared."

Which could mean all sorts of nasty things, from killing them outright to subtler but just as unpleasant fates, such as wiping their memories and dumping them in a military prison.

"They helped us," I reminded him. "They didn't have to."

"And they're both very good at their jobs," Vicky said. "Besides being a bit of a prick, Dunstan is one of the best pilots I've ever known. And Fargo is cool under pressure, never lost her head once."

"Or her sunny disposition," I added, trying not to make it sound like a criticism.

"If we do include them in this task force," Hachette warned, "you'll be responsible for their actions. They fuck up, it's on you two."

"Understood, sir," I assured him, trying to sound confident. The idea of my continued career being contingent on Dunstan not fucking up was more frightening than facing a thousand Tahni High Guard.

Hachette shot Top a look.

"Bring them in."

Top touched a control on her 'link, presumably sending a message, and the hatch to the Ops Center slid aside. Dunstan and Fargo were ushered in by a Marine officer I recognized from our previous stay on the *Orion* as Captain Solano, the company commander of the Marine Drop Troopers stationed on the ship. It struck me as amusing that Top got to sit in on the meeting while a captain was reduced to babysitting Dunstan and Fargo, but at least he got to stay once they shut the door behind them.

"So, it's official?" Dunstan asked, face lighting up when he saw us. "I'm in?"

"You both are," Vicky said, offering Fargo a reassuring smile.

"Provisionally," Hachette added, his expression hardening. "Captain Dunstan, I happen to have access to your records, so I know *exactly* why you were not retained in the service after the war. And if those proclivities reassert themselves at any point in the future, well...this is a classified, compartmentalized operation. You won't be discharged, and you won't be thrown in the brig, either. Do you understand what I'm saying?"

"Aye, sir," Dunstan said, bracing to attention, sounding serious for once in his life. "I won't let you down." The *this time* remained unspoken, but we all heard it anyway.

"Sit down," Hachette told him, then nodded to Fargo. "You, too."

Captain Solano took a seat beside them, though he hadn't been mentioned, and I began to wonder if Hachette didn't care for the man. The Marine officer didn't seem overtly objectionable. He was a cookie-cutter Drop Trooper, down to the depilated head and the generic, clear-eyed expression straight out of a recruiting commercial, quiet and professional and probably no older than I was.

"Our situation has changed," Hachette declared without any sort of segue. "It will be difficult for you to go back to the CSF and pretend you're still loyal." He shrugged. "Not impossible. We do, after all, have Captain Dunstan and Corporal Fargo to corroborate whatever story we concocted. But we also have thousands of potentially damning witnesses on Portent who might betray you, given a sizable enough bribe. But thanks to your efforts in the shipyard, we may not require an intelligence source inside the CSF anymore."

He touched his 'link and a holographic image appeared above the table, a small compartment with a restraint chair at its center. Locked into the seat was the Tahni technician we'd captured, his broken arms repaired, though otherwise, he looked pretty miserable. They wouldn't, I was fairly sure, be using physical duress against the Tahni, but the interrogation drugs and the psych-probe process wouldn't be at all pleasant. His head sagged against the strap holding it in place and sweat stained his uniform fatigues, his mouth hanging open with strands of drool trailing out of it.

A couple of medical technicians monitored from a portable display set up behind him. Standing over him were Wade Cunningham and Major Kyari, the dumpy, unassuming little man we'd first come to know as Ogbah, before we found out he was an Intelligence officer.

"Hey Cam, Vicky," Wade said, grinning. "Glad you guys are okay."

"Good to see you, Wade," I told him. I even meant it, despite the fact that he'd lured us into working for the CSF without bothering to tell us he was doing it undercover for Fleet Intelligence.

"Major Kyari," Hachette cut in, an edge to his tone that spoke volumes about how little patience he had with our senti-mentality, "has the prisoner confirmed the data the netdivers recovered from the drive mirror on Captain Amendola's 'link?"

"He has, sir," Kyari said, nodding. "Zan-Thint is hiding his forces in what used to be Tahni space, on a world our charts list as Fomoria in the Firbolg system." He sniffed an amused half-laugh. "The Tahni had another name for it, but I'm not going to try to pronounce it."

Another window opened up in the holographic projection, a star chart with the system in question highlighted in red. It meant nothing to me except in relation to the Tahni home system, outlined in blue, a dozen or so light-years away.

"The reports from the Scout Service don't show any habitables in the system, though there was a small Tahni outpost there. No reports on it since the war. Not a bad place to hide a fleet. Or that last Skrela pod."

I frowned, something he'd stayed sticking in my mental craw. I wasn't going to say anything, but Hachette must have noticed the change in my expression.

"Problem, Lt. Alvarez?" He cocked his head to the side, waiting for an answer, so I couldn't get by with just shrugging it off.

"Something doesn't track with this for me, sir," I admitted. "Why does Zan-Thint need a fleet if his plan is just to unleash the Skrela on the rest of the galaxy?"

"Well, not the *whole* galaxy," Dunstan pointed out. "He can't reach the whole galaxy." I cocked an eyebrow his way, showing my incomprehension. He spread his hands like he couldn't believe I didn't know. "Don't they teach you Marines anything about star travel?"

"Yeah," Vicky replied, sneering. "They teach us to get in the troop ship and let the Fleet chauffeur us around to the next place we're supposed to fight."

"Come on, I mean, you gotta know about Transition lines, right? Gravito-inertial lines of force between bodies of sufficient mass that act like highways through Transition space? That's why you can't just go *anywhere* using the Transition drive, you can only go to systems connected through the Transition lines...

like from one star system to another, not just out in empty space."

"I guess," I said, shrugging. I'd probably been told that at some point, but the only technical details about the Transition drive I'd bothered to learn in detail were the ones about how far away from a planet you could jump in.

"Then you should know that we can't *reach* a big part of the galaxy—most of the galaxy, actually—with the drive, at least not yet. We're in a bubble of connected stars a thousand or so light-years across. I don't know what the scientists call it, but every pilot I know calls it the Cluster. Everything outside that might as well be in another universe. Hell, ever since we figured that out, every independent mineral scout has been hunting high and low for the one Transition line that leads out." He snorted. "They call it the Northwest Passage, but no one even knows if it exists."

Hachette's face was turning an interesting shade of red, and I sensed an eruption coming from the man any second, so I steered the conversation back to the subject.

"Good to know, but the question remains. Why is Zan-Thint bothering to build a fleet?"

"Maybe," Fargo suggested, with more insight than I'd expected from someone who'd stayed a corporal as long as she had, "he thinks that the Skrela and the Commonwealth will, like, take each other out, and whatever's left will be weak enough for him to come in and take over?"

Vicky answered, which was good, because I was afraid Hachette would rip into her and she didn't deserve it.

"The Predecessors could move planets and create jump-gates, and the Skrela supposedly killed them off. I don't know how Zan-Thint thinks we'd be more than a speed-bump to them."

"According to what Zan-Thint told us on Bathala," I said,

"the Skrela didn't kill off the Predecessors, they just chased them away. Maybe he really does think we can take out the Skrela before they spread too far. He might be nuts to think that, but...." I shrugged. "Well, he *is* nuts."

"We can ask him when we get there," Hachette declared. "If he's inclined to answer questions after I shoot him in the head."

"You think we have enough firepower to take on his entire force?" I asked, ignoring the bravado and the remote likelihood that an Intel spook would be the one to kill Zan-Thint rather than a Marine grunt.

"I think we have as much as we're going to get." He pushed up from his seat and the rest of us stood as well, Dunstan taking perhaps a second longer to remember his military decorum than the others. "Make your preparations, boys and girls. We arrive in the Firbolg system in one hundred and thirty hours."

His lips skinned over his teeth in a wolf's hunting grin.

"It's time to finish this."

CONTACT FRONT
KINETIC STRIKE
DANGER CLOSE
DIRECT FIRE
HOME FRONT
FIRE BASE
SHOCK ACTION
RELEASE POINT

Start a new adventure today!

RICK PARTLOW is that rarest of species, a native Floridian. Born in Tampa, he attended Florida Southern College and graduated with a degree in History and a commission in the US Army as an Infantry officer.

His lifelong love of science fiction began with Have Space Suit---Will Travel and the other Heinlein juveniles and traveled through Clifford Simak, Asimov, Clarke and on to William Gibson, Walter Jon Williams and Peter F Hamilton. And somewhere, submerged in the worlds of others, Rick began to create his own worlds.

He has written a ton of books in many different series, and his short stories have been included in seven different anthologies.

He currently lives in central Florida with his wife, two children and a willful mutt of a dog. Besides writing and reading science fiction and fantasy, he enjoys outdoor photography, hiking and camping.

www.rickpartlow.com